TRAPPED

SINNERS OF BOSTON
BOOK 5

VANESSA WALTZ

Copyright © 2024 by Vanessa Waltz

All rights reserved.

No part of this book may be reproduced in any form or by any electronic or mechanical means, including information storage and retrieval systems, without written permission from the author, except for the use of brief quotations in a book review.

Cover by Kevin McGrath
Photography by Michelle Lancaster @lanefotograf

ISBN: 9798340858818
Imprint: Independently published

DELILAH

I hurried down the church steps.

The wind kicked up my dress, the long train billowing toward the bright sky. A couple strolling down the street stopped, staring at me. Faint organ music played behind me from the church I'd just fled. My now ex-fiancé stood inside, waiting at the altar. In a few minutes, he'd realize something was wrong.

I reached the bottom and raced down the sidewalk past the *Just Married* BMW decorated with streamers and white balloons. As I scanned the street, panic gripped my throat. Santino's friend was supposed to be here. Where was my escape?

A car pulled onto the tree-lined street, halting in front of me.

The invisible hand on my throat tightened as a man in a jean jacket exited the driver's side and opened the door. He gestured with his head.

"Get in, Miss Romanov. Santino sent me."

I'd never seen him before, but I barely glanced at him as I stuffed myself in the backseat. I seized the handle and yanked. It didn't close—damned dress. I opened the door again, yanking the fabric inside. Then I slammed it shut.

"Name's V," said the man as he got behind the wheel.

"Delilah." I buckled my seatbelt. "Get me the hell out of here."

The car accelerated, knocking my head back. A black fear swept through me as the church doors opened. Men in suits spilled out, one of them wearing the white lily boutonniere I'd picked from a catalog.

I raised my hand in a mock salute.

Goodbye, Dimitri.

ONE
DELILAH
FOUR WEEKS EARLIER

I sat on a barstool, my gaze glued to a man I'd only heard rumors about. I wasn't the type to stalk a man. It felt weird, but my situation called for desperate measures. Men hunted women all the time. At least I wasn't planning to hurt him.

Santino Costa had no idea I'd been watching him for the past hour. From his corner of the VIP section, he lounged in a chair, his drink barely touched. His face was hard to make out in the dim club light, but his magnetic presence lured more than one woman to his table. His bodyguards hung around him, radiating menace.

"Need a refill?" asked the redheaded bartender.

"Yeah, please."

I pushed my empty glass toward her, looking away from Santino as a girl my age prepared another vodka on the rocks.

"Do you know Santino Costa?"

She smiled. "A little."

"You dated him?"

"He doesn't date. Just flings. Which worked for me until it didn't." She sighed and garnished the cocktail, sliding it in front of me. "He wasn't interested in taking things further, so I moved on."

"So, he's a player."

The bartender leaned in, her red curls spilling over her shoulder. "Player is putting it nicely. He doesn't take no for an answer. Knows what he wants and gets it. If you want a serious relationship, I'd keep my distance."

"What *does* he want?"

A pitying smile spread across her face. "A girl to call his for a while. He'll make you feel like the only woman in the world but by sunrise? You'll be yesterday's news."

"Sounds like my kind of guy."

She arched a brow.

I wasn't after love, just a man dangerous enough to protect me from my fiancé. I'd spent weeks studying the Costas, no easy feat considering they were the most powerful mafia family in Boston. I'd done my homework, weeding out the married guys first. I had no interest in becoming anyone's side piece. Then I sorted through the single ones by rank and status. I hated it, but I had no other way out.

"What do you think he'd say if I asked him for a favor?"

Her brows shot up. "Depends on what it is. But trust me, nothing comes free with Santino."

Not surprising. I'd grown up around men like him. They never gave without expecting something in return, and the price was always steep. But if I was going to survive, I had to be willing to pay. Staying with Dimitri was no longer an option.

I glanced at the broad-shouldered silhouette bathed in shadows. I had to make my move soon.

Glasses clinked as the bartender loaded a dishwasher. She closed the door, the snap jolting through me. Her wary gaze settled on mine again.

"Look, I don't know what you're planning, but be careful. He isn't easy to walk away from."

I forced a smile. "I'll keep that in mind."

Walking away was the least of my problems.

I took out my phone, scanning the list of missed calls from one number. Dimitri was supposed to be at a poker game with his friends. He must've found out I'd ditched my guards because he'd left me a string of colorful messages.

> **DIMITRI**
> Did you forget who you belong to?
> Don't make me come find you.
> This is your last warning.
> Just wait until you get home.

I rolled my eyes and paid for my drink. Soon, I wouldn't have to deal with this asshole. My fingers shot off a quick text, and I slid off the barstool and headed for the exit.

I drove back to Providence.

I lived in a duplex owned by Dimitri. Months ago, I'd moved in with my father's encouragement. The ceilings were low and it was thirteen hundred square feet, small compared to my father's mansion. Barely any sunlight touched the dreary walls. It felt like a dungeon.

Ivan, one of my fiancé's henchmen, waited in the driveway. He bristled when I got out of the car. It probably stung that I'd outsmarted him again. I hurried past him and approached the front door. I dug out my keys and unlocked it.

Pushing it open, I stepped inside. My heart thudded as my gaze swept over Dimitri's bland furniture. My breathing hitched as I dropped my purse onto the kitchen counter and dashed into the living room.

Oh no.

Racks of clothes I'd collected over the years—sourced from estate sales, thrift shops, and online auctions—were ripped to shreds.

All of it.

Metal stands and hangers were scattered on the floor. My hands shook as I kneeled, running my fingers over strips of ruined fabric. The air smelled faintly of something burnt. My throat tightened.

I rushed to the bedroom, praying he hadn't destroyed *everything*. I threw open the closet door, choking back a cry. The shelves holding boxes of carefully preserved vintage fabrics, accessories, and handbags were bare. Only a few tattered pieces lay in the corner, half crumpled as though he hadn't cared enough to finish his destruction.

A deep anger settled in my chest. The hours I'd spent

building this collection, dreaming of my boutique, my escape, my future—all of it, gone in one vicious sweep.

And I couldn't do anything about it.

Because I'd agreed to marry Dimitri.

It had *always* been about pleasing the Pakhan of the Bratva. My father had orchestrated this engagement like a business deal. He made it sound like an honor. Marrying Dimitri would keep the family strong, reinforce alliances, and cement my place in the organization. I'd only said yes to please my father.

But I hated Dimitri.

I hated the way he looked at me. How he flaunted me to his friends but never respected me behind closed doors. How he used my father's power as a leash.

The door creaked, and footsteps clicked over the hardwood floors. Dimitri walked in, wearing a smug smile. Dressed in a tailored suit, he didn't bother looking at the mess he'd created. His cold eyes shot at me.

"You're home," he said, as if he hadn't just demolished everything that mattered to me.

"What did you do?" My voice cracked, but I stood up.

"I did us both a favor. This—" he gestured lazily to the empty racks, "was a distraction."

"A *distraction*?"

"You've spent more time on this bullshit than on your fiancé."

Heat bubbled in my throat. "This was my collection. It was my future. My boutique—"

His mouth twisted, and he waved his hand. "Drop the

little girl dreams and start acting like a woman. Your only job is being my wife."

His venomous words were wrapped in velvet. He always made his control sound so reasonable, but he destroyed anything that gave me independence. He wanted me to rely on him.

So did my father.

Dimitri is perfect for you. He is a very strong man, he'd said months ago. *You'll learn to be grateful for that. You're not some American girl who gets to run wild, Delilah. You marry for the family. Dimitri knows how to keep his house in order, and you will be part of that.*

My father respected men like Dimitri, who saw love as something to conquer. A good husband wasn't measured by kindness but by how well he controlled his wife. Turning me into a demure Bratva wife had been my father's plan for years, but I'd never been the obedient type. I fooled myself into thinking I could embrace it, hoping to buy a fraction of my father's love. It was a terrible mistake I couldn't take back.

Dimitri stepped closer. "You didn't think I'd let you go through with that ridiculous little shop, did you?"

"I never asked for your *permission*."

His lips curved. "I don't need you to ask. I make the decisions now."

"You don't decide anything for me!"

"The sooner you accept that I'm in charge, the better off you'll be."

"These were one of a kind. *Irreplaceable*."

"Maybe next time you'll answer my calls."

My eyes burned. "You had no right. They were mine."

"Nothing is yours," he said smoothly. "Not the slutty clothes you wear. Not even *you*. Don't forget that, *kotyonok*."

I fucking hated him.

Dimitri smiled. "You'll thank me later."

He patted my cheek and left the room.

I stood in the wreckage of my dreams, my stomach boiling. The tears I held back dissolved. Dimitri thought he'd won, that he'd crushed me, but he was so wrong. Destroying my boutique didn't break me—it only lit a fire.

I couldn't live like this. He would strip me of everything I cared about. I needed to escape, and I knew exactly how.

Santino Costa.

He wasn't a good man either, but he could free me from Dimitri's grip. Tomorrow night, I'd go to him. I didn't care what I had to do. Santino was my way out, and I'd trade my soul to take it.

I'd turn into a woman he liked—beautiful, willing, and in need of something only he could provide. Then I'd offer him the one thing he couldn't resist:

Me.

TWO
SANTINO

Vitale shoved the man forward.

Joe caught himself on the back of the chair, wincing. His shirt was torn. His lip, busted. Blood dripped onto his chin. Pathetic.

I'd seen that before too many times. My father used to stumble through the front door after losing everything at the poker tables. He'd head straight for the bottle. The electricity bill would sit on the kitchen table, unpaid, while my mother cried in the bedroom.

The sound of the door slamming meant my father was home. I'd take my little brother, Kill, into the closet and hide while my oldest brother, Romeo, took the brunt of my father's rage. When Dad sobered up, he'd promise the big score was around the corner. It never was.

This guy was another loser who thought he could talk his way out of a hole he'd dug himself into.

I watched Joe mop up his face. "You remind me of my father."

Joe perked up. "Oh yeah?"

"That's not a compliment."

Joe said nothing. He shifted in his seat like he knew the noose was tightening.

I looked him over. "You know what your problem is? You think I'll forget that you fucked up. Somehow, you'll convince me that things will get better. This is just a rough patch. I've heard that before, Joe. I grew up listening to it."

Joe swallowed hard, but I wasn't done.

"My old man used to come home like you. Face fucked up. Disheveled clothes. Talking about how he'd almost won thousands of dollars. Always the same shit. You know where he ended up?"

Joe paled, his head shaking.

I leaned back again. "I'm not in the business of giving second chances. Make this right, or I'll take everything."

If I learned anything from my dad, it was to never bet on people who couldn't pay their debts. This was my favorite part of the job. When it dawned on them that it didn't matter, the game was over, and I held all the cards.

I didn't have to raise my voice for this guy to sweat bullets. I broke men like him, and they still came back to kiss the ring. That's what it meant to be Santino Costa.

"I just need ten more," Joe begged. "I have an opportunity lined up. Luxury goods. Double the investment, I swear. Just give me a little more time."

"What's your backup plan when your deal goes sideways?"

He wiped blood off his cheeks. "It won't."

"That's not what I asked."

"I'll—I'll get it. I've never been late before, have I?"

"No, but I don't trust people who bet on things they can't control."

His mouth opened and closed, but nothing came out. I watched him squirm, making sure he understood how thin the ice was beneath him.

"You want ten grand, fine," I said after a long pause. "But it'll cost you."

He blinked. "How much?"

"Twenty points."

Joe's face fell. "Twenty points? Mr. Costa, that's—"

"That's the deal. Twenty points on top of what you already owe. You miss one payment, and I own everything. Your business, your car, all of it. Take it or leave it."

He hesitated. Then, slowly, he nodded.

Desperate fool.

I smiled, standing up. "You'll have the money by tomorrow."

Giorgio shouted.

What now?

I glanced at the velvet rope separating the VIP section. A beautiful girl walked past my bodyguard, ignoring his shouts to come back. Didn't even glance at him.

Giorgio caught up to her.

I held up a hand. "It's okay. Let her through."

She wrenched out of his grip, smirking, and marched toward me. Confidence poured off her in waves. She knew exactly where she was going. A woman like her didn't need permission to jump the line. Her looks were the ticket. Her bold eyes locked on me. They grabbed me by the balls.

I sat up straighter.

She stopped in front of me, beside the tool I'd made a deal with. I waved him off, and he disappeared. She wore a tight gray skirt that hugged her curves, cutting off above mid-thigh. Her legs seemed to go on forever. A black belt cinched her waist, accentuating her hourglass figure. But it was the top that got me. A polo shirt, of all things—something that would've been conservative, except she'd undone the buttons to tease her cleavage.

"I need to speak to you. Privately."

Her frigid tone caught my attention. I leaned forward, taking her in. Most women who came through here wanted money. They'd flash me their tits, smile, and try to sit on my lap. She acted like she already had what she needed.

Now I was intrigued.

I motioned to a chair. "And who are you?"

She didn't sit. Darkness lurked in her gaze. "Delilah Romanov."

That name socked me in the ribs. I stared at her. The Romanov family carried a history I couldn't forget. My chest tightened.

I gave her a hard look. I had every reason to hate the Romanovs. Old wounds I'd rather keep smothered in denial broke apart, stitch by stitch.

I sat back, crossing my arms. "So, you're one of *them*."

"I am."

She wasn't even *trying* to charm me. No attempt to smooth over the tension she must've felt radiating off me. She stood there, proud, as if she hadn't dropped a name I'd spent my whole life hating. Why was she here? Why me?

"Let me guess. You're here to make peace, right?"

She shook her head. "No."

I raised an eyebrow. "Then why the hell are you here?"

"Because I need your help."

I laughed. "You're lucky I haven't thrown you out."

She didn't waver, and that surprised me. Most people would've buckled. Maybe tried to backpedal or offer some pathetic excuse.

"You won't," she purred. "You're too curious about me."

She put her hand on my arm. Her fingers skimmed my jacket, but a shot of adrenaline went straight to my chest. I watched her, heat twisting in my gut. Seduction was such a cheap trick, but damn if I wasn't already imagining her on my desk.

I clenched my jaw. "You know what you're doing, sweetheart?"

Her mouth twitched. "I do."

My attention flicked to her deep red lips. *If you think you can use me, you better be ready to pay up.* I stood, palming the small of her back.

"Let's talk in my office."

She smiled. "Lead the way."

THREE
DELILAH

Breathe.

I forced myself to inhale as I followed Santino into a small office. The air felt heavier in here, but the suffocating feeling didn't come from the room.

He was gorgeous. No one told me Santino had an athlete's body honed from years of brutality, or that he stood at an imposing height that made the office seem smaller. His tanned skin was tempting, and his voice was like silk. His raven black hair blended into the shadows.

Get a grip, Delilah.

But getting locked in a room with him wasn't doing anything for my nerves.

Santino's palm slipped from my back as he shut the door with a soft click. He turned around, his movements rigid. His expression clouded with suspicion as he gave me a once-over. Then his glance fell to my legs, and his mouth softened.

He pulled out a chair. "Sit."

I sank into the wooden chair.

He stepped around me and shrugged off his jacket. A white dress shirt clung to his chest, stretching over broad muscles. He folded the jacket over the chair and sat. He rolled up his sleeves. Each roll exposed thick forearms, corded with veins and tattoos. My heart throbbed as I studied them.

"So, what can I do for you?" he asked.

"I need help leaving my fiancé."

Santino's brow lifted.

I swallowed, my fingers tightening around the edge of the chair. "I was pushed into an engagement. My father doesn't care about what I want. His only concern is how it'll benefit the Bratva, but I can't go through with it."

He darkened. "Why?"

"My fiancé is an abusive piece of shit."

"What's his name?"

"Dimitri Petrova."

He crossed his arms. "You don't look like a woman who needs saving. What's stopping you from walking away?"

"Dimitri will kill me. And if he doesn't, my dad will do it for him."

"Who's your dad?"

"Mikhail. He's Pakhan."

His stare drilled into me. "You know what kind of risk you're taking just being here, right?"

"I don't have a choice."

"You've picked a dangerous one."

"I'm willing to do whatever it takes to get out."

He stared at me. Then he stood up, rounding the desk and leaning against the edge.

"Out of all the people in Boston you could've run to, why me?"

"Nobody can protect me like you."

"Someone else could've found you first. They would've kidnapped you off the street and locked you up. Or worse, sold you to the highest bidder."

"I know the risks."

"You don't. You think you're desperate now? Some men wouldn't have thought twice about raping you the moment you asked for help. They wouldn't have stopped until you were broken. I could be one of them."

My stomach clenched. "But you're not."

"How the hell would you know?"

"Because I'm not an idiot. I didn't pick you randomly. I asked around. I watched you."

"You *watched* me?"

"I came in here a few times. I followed you to the deli once."

His lips curled. "And what did you find out?"

I wiped my palms on my skirt. "You don't tolerate disrespect. Nobody crosses you without paying a price."

"You've got me all figured out, huh?"

"No, but I know enough."

He grabbed my chair, caging me within his arms. Then he lowered his head, so close that his scent swirled in my nose. His proximity alone set me on fire, but I wanted to bathe in his smell.

"You know nothing," he said, his growl settling deep in my bones. "If I wanted to, I could ruin you right now."

"Then why don't you?"

"Because I'm intrigued. You walked into my world, knowing exactly who I am. That takes guts."

"I'm desperate. Is that a dealbreaker for you?"

His scowl darkened. "Being a Romanov is."

A lump formed in my throat. "You don't understand what they'll do to me."

"What makes you think I'll be any better?"

"You don't kill women. You play with them and let them go."

"What if I don't? What if I end up liking you more than you bargained for?"

"I-I guess I'll deal with it."

A merciless smile carved into his face as I stammered my response. He was thoroughly enjoying himself. At least he was entertained.

His hand skimmed over the back of my chair, brushing the side of my arm. I tensed but didn't pull away. He was testing my limits.

"You don't know the first thing about what you're asking for. You can't handle me."

I met his gaze, refusing to cower. "Yes, I can."

"All it'll take is one wrong move, and you'll regret ever walking into my office."

My pulse raced. "Then why haven't you kicked me out?"

He shot me a wicked smirk. "Because I'm having fun.

You knocked on the devil's door, and now you're wondering if he'll release you."

"I knew what I was doing when I came here."

He arched a brow. "What's your plan if I decide to take advantage of you?"

I faltered, and his grin deepened. "I'm counting on the fact that you like a challenge."

"You're more of a damsel." He traced his fingers lightly over my wrist, the contact searing my skin. "Running to me for help."

I clenched my fists. "You're the only one who can help me, Santino."

"That's what makes this so interesting. You're desperate enough to approach a man like me, even though you know I could hurt you for the fuck of it."

"I'm not scared."

"You should be. Because now that you're here, I'm not sure I want to let you leave."

"Then don't. Keep me."

Santino's smile vanished, replaced by something darker. He looked like he was genuinely considering it. The idea of claiming me wasn't a game anymore.

"Are you sure this is what you want?"

"Yes," I choked out. "Help me. Please."

"No more begging, Delilah."

The cold edge in his voice faded enough to make my breath hitch. He reached out, his fingers brushing my cheek, a touch so soft it broke me. The walls I'd built up buckled. Tears burned before I could stop them. I turned my head, trying to escape him. I hated showing weakness, especially now. I couldn't hold it back. My breathing shallowed and my vision blurred. I blinked furiously.

Oh God, I was unraveling right in front of him.

Santino grabbed a small box of tissues and pushed it into my hands. There was no pity in his gaze, just understanding.

I snatched a tissue and dabbed at my eyes.

Santino disappeared, and glasses clinked. He sank into the seat beside me, handing me a glass of dark amber liquid.

I lifted it to my mouth and drank.

Santino sipped his drink. "This won't be simple."

"I know."

He balanced the glass on his knee. "Do you? Because this isn't something I can do with a snap of my fingers. Not when you're tangled up with people like your family. It's gonna cost you."

"What do you want?"

"*You*. In every way a man can have a woman."

Tingling pitted my stomach. "One time?"

"I'm not risking all this to get laid once. I'll have you as often as I want."

I balled the tissue in my hand. "For how long?"

A feline smirk tipped his mouth. "To be determined."

"I need a timetable. I can't be your plaything indefinitely."

"You don't make demands with me," he warned, still smiling.

"What happens when you're bored? I'm on my own, as far as Dimitri is concerned?"

He frowned. "I don't take care of someone only to throw them away."

My cheeks flushed. Hopefully, he'd blame it on the alcohol. My skin was too hot, and my mind kept racing. Did he mean that?

I drained my drink, and he refilled it. As soon as he finished pouring, I grabbed the glass and drank from it deeply.

"And when you're done with me?" I asked.

He shrugged. "We go our separate ways."

"But you'll protect me? That's...reasonable."

"Nothing about this will be reasonable. I don't share. I'm a jealous asshole. Once you're mine, no other man so much as breathes near you. Also, this isn't a business transaction. You don't get to walk away when it's convenient for you."

I bit my lip. "And if I agree?"

"You'll never see Dimitri again."

"That's all I want."

His gaze didn't leave mine. "Then it's not a hard decision."

It *was*, though.

Santino made it sound simple, like all I had to do was nod and my life would be fixed. I'd never have to face Dimitri or worry about my father's wrath, but this clearly wouldn't be an equal partnership.

What choice did I have?

I took a deep breath, reaching for the drink. I downed the rest in a gulp. My eyes met his again.

"When can you get me out?"

FOUR
DELILAH

Today was my wedding, but the man I planned to abandon at the altar barely crossed my thoughts.

I sat in my bedroom, playing with my phone. Inside the case was a slip of paper with a number I had to call but couldn't. My soon-to-be ex-fiancé didn't tolerate other men in my life, especially Italian men with seductive grins who lurked in dark corners.

Santino.

After I'd agreed to be his, he told me in explicit detail what he wanted. Santino hadn't bothered with sweet words. He'd laid out his terms with all the subtlety of a sledgehammer. It would happen tonight after he whisked me away from the wedding. I had to confirm that we were good, but I couldn't contact him. Not with Zofia hovering and Dimitri's men outside my bedroom.

I put my phone down. The stylist doused me in hair spray as I grabbed a half-filled bottle of vodka and swallowed a mouthful.

The key to daytime drinking was doing it slowly. Little sips of alcohol, all day. Sometimes, I didn't realize how wasted I was. I'd grab a cup, miss it, and never feel drunk because being drunk was normal. Sober was chaos. Sober was panic attacks.

My stepmother, Zofia, a tall blonde in a form-fitting black gown, scowled at me. "Don't drink too much. A Romanov woman doesn't slur her vows."

"I'm not planning on slurring anything."

Zofia lifted the bottle from my hands and set it on the vanity. "All eyes will be on you. Our family, your future husband's family. If you bring shame to us, there is no coming back."

"I know."

I'd given a lot of thought to how Dimitri's people, his colleagues, and even the side piece he assumed I was clueless about would witness his humiliation. After today, he'd be the laughingstock of the Bratva.

The promise of his destruction kept me sane, making me keep my mouth shut when Dimitri talked down to me. He could do whatever he wanted. I had the best revenge planned for him.

But this morning, when I woke up to fresh bruises on my arms, doubt slithered in my head like a cold snake. If my deal with Santino didn't go through and Dimitri caught me trying to escape, the damage he'd inflict on me could be permanent. It could be fatal.

The stylist backed off, and the makeup artist took her place. She squirted foundation onto her hand, dabbed the brush into it, and swiped it across my face.

She paid particular attention to the hollows under my eyes.

Zofia checked her Rolex, sucking in her cheeks. She'd been a nightmare all week. Dad had ordered her to watch me, and she stuck to my side, pestering me about last-minute changes to seating arrangements, makeup trials, and picking a hairstylist.

"I hope you're not getting any ideas about backing out. Because there's no walking away from this. Not without consequences. Cover that up," she barked to the makeup artist, pointing at the faint purple marks on my arm.

The girl continued her work in silence, her brush strokes methodical.

The door creaked open, and a young girl peeked in. "Are you ready for the dress?"

"Bring it in," Zofia commanded, her tone brooking no argument. The girl disappeared and returned moments later, struggling with the weight of the gown. The dress was ridiculous, as if someone had tried to trap a wedding in a cage.

Zofia took it from the girl and held it up, inspecting every inch and seam. "This is what a Romanov bride wears. Strong, elegant."

The dress seemed to mock me with its pristine white fabric. A symbol of commitment when all I felt was trapped. This wasn't the dress of my dreams. I'd always wanted something vintage, with delicate lace. But no, they had insisted on this modern monstrosity.

"It's beautiful," I lied, my voice hollow.

She smiled. "Now, let's get you into it."

I was dying to tear the dress apart, but any defiance would cost me. So I stood there as Zofia manhandled me into the gown.

"There." Zofia stepped back, her lips curving slightly. "*Solnyshko*, you look perfect."

I looked like a doll. I was Dimitri's flawless bride, dressed to play the part while planning my escape.

I pasted on a smile and met Zofia's gaze in the mirror. "Thank you."

"Come on," Zofia said, her tone softening just a fraction as she smoothed a wrinkle in my skirt. "Your guests are waiting."

I followed Zofia out, the satin and tulle rustling. The cold weight of her hand on my back reminded me I was being pushed, not led.

Downstairs, the sound of distant chatter grew louder. I kept moving, but all I thought about was the man I'd be throwing myself at. Was Santino a better choice than Dimitri? Would he even come? What if he decided not to and left me here to face Dimitri's wrath?

I needed to call Santino.

I mingled with guests for as long as I could stand and then headed to the bathroom. I stuffed myself in and locked the door. Finally alone, I pulled my phone from a hidden pocket in my dress, my hands trembling as I dialed Santino's number.

The line connected.

"Delilah?"

His velvety murmur stroked my ear.

"Yes. It's me. I have to keep this short. They're

watching me." I dropped my voice. "So you'll be outside the church?"

"I won't be. Got a friend handling that part."

"How do I even know this is real?"

He released an exasperated breath. "You asked for a way out, and I'm giving you one. My guy's solid. He'll get you out of there."

"I don't like this," I whispered. "If anything goes wrong, I'm dead—"

"*Hey*. You think I'd waste my time setting this up to watch you marry your prick of a fiancé? I've got a lot riding on this, Delilah. Stick to the plan."

"You don't understand the risk I'm taking. Dimitri will kill me."

"I won't fail you."

I gripped the phone tighter. "I'm supposed to trust a random guy whose only interest is fucking me?"

A dark chuckle rumbled through the speaker. "You don't have to trust me. You just have to do what I say."

I gnawed on my lip. "And what if I decide not to?"

"I don't need to remind you what'll happen if you stay with him. I'm offering you an opportunity so you don't end up six feet under or wishing you were. All you have to do is give me what I want. You should thank me."

My cheeks burned. "For what, using me as your plaything?"

"Pretty much."

I despised the idea of giving in to him, but the alternative was far worse. Dimitri was cruel, controlling, and dangerous. But Santino? He didn't want to hurt me. He wanted to play with me.

"Do we have an understanding, or are you gonna keep playing hard to get?"

I laughed bitterly. "You're not making this decision easier."

"You want out? This is how it'll work. You're going to calm down. You'll pretend to be a blushing bride. You'll smile. Pose for pictures. When you're at the church, use the side door, and my guy will be waiting at the curb. He'll bring you where you need to go, and then...you and I will have a nice time together."

"Right."

"This is your chance. Either take it or live the rest of your life as Dimitri's possession."

"Fine," I snarled. "But if you screw me over, I'll—"

A fist hammered the door.

I ended the call and slipped the phone in my pocket. The door's lock unlatched, and Zofia stood there, her black eyes glittering with suspicion.

"Were you drowning in the sink?"

I glowered at her. "I needed a minute to myself."

Zofia grabbed my arm and steered me out of the bathroom. "This is your wedding day. Mingle. Talk to your guests!"

"Stop yanking me."

Zofia halted, her bony fingers still clamped around me. "I heard you in there, *solnyshko*. You were talking to someone. I *hope* it wasn't another man. Dimitri would be very unhappy to know this."

"Of course not," I snapped. "Why would I do something so stupid?"

"You've been sulking like a little child for weeks."

I forced myself to hold her gaze. "I've done everything my fiancé has asked me to do. I just needed a moment to myself."

"For what?"

"To be *alone*. Weddings are stressful enough without you breathing down my neck."

She released me and held out her palm. "Give me your phone."

I handed it over. A sickening pulse throbbed in my stomach as she unlocked it, her thumb clicking my recent calls list. She bared her teeth as she stabbed Santino's number and hit the button for speakerphone.

Please don't pick up.

I swallowed hard, trying to look bored. Zofia glared at me as she waited for the call to connect. My heart slammed against my ribs. If Santino answered, it would all be ruined.

The phone rang once, twice, and then—

"Hello?" A woman's voice echoed through the speaker.

Zofia's brows arched. "Who is this?"

"This is Julia from Bliss Bridal."

"Why did Delilah call this number?"

"Um...just following up about the gown and last-minute alterations."

I stared at Zofia, praying she would buy it. She frowned. "Shouldn't you be speaking with the wedding planner?"

"Oh, I do apologize. There was a minor question

regarding the fit, and I wanted to make sure it was perfect for the big day. It's a quick follow-up. We want Delilah to look her absolute best."

Zofia hesitated. "Well, go through the proper channels in the future."

"Of course. Thank you so much for understanding."

Zofia hung up and thrust the phone into my hand. I slipped it into my dress, slowly letting out a tense breath. *Thanks, Julia, whoever you are.* Luckily, Santino had planned for this situation weeks ago.

As I returned to the party, Zofia's stare bored into my head. I had to be careful. Any slip-up and Zofia would pounce on me.

The ride to the church was a blur, with Zofia sitting beside me, watching. When we arrived, my throat was so tight I could barely breathe. The massive doors loomed ahead, the steps lined with white lilies. Guests had already filled the pews.

Zofia grabbed me as I stepped out of the car.

I allowed myself to be led up the steps and into a small antechamber where various family members picked to be my bridesmaids waited. Soft chatter filled the room as the girls adjusted their tulle skirts, making last-minute touch-ups to their makeup. When we entered, the room quieted.

Natalia, the wedding planner, shepherded women into place. The girls fell into line, their pastel-colored dresses swirling as they moved. Zofia stood at the door leading to the church, her arms crossed.

"You should get to your seat," I told her.

Zofia nodded. "Remember, Delilah. No foolishness."

She disappeared inside. Minutes later, the organ music swelled to life. One by one, bridesmaids filed down the aisle.

A door creaked, and I gritted my teeth. Natalia poked her head in.

"It's time," she whispered. "Are you okay?"

I forced a smile. "Just need a moment. I'll be right out."

She hesitated but nodded and slipped out, closing the door behind her. I let out a shaky breath and wiped my palms on my dress.

This was it. Now or never.

Trembling, I reached for the door that led out. It opened, revealing a brilliant sky. I stepped outside and didn't dare look back.

I was free.

FIVE
DELILAH

Two hours later, V parked the car at its final destination—an upscale hotel in the heart of Boston. V stood outside, talking to the valet.

I stayed rigid, my fingers clawing the seat. I kept second-guessing what I'd done. Imagining the hell storm of Dimitri's fury when he realized I'd slipped from his grasp. He wouldn't find me. Not for a long while, and once he did, it'd be too late. I'd already belong to another man.

One even more powerful than Dimitri.

The door yawned, and V's boyish face poked through. "You coming?"

I unbuckled the seatbelt. I grabbed his hand as he helped me exit the car. People stared as I gathered my skirts and headed into the hotel, following V. No doubt, we looked weird together. Him in his jean jacket, black commando boots, and pants. Me in my wedding dress.

The fabric itched as we rode the elevator up. I couldn't wait to rip it off my body. Despite my relief, the panicky feeling returned as the bell dinged. The man waiting for me in room 1514 scared me a lot less than my ex-fiancé, but I'd still traded one devil for another.

The elevator doors opened, and V led me down a carpeted hallway. My heart pounded with each step. No turning back now.

We halted in front of a door, and V knocked twice before stepping aside. It opened, revealing a man in a suit.

"Everything work out okay?" Santino asked V, who nodded. "You weren't seen?"

"Nope."

Santino handed an envelope to V. "There's a bonus inside."

V opened it, flipping through the bills. "I appreciate that."

Santino jerked his head down the hall. "Now get lost."

Tucking the envelope in his pocket, V strode down the hallway. Santino's dark eyes locked onto mine. A smile crept across his face, dragging ice down my spine.

"Come in."

I stepped inside, the room's opulent décor barely registering as I focused on him. Santino closed the door behind us, sliding the button over Do Not Disturb before turning around. His eyes blazed as they traveled up the dress to the bodice and my boobs on display from the plunging neckline. This dress hadn't been my first choice, not that anything about the wedding had been up to me.

Santino's gaze lingered on my chest.

I didn't call him out on it. He could do whatever he wanted. The man I'd left behind terrified me, but this one surprisingly didn't. And yet, my abdomen tensed when he approached me.

He stopped inches away. "It's been a long month for you, hasn't it?"

"Yes."

"It was an agonizing wait for me, too."

Of course, he'd been looking forward to it. He got free pussy in exchange for whisking me out of Providence. For weeks, I'd dreaded this moment.

At least he'd dressed up for the occasion—fitted suit, leather shoes, cream button-up shirt. He'd styled his hair with the perfect amount of pomade that didn't look crunchy. The man knew how to dress. He smelled nice, too. Notes of his cologne swirled in my nose—citrus and sea salt.

Santino's thick brows furrowed. "What's that on your arm?"

I didn't have to look. "Bruises."

"From what?"

I shrugged. "Dimitri was angry about the seating arrangements. We argued. He grabbed me."

I had a whole routine down for covering up bruises. Smoky eyeshadow to cover up a black eye and deep red lips to hide a busted mouth. But some things were harder to conceal than others. Even foundation wasn't enough to completely hide them.

"Did he hurt you anywhere else?" he demanded.

"No."

Santino brushed a finger over the purple shadow. "How many times has he done this?"

"We don't have to talk. I'd rather you just ripped off my clothes and got it over with."

"You don't call the shots," he said coolly, crossing the room to a console table. He splashed whiskey into a tumbler.

I swiped the glass before he gave it to me, inhaling the alcohol. An earthy taste rolled over my tongue. Not my favorite, but it did the trick. I glanced at the label. Top-shelf brand. So he wasn't cheap. Good.

I set the glass down. "Thanks."

He poured himself a drink. "You know, I wasn't sure if you'd go through with it."

"I had no choice."

He grunted. "It went okay?"

"Aside from my stepmom calling you, yeah. I woke up early this morning. Around three. Couldn't sleep. I was worried it'd all go wrong. A bridesmaid would find out and report to him. Maybe you wouldn't show up."

He refilled my glass.

I gulped the alcohol down again, savoring the exquisite burn. As soon as it faded, my body screamed for more. I reached for the bottle, but Santino dragged it away from me.

"That's enough for now."

A ribbon of anger worked through me as I stared at the mostly full bottle. "It'll help with my nerves."

"You seem fine."

I snorted. "I'm about to have sex with a man I hardly know."

Santino drank his whiskey, setting down his glass with

a grunt. He stepped closer, and I fought the urge to back off. His eyes were so dark, and they kept eating me up. He leaned in, his breath ghosting my ear. Then he inhaled. I listened to the air whistling in his nose.

Was he smelling me? What a freak.

He reached out, his fingers brushing a strand of hair from my face. Santino's hungry gaze watched me, his expression ravenous. Some of Dad's men had looked at me like that. It always creeped me out, but with Santino, the effect was muted. Maybe because he was so handsome. He had a strong jaw and an insanely sensual mouth. His teeth were white and straight, and when he smiled, a dimple popped in his cheek. He was beautiful, but his presence was a loaded gun with a whisper for the trigger.

"So we're spending the night together, and then what?" I pressed.

"Tomorrow morning, I'll take you to your new apartment."

"How can I be sure it's real?"

"I'm a man of my word, Delilah."

I met his gaze. "That's what they all say. Sending a car to deliver me here doesn't prove much."

"It's a little too late to back out."

"I'm not backing out. I'm clarifying terms."

He shot me a twisted smile. "You don't get to demand last-minute changes."

I lifted my chin. "Then find another girl to be your sex slave."

Inwardly, I cringed.

You didn't talk to a man like that, especially after he

saved your ass. I grew up watching Dad smack Mom down after a snarky comment and decided I liked not being hit more than I enjoyed being right.

But I couldn't stand being at Santino's mercy. I needed more than his protection if I was going to thrive in Boston. Living wasn't enough. I wanted to grow something of my own. And I couldn't do that without money.

Santino seemed to find my gall amusing. "What exactly do you want, principessa?"

"An allowance. Five thousand a month. And if I'm going to be your full-time mistress, all my expenses will be paid for."

His eyes sparkled. "Done."

"Just like that? No negotiation?"

He lifted his shoulder in a shrug. "I've already rented out an apartment in my name. All your bills will be forwarded to me. I'll throw in another grand for food, too. I assume you don't cook."

He assumed wrong, but I wouldn't talk myself out of more money.

He reached into his wallet and grabbed a thick clip of cash. Licking his thumb, he counted the bills, piled them in a neat stack, and gave it to me.

"That's only half. I'll give you the rest in a couple weeks."

Jesus. "Oh. Okay."

"We good?"

I inclined my head. I didn't expect that to work. Shaking, I took the bills and braced for him to slap it out of my hands. When he didn't budge, I slipped the cash into my clutch. The snap of it closing jolted through me.

"So, what now?" I asked him.

"Now," he murmured, taking the empty glass from my hand and setting it on the table. "We take off your dress."

Santino stepped behind me. His hands drifted to the back of my gown, undoing the buttons. I stood still, my pulse pounding. The fabric slid down, revealing the crotchless bridal lingerie and open-cup bra.

"You wore that for me?" he said huskily, moving in front of me.

My heart hammered. "Dimitri picked it out."

"I'll have to thank him."

I blushed from my ears to my neck, and he grazed a finger across my burning jaw.

"Are you a virgin?"

"No," I whispered as he cradled my chin. "Is that a problem?"

"Of course not, principessa."

His voice stirred the darkness inside me.

"Why do you keep calling me a princess?"

"Because you're delicate but very demanding. Isn't that what princesses are?"

I scoffed. "I'm anything but delicate."

"Well then, you're something precious that needs to be protected."

I opened my mouth, but my breathing stopped.

He let go of my face, his touch drifting to my waist. I shivered. His fingers skimmed my skin as they began tracing the bra band. His thumb brushed the cutouts of my bra with feather-light touches.

"I'm going to take my time with your body," he purred, drawing curlicues over my breast. "If you're a good girl, you'll get my mouth. If you're bad..."

His palm had reached my pussy, and he slapped it.

An unexpected jolt joined the smarting pain.

"Touch me," he demanded.

"Where?"

"Anywhere you want."

I put my hand on his chest, feeling his muscles through the jacket and dress shirt. Then I linked my arms around his neck, my heart hammering. He made me nervous, and it was harder to hide that up close. His hands slid down my back, grabbing my ass.

Then he lifted me.

I went into the air with hardly any effort. Santino looked comfortable with me in his arms. The sheer strength and size of him was a reminder of what he could do to me. How useless it would be to fight. He laid me in the middle of the bed, unlinking my arms from his neck.

"Get on your hands and knees."

Feeling foolish, hot, and confused, I obeyed. I bunched my fingers into the sheets, waiting for him to climb onto the mattress and stab himself inside me.

Instead he walked around the bed, touching me here and there like a man assessing a recent purchase. I held my breath as he repositioned me, pushing my knees further apart and arching my back toward the bed. He grabbed my ass with both hands, and his thumbs pressed into my lips and pulled, opening me. I'd never been so vulnerable in my life.

"What a perfect girl," he murmured, his praise stroking me like hot feathers. "Beautiful and brave."

My face flushed. "I'm not perfect."

Santino lightly traced my clit. "You're exactly what I want."

"Fine, but I'm not perfect."

"You're whatever I say you are."

Was this supposed to make me feel comfortable? Because it didn't. I wasn't used to being showered with compliments. My only sexual experiences had been one-night stands with men who didn't give a damn about me.

"Turn around," he rumbled.

I complied, lying on my back.

Santino stood at the foot of the bed, the wool of his pants tented with his erection. "Show me your pussy."

I opened my legs a fraction, the bridal lingerie leaving nothing to the imagination. Santino knocked my knees apart and lowered himself between my thighs, his gaze riveted on me. His hands curled around my thighs, and he brushed his lips across the sensitive skin. His hungry mouth blazed a trail closer and closer.

My cheeks burned.

He must've liked what he saw because he pressed his lips to my clit. Heat flashed through my body before it went taut and seized again as he licked.

I made a strangled sound.

He caught my eye, winked, then resumed licking. I had no measure of time, but it felt like an hour passed while a stranger's mouth sucked me, his perfect tongue flicking my clit, pressing his nose flat to tongue-fuck me. With his finger, he played with the swollen nub.

I couldn't breathe. I fisted the sheets.

Pleasure crested, and then he added a finger. My breathing hitched as he plunged in and out, working me into a frenzy. His eyes never left mine, the intensity in them making my head spin.

"Such a good girl, taking me so well."

I couldn't form words.

Santino's finger worked magic inside me, and I felt an orgasm building. His thumb stayed on my clit, rubbing in slow circles that made me arch off the bed. "That's right," he growled, adding another finger and increasing the pace. "Come for me."

My world shattered as I came, my body shaking.

His touch disappeared as I squirmed on the bed.

Santino unbuckled his slacks and shucked off his clothes. He was such a man. Curly hair dusted his built chest and trailed down a sculpted abdomen. My gaze darted to his thick cock, fully erect and veiny, just as perfect as the rest of him.

This is happening.

A dark thrill ran through me that felt too much like excitement. I'd spent at least a decade listening to my dad complain about Italians. How they were dirty, lying, cheating thugs, and now I was about to sleep with one. If my father ever found out, he'd strangle me in my sleep.

The bed dipped as Santino climbed on.

He urged me onto my hands and knees so that I faced the headboard.

I breathed in sharply. "I'm not on birth control."

He shushed me and kissed the nape of my neck. The room was charged with a dangerous energy as he positioned himself behind me. His hands roamed over my back and down to my hips, pulling me closer to him.

I swallowed hard.

I felt him sliding on my slick pussy. He entered me, stretching me inch by inch. *Oh my God.* It was overwhelming, like he was splitting me apart. Was that his cock or a baseball bat? I gritted my teeth against the ache and winced as he seated himself completely. Santino stayed buried inside me, his fingers digging into my hips. He stroked my curves, giving me a few moments to adjust.

Then he moved. He was so big that his slow rhythm had me gasping. His hand gripped the back of my neck, holding me in place. His thrusts were powerful, like ocean waves battering rocks.

Over and *over*.

My eyes watered as pain rushed over me, ratcheting my pleasure higher. His cock dove in and out of me—*no condom*. Even if I wanted to, I couldn't stop this. Every stroke bound me tighter to him, stoking flames that would consume us both.

SIX
DELILAH

My alarm clock this morning was Santino's face, shoved between my thighs. His tongue soothed the ache from being railed all night. He played with me until I gave up and whimpered for more. Then he flipped me on my knees. On my back. Over the desk.

Everywhere.

Santino had sex like he'd lost his mind and could find it inside me. He was feral. I'd never seen a man so determined to make me come. Not just once. Countless times.

At some point, Santino ordered room service. We ate breakfast. He poured me coffee and asked how I liked it—two sugars, lots of milk. After breakfast, I realized that I didn't have any clothes and would have to do the walk of shame in a wedding dress. Until Santino grabbed a set of women's size medium leggings, a shirt, and sandals from his suitcase. He'd figured I wouldn't have anything on me, an alarmingly thoughtful gesture.

Santino didn't say much the whole morning, but he

laughed when I dropped Dimitri's engagement ring into a homeless person's cup on the way to his car. He opened the door for me, like a gentleman. When he got into the car, he stared at me and barked one word.

"Seatbelt."

I put on the damned seatbelt, still feeling like I was floating in a strange dream. This gentlemanly side of him confused me. I spent the drive to my new place obsessively analyzing him. I'd expected rough, impersonal sex with Santino, but a business transaction wrapped in heat was *not* how it felt.

My fingers dug into the seat, the ache between my legs still throbbing. The way he'd touched me still warmed my skin. How my pussy clenched when he'd whispered filthy things like: *swallow my cum, principessa*. Even as he lined up his cock to fuck me, I never felt like I was being used for his pleasure. I'd enjoyed myself too much.

What was wrong with me?

I glanced at Santino. He stared ahead, eyes on the road. He looked bright-eyed and ready for the day, and not like he'd spent the last six hours screwing me. Was this not a big deal for him?

"Where are we going?"

"Your new place," he said.

I fidgeted in my seat. It'd been too long since my last drink. Before we left the hotel, I'd snuck some bottles from the minibar into my purse, but I couldn't drink them now. People rarely reacted well to my drinking.

Twenty minutes later, I stepped into a stunning apartment with floor-to-ceiling windows that offered a breathtaking view of the city. The place was sleek, all glass and steel, and it screamed luxury.

I turned to face Santino, my heart racing. "This is my apartment?"

"Yeah. You like it?"

It was beautiful. An apartment I'd only dreamed of living in. I crossed the room, running my fingers along the polished marble countertops. "I would've been fine with a less expensive place."

Santino gave me a shrewd look. "Did you expect me to throw you in a dump?"

"No, but...I'm not a girlfriend. I'm only your mistress."

"This is where you'll stay," he said, sliding a set of keys on the counter. "No one can touch you here. You're safe."

I curled my hand around them. "Thanks."

He took an envelope from his jacket and placed it next to the keys. "That's the money we agreed on."

Santino leaned on the counter as I grabbed the envelope. My breath hitched as I thumbed through the crisp bills, my mind racing with the possibilities. He'd really given me the money. For the first time in months, I felt a spark of hope. Maybe this arrangement with Santino wouldn't be as painful as I'd thought. Maybe it wouldn't be painful *at all*.

That blew my mind. I could rebuild everything Dimitri had destroyed. My vintage boutique had been more than a dream. It was supposed to be my chance to have something of my own. I'd been working on it for years, collecting clothes from different eras, carefully preserving each piece until Dimitri decided it was all "a distraction" and wiped it all out in one tantrum.

But with this money? I could start again.

I pictured the boutique I'd always imagined. The soft lighting, rows of beautiful dresses lining the racks, customers coming in to find their perfect piece. Santino could fund it, make it happen. If I played my cards right and kept him satisfied, I could have my boutique back.

Excitement buzzed under my skin. This wasn't just about getting away from Dimitri anymore. It was about reclaiming my life.

I looked back at Santino, my heart still pounding. He stood there, arms crossed. Did he know what this meant for me? Could he see the flicker of hope he'd just lit?

"What are you thinking?" he asked, his voice low and rough.

I shrugged. "I'm imagining all the stuff I want to buy."

"Good. You should be."

I stared at Santino, incredulous. This was too easy. Too good to be true.

"What's the catch?" I asked.

"You know the catch. You're mine."

"But this... all of this—" I gestured to the luxurious apartment, still holding the envelope. "It's more than I expected."

"You asked me to keep you safe."

"Yeah, but it seems like there's strings attached."

"The only string is me, principessa. You belong to me now. As long as that's true, you'll live like this. But if you betray me or try to run, this goes away."

Santino's gaze stayed steady on mine, his dark eyes flickering with...possessiveness? Amusement? It unnerved me the way he claimed me so easily.

I steadied my breathing. This was what I'd signed up for. Santino had never hidden who he was or what he expected. I'd prepared for a less intense version of Dimitri.

"I won't."

He shrugged. "Then you've got nothing to worry about."

Why was he so generous to a woman he used for sex? Sure, he was getting what he wanted—my body, my compliance—but there had to be more to it. No man handed over this kind of luxury without expecting something bigger in return. He could've just given me a cheap apartment, tossed a couple of bills my way, and still had the control he wanted. But this... this felt like more than an arrangement. It felt calculated.

Maybe he enjoyed making me feel indebted to him, keeping me on edge, wondering when the price would be paid. Or maybe he liked the idea of me depending on him for everything.

"What's the real reason?" I asked.

"For what?"

"For all of this."

His smile flipped my stomach. "What makes you think I need a reason beyond what I've already told you?"

"Because men like you don't do *anything* without a reason. You could've given me a lot less. Hell, you could've skipped renting an apartment."

He stepped closer, his hand brushing my waist. "I like taking care of what's mine."

Heat crept up my neck. He said that like he meant it, which was crazy, but here I stood in an expensive apartment that he'd paid for. He liked paying my bills?

I could work with that.

I could even come out *on top*. If he liked me enough, maybe the gravy train would last for a while. I'd pretend to be perfect, keep him hooked, and hide my glaring flaws. Staying with him was in my best interests, but it'd require a delicate balancing act. I *never* wanted another serious relationship again.

I plastered on a smile, letting my fingers trail his chest. "Well, I guess I'd better be a good girl."

Santino leaned in closer, his breath warm and teasing as it brushed my lips. He kissed me, and I swept my tongue across his lip. He tasted clean and sharp, like citrus. I cradled his face in my hands, pulling him closer to me, and he groaned. He seemed to like that, so I gripped the back of his neck and fisted his hair.

The kiss turned feral. Santino pushed me against the wall, hands on my waist. His growl vibrated into my fingers.

Santino broke the kiss, panting. "You're going to make me miss every appointment this week."

I smiled, tracing the sharp line of his jaw. "We could stop."

"Fuck that."

He crushed his mouth against mine. His hand slipped under my dress, palming my ass. Gathering my panties in his fist, he ripped them off. His eyes darkened when he felt how wet I was. His touch disappeared, and then he lifted me into his arms. He carried me into a dark room, tossing me onto a king-sized bed.

This arrangement would work out better than I thought. Everything was falling into place. With him, I could rebuild my life on my terms. I could handle him. If I played the part, I'd be the one in control. As long as he never noticed how much I drank.

SEVEN
SANTINO
TWO MONTHS LATER

I wished Delilah were here.

Spending time with Delilah was more fun than holding court in Afterlife. My bodyguard waved a line of peasants forward, and a man stepped in front of me, clutching a Red Sox baseball hat.

"Good evening, Mr. Costa."

I nodded. "Who are you?"

"Greg, sir. Greg Cafaro." His voice was so low, I leaned closer to hear him. "I appreciate the opportunity to meet you."

"What do you need?"

Greg swallowed. "To borrow some money. Six thousand. No, *eight*."

"Is it six or eight?"

He grimaced, shaking off something. "Eight."

"What's it for?"

"My restaurant's floor is wrecked. We had a fire next

door, and water flooded in from upstairs. Completely ruined the hardwood."

"So file a claim with your insurance."

"I did, but it's not enough. I'm dealing with damage from street gangs. Spray-painted doors. Smashed windows. The other week, they stole our point-of-sale systems. It's addin' up."

I sighed, well aware of the street gangs infesting Boston. The Animals. 12th Street Gang. Mayhem. Some of them sawed catalytic converters out of cars and sold them. Others broke into small businesses, stealing everything that wasn't nailed down.

"You should've paid us for protection."

He flushed. "I can't afford it."

"Then quit."

"I can't, Mr. Costa. The restaurant's been in my family for generations."

"How will you pay me back?"

"As soon as I'm open, I'll make what I owe you in a month. We've just been unlucky," he mumbled, rotating the cap in his hands. "It's been delay after delay. It took weeks for everything to dry, then supply chain issues. Now I'm burning cash just to keep my staff—"

"What's your restaurant?"

"Vito's."

Ah, the swanky steakhouse with *Godfather* vibes. Black leather booths. Jazz singers crooning into microphones. An exclusive dining room called The Cougar Room because it featured a real stuffed cougar. I'd been there a couple times. The food was all right.

"And you've been closed for how long?"

"Six months," he said, his voice catching fire again. "But we're one of the best restaurants in Boston. We'll get back on our feet. I still have my employees."

"Go to the bank. I'm your worst option."

"Can't, sir. They won't approve me for a loan because I've already taken a second mortgage on my house."

Idiot. "Risk-taker, huh?"

"I've gotta save the family business."

I smiled indulgently. Greg was the kind of desperate fool I thrived on. Normally, I'd set him up, but there was no way he'd make the money back, and I didn't feel like sending Kill's crew to mop up this guy. Lending him capital might as well be flushing it down the drain.

I *did* like the idea of owning his property. Its location on Newbury Street gave it an ideal mixture of high foot traffic, retail establishments, and homes. Perfect for a luxury residential development.

I pretended to think it over. "Here's what I'll do for you, Greg. I'll lend you the eight thousand, but it's going to be at two points a week. You've got three months. And I'll need collateral—your restaurant."

A spasm of panic crossed his face.

I shrugged, giving him a harmless smile. "If you can't pay, I take over the property. But if you can, you keep your legacy. That's the best I can offer, given the circumstances."

He bit his lip. "Okay."

"Do we have a deal?"

"Yes, Mr. Costa."

He shook my hand.

I gestured to my bodyguard. "Hook him up."

"Thank you so much, Mr. Costa. This is gonna change my life."

"I suggest you concentrate on making money."

I waved him off, watching him slink away. Same story, different face. People like Greg—and even Delilah—were my bread and butter. Their desperation kept me thriving.

The next guy mumbled about protection, but all I could see was Delilah. Her laughter, her smirk, how her eyes lit up when she got what she wanted.

A text buzzed on my phone.

> PRINCIPESSA
> Guess what came in the mail ;)

A photo of her in the lacy lingerie I bought two days ago popped under the message. Thought it'd look hot on her, and I was right, judging by the mouthwatering image she sent me.

She was bent over, the phone between her bare legs. Her head hung upside-down, and she wore a coquettish grin. The lingerie clung to her curves perfectly. A thin strip of fabric barely hid her pussy, and her free hand gripped her ass.

Damn.

Heat curled below my waist. I saved the photo to a private album and scrolled through the others, blood rushing to my cock. Only she could get me hard while men surrounded me.

> Wear it tonight. I'll pick you up at 8.

> **PRINCIPESSA**
> OK.
>
> Thank you. <3

I tightened my grip on the phone before shoving it back into my pocket and standing, signaling for my bodyguard to take over. The cool night air slapped me awake as I stepped out of Afterlife.

The day we'd met still blazed in my mind. Delilah was unforgettable. With the bold red lipstick and winged eyeliner, she was a walking advertisement for a gun moll.

Colpo di fulmine.

It meant getting struck—like a bolt of lightning. My Nonno used to talk about it, said it made him steal a capo's woman. He'd called it a curse, even though he spent the rest of his life with her. He'd laugh about how he didn't have a choice. The second he laid eyes on her, it was like a fire lit under his skin. Couldn't breathe. Couldn't think.

I always figured it was his clogged arteries.

I never thought it would hit *me*.

Then she walked into Afterlife.

Struck.

She was too perfect to ignore, and she needed me.

I had no love for the Romanovs, but something about her made me hesitate. A Russian princess begging her enemy for help.

As I climbed into my car, I fantasized about Delilah. Her smile, her body, the way she made me feel. I gripped the wheel, my knuckles white against the leather.

I couldn't afford to lose control.

Not with vengeance within my grasp.

EIGHT
DELILAH

Santino fucked me on the bed.

The sheets were a tangled mess on the floor, pillows were thrown about, and the room reeked of sex. My muscles ached as though I'd scaled a rugged mountain.

Rough hands repositioned my hips. Santino stuffed a pillow underneath me. The new angle pierced me so deeply that I curled my fingers tighter into the sheets. Each thrust pushed a moan past my lips. Gritting my teeth, I focused on the banging headboard and not the gorgeous, six-foot-two man claiming me over and over.

"Come for me."

His delicious whisper stroked my ear, and his finger landed on my clit. He teased it as he drove into me, coaxing more pleasure until I teetered on the brink. Waves of glowing heat joined the ecstasy from his thrusts, but I fought the urge to come. Every orgasm felt like surrendering a piece of myself I'd sworn to keep hidden. He owned enough of me. I wouldn't allow him to have this too.

But he was relentless.

"Give me what I want, Delilah."

The dark threat delivered the final spark, and I detonated. I let out a gasping cry and collapsed. Sweet relief rolled through my body.

Santino groaned. The hot release of his orgasm filled me up, joining the three other cum shots he'd left inside me. His thighs jerked as he gripped me tightly, pulling out only to collapse beside me, dragging me into his chest.

I sank into bliss. When he held me, too spent to move, I almost forgot who we were.

He nuzzled my neck, breathing hard. "You okay?"

I ran my fingers through his hair. "Tapped out."

All night, I'd been tossed around. Devoured. Santino fucked like a madman—his brow slicked with sweat, his sides heaving. I was his toy, and when he finished with me, I felt thoroughly used. Sucked, licked, pounded, my body marked with his teeth. In return, he paid me every week with envelopes stuffed with cash. He gifted me jewelry, trips to Nantucket—anything I wanted. I'd been funneling his money into a business account for months, planning for a brick-and-mortar vintage clothing store. Retro Rose Boutique.

He lingered tonight, which was rare. Usually, Santino was out the door as soon as he composed himself. With a quick fix of his appearance, he returned to the untouchable mafioso who ruled his world with an iron fist. But this morning, he stayed, his breathing syncing with mine, and the soft rise and fall of his chest touched my back. His presence cocooned me in an unnerving comfort.

Santino traced his fingers along my side. "You're quiet."

"I'm thinking."

"About?"

"How I ended up here."

Santino leaned in, kissing my shoulder. "Just be with me."

That was the problem. It was too much like being in Providence, trapped in a cycle of being owned by a man. I couldn't depend on Santino forever.

"What time is it?" he murmured.

I grabbed my phone from the bedside table. "Ten-thirty."

Santino cursed.

He uncoiled himself from me and slid off the bed. I'd seen him naked many times, yet still, a flame flickered between my legs at the sight.

I rolled out of bed and made my way to the bathroom, catching a glimpse of myself in the mirror. I was a mess. My hair was tangled, and his cum stuck to my thighs. I probably tasted like him, too. We'd partied hard last night. Santino knew I liked to drink, so he traded me sips of Dom Perignon for my lips wrapped around his cock. All evening, I'd gone back and forth between him and the bottle.

Santino took my hand and led me into the bathroom, turning on the shower. Once the water was hot enough, we both got in. He soaped up his hands and massaged me, then put shampoo in my hair, his fingers soothing on my scalp. My eyelids fluttered. He was so gentle. After washing the suds from my head, his lips touched my face, brief and sweet.

I tensed.

Maintaining boundaries was easier when Santino kept to the script—fuck me, pay me, leave. Anything more than that threatened the delicate balance I'd managed to maintain.

"Santino, we should talk."

He traced small circles on my hip and shifted, drawing me closer. "No talking. Isn't that what you said when we first started this? No talking, just feeling?"

A lump settled in my gut. "Yes."

"No talking, principessa. I want to enjoy you."

I held my breath, caught between leaning into his touch and pulling away. "I—"

He kissed the sensitive skin behind my ear. "Shh. It doesn't have to be complicated."

But it was. Everything about us was tangled in power dynamics. How could it not be? I came to Boston to escape one prison, only to trap myself in another wrapped in silk sheets and easy money. I couldn't allow myself to sink into this. Because whatever it was, it had strings attached that tugged at parts of me I'd closed off.

My throat tightened. "Are you trying to get me pregnant?"

He laughed, a deep, careless sound that echoed off the tiles as he rotated his head under the spray.

"*Answer me.*"

He sighed, shutting off the water. "Why are you asking that?"

I stared at him. "I told you, I'm not on birth control."

"I'm aware. Don't worry about it."

He sounded so confident as he stood there, swiping water out of his hair.

"Santino, I need you to take this seriously."

"We'll handle it if it happens."

His confidence didn't match the panic stabbing my chest. He handed me a towel, his movements brisk. He rubbed himself head to toe, then folded the towel and hung it on a drying rack.

My hair dripped on my shoulders as I followed him into the bedroom. He picked his clothes up and put himself together, piece by piece. Briefs. Slacks. Wrinkled white shirt. Italian leather shoes. Finally, he slapped a vintage watch on his wrist.

"Santino, you don't want a kid with me."

He paused slightly as he pulled on his jacket. "I'll see you later."

"Wait—"

He kissed my cheek. "I gotta go."

He was at the door when I asked, "What do you expect me to do if I'm pregnant?"

He grabbed the doorknob. "I guess you'd have to marry me."

He didn't even look back to see how his words landed. He stepped out, closing the door behind him like the gavel in a courtroom.

Marry him?

That hung in the air, mocking me. I glared at the wall, imagining him laughing as he got into his car. He didn't mean it. I was just the girl he fucked.

Before I escaped Dimitri, I knew I had to attach myself

to a powerful man. Santino seemed like the perfect choice—dangerous, extremely jealous, and rich.

I was his mistress. That role suited me fine.

But he'd gotten too comfortable. Forgetting to use condoms. Jokes about marriage. Sweet kisses in the shower. This couldn't continue. Our worlds didn't mix. They couldn't.

The knot in my stomach tightened. I had to draw a line and reclaim the control slipping away. The more I let him in, the more I risked losing myself. I couldn't let that happen.

Not again.

I needed space from a room that smelled like him. I combed and blow-dried my hair. Pulling on my heels, I seized the envelope he'd left on the console table. The hallway blurred as I headed outside. I locked my brownstone's door and descended the steps.

Sunshine bathed the streets in gold, highlighting the heat rising from the pavement. People rushed the sidewalk with their coffees, heads down, the world narrowing to the glow of their screens. A stroll to the Boston Common would do me good.

I took a deep breath, steadying my nerves.

A strong hand clamped down on my shoulder, the grip so tight it sent a jolt of fear through me. I spun around, my pulse quickening, and stared into the hollow eyes of a sallow-faced man in a worn jean jacket. One of Dimitri's men.

He found me.

NINE
DELILAH

Ice stabbed into my stomach.

Ivan was an alley cat, rough and lithe. Dark scars marked his weathered face, trophies from a life spent in back alleys and bar fights. Since I'd known him, he'd been a rotten bastard. I couldn't count how many times he'd watched Dimitri slap me around. If he was here, my ex wasn't far behind.

He could be watching me now.

Ivan's grip tightened, smirking. "Delilah, fancy meeting you here. You look tired. Santino ride you too hard?"

I flashed him a wintry smile. "What brings you out of the gutter today?"

He gestured to a car at the curb. "Let's talk in private."

"Let's not."

Sneering, he wheeled me toward the Mercedes. "Your fiancé is still looking for you. And unless you keep me happy, he'll find out where you've been hiding. So be a good little whore and come quietly."

Whore.

The word was a spark in the oil well of my self-loathing.

"Go fuck yourself, Ivan."

Ivan's hand shot out, and a blinding pain struck my cheek. I stumbled and fell. People around me either pretended not to notice or were too cowardly to intervene. *Story of my life.*

I picked myself off the street. Tiny rocks had embedded themselves in my palm. I brushed them off, wincing. Ivan grabbed me by the hair, leading me through a packed intersection and nudging me toward the parked car. A man got out and opened the door.

Shit.

I kicked and slapped, screaming, but he forced my head down. Then he shoved me, and I tumbled into the car. I launched myself to the passenger-side door and yanked on the handle—locked. I lunged at the driver, but the man in front pulled out a gun.

"Sit."

I threw myself back, breathing hard.

Fuck. This was fine. I'd dealt with worse.

Ivan slid into the seat next to me, slamming the door shut. He laughed, shaking his head, a chilling sound. "You're a tough bitch, I'll give you that."

The car moved.

"Let me out," I snarled.

He winked at me, and my heart pounded.

"Poor Dimitri," Ivan tsked. "He'll be so disappointed. He's been so sure you were kidnapped."

I scoffed. "Is that what he's telling everyone?"

Ivan leaned in, his breath reeking of cigarettes. "Oh yeah. He's playing the heartbroken fiancé, searching high and low for his abducted bride. Meanwhile, you've been spreading your legs for Santino and fuck knows who else."

I glared at him. "You don't know anything."

He chuckled. "We all saw the street camera footage of you *running* out of the church."

"How did Dimitri take it?"

He made a face. "He's lost his mind. He thinks you were taken against your will, but everybody's talking about how you left him at the altar. You're the girl that ghosted the Sovetnik of the Providence Bratva. Dimitri's a laughingstock."

"Good."

He grinned. "He's going to make your life a living hell when he catches you."

"What do you care?"

"I'm the only reason Dimitri hasn't found you yet. So if I were you, I'd be a little nicer to me."

"All you're doing is giving Santino more reasons to kick your ass."

"You're nothing more than a hole to warm his dick."

I cocked my head. "Want to test that theory?"

Ivan's smirk faltered. The car turned sharply, throwing me against the door. I bit back a cry and squared up against him.

"Stop the car. You should know better than to mess with Santino's property."

"Property," Ivan mused, tapping his fingers on his knee.

"That's what you are, huh? A possession. But possessions can be exchanged."

I swallowed hard, hating how true his words felt. "Santino would never trade me."

"You sure about that?"

No, not really.

I didn't trust men. At the moment, Santino liked me enough to keep me around. What happened when he discovered I wasn't the dream girl he'd constructed in his head?

I bit my lip.

"Look, all I want is information. You're close to Santino. I need details about his operations. Anything that's leverage over Dimitri."

I laughed bitterly. "Planning to take over?"

"He's on his way out."

"Santino will kill me if he even suspects me of betraying him."

"Not if you're smart about it. You give me what I need, and Dimitri stays in the dark about your location. We both win."

"And if I refuse?"

Ivan's grin widened. "Then you'll be on your own. And believe me, Dimitri's men are already circling. It's only a matter of time before they get you."

I leaned in, close enough that I could smell his sweat mixed with cheap cologne. The intimacy of the space made my skin prickle, but I forced myself to hold his gaze.

"I'm not snitching on Santino."

His face darkened, his hand twitching as if he wanted

to strike me again. "You have until the end of the week. Either you cooperate, or Dimitri gets a very interesting call."

The car stopped, and the doors unlocked.

I opened it and spilled onto the street as the Mercedes sped off.

I got home and poured a drink.

Fire slipped down my throat. I needed to kill Ivan. *Son of a bitch. Bastard. Gangster flunky.* I ripped open the fridge, staring at a Styrofoam box filled with leftovers. I grabbed it, barely tasting its contents, and then washed it down with vodka.

Growing up in Providence, I'd never been more than a pawn. Dad didn't see me as his child, just another asset. Mom died when I was little, and the woman he replaced her with treated me like a rival for my father's affection.

He always picked her. Love was a transaction, and I didn't have enough to buy it. My only friend was Luca, a boy I'd met when I was ten.

When I turned twenty-three, Dad handed me over to Dimitri, a monster who wore cruelty as easily as his Brioni suits. Running away wasn't just about escaping a bad marriage. Luca said it was more about breaking free from a life that never belonged to me. Boston was supposed to be different, but here I was, still haunted by the men who tried to own me.

The urge to obliterate myself yanked at my navel. I

wanted to smash all the glass in my apartment, but I had things to do.

I moved to the kitchen table, where a stack of sketches for Retro Rose Boutique awaited my attention. The boutique was my escape from my dad's violent world, and I wouldn't let anything derail my plans.

I pulled out my laptop and opened a message from my interior designer, Claudia. She'd sent mock-ups for the boutique's layout, each design more beautiful than the last. I clicked through them, making notes on what I liked and what needed tweaking. The vintage aesthetic I envisioned was coming to life.

The next email was from a potential supplier, confirming the availability of vintage pieces I'd been eyeing for months. A smile tugged at my lips as I replied. Every small victory in setting up the boutique felt like a step toward something normal.

As I worked, my thoughts drifted back to the encounter with Ivan. Adrenaline still throttled my veins. I wouldn't let fear dictate my actions. Retro Rose Boutique was my future.

I picked up my phone and texted Claudia.

> Just reviewed the designs. They look fantastic, but I have a few suggestions. Can we meet tomorrow to discuss them?

As we set up a meeting, I breathed easier. No matter what happened, I'd see this through. Hanging up, I started organizing the paperwork: invoices for merchandise, and contracts with suppliers. I ordered a grilled chicken salad for dinner and wolfed it down.

My phone buzzed.

I glanced at the screen.

SANTINO

How are you?

Answer me.

The phone's screen felt like the only light in a freefall into hell.

I'm good. <3

What about you, handsome?

SANTINO

Still out.

Ooh. Handling business or causing trouble?

SANTINO

Both. Keeps life interesting.

Life with you is never dull. Not sure if that's a good thing.

SANTINO

It's only a problem if you can't handle excitement.

Maybe I add a bit too much of that to your life…but you like it, don't you?

SANTINO

You're mine. I'll decide what's too much.

I smiled, warmth blooming inside me. Even through text, Santino's words dripped with a dark intensity that thrilled me. After that messy fight with Ivan today, part of me was here for this—*yes, claim me, protect me, kill for me.*

I had to tell him about Ivan.

I typed a message on my phone, my fingers trembling.

> When am I seeing you?

SANTINO
> Whenever you want.

> How about tonight?

His reply came a few seconds later.

SANTINO
> I'll send a car to your place.

TEN
DELILAH

Santino's driver brought me to an abandoned warehouse on the South Boston waterfront. Inside was a cacophony of primal roars and the sickening smack of gloves against skin. Blood, sweat, and the metallic tang of fear mingled in the air, a pungent cocktail that filled the arena. Men crowded the ring, cheering the bloodbath.

Santino's fighting ring was a powder keg of testosterone, but people kept a respectful distance. Everybody knew I belonged to Santino, and if they didn't, the guard standing by my chair reminded them.

I glanced at a tall man in a suit, one of Santino's soldiers. Vitale was a quiet guy who expressed as much emotion as bark on a tree.

"How are you doing, Vitale?"

"Good."

"Any plans this weekend?"

He shrugged. "You?"

"I guess that depends on your boss."

Vitale's attention returned to the crowd. "Santino will be here in a minute."

I sipped my drink, trying to settle my frazzled nerves.

As the frenzy in the crowd grew, my mind drifted to the clink of hangers moving across racks in my boutique.

A grizzled man in his forties bumped into my table. His cup jolted, sending beer sloshing over the rim and onto his shirt, darkening the fabric. He hardly noticed, his boozy gaze diving into my cleavage. He barked something, his words lost in the noise.

I leaned forward. "What?"

"I said, you look like you could use another!" He belched, adding, "Let me buy you a drink."

I could use a refill. Santino kept me on an annoying two-drink maximum for reasons he'd never spelled out, but I liked to indulge.

I smiled at the man. "That'd be nice, thank you."

He grinned back. "Comin' right up."

Vitale's bulk slid in front of me, blocking the man's view.

The drunk man scowled. "What do you want?"

Vitale's posture hardened. "No one talks to Santino's girl."

No one?

Well, that explained Vitale's curt response to my every question for the last month.

Drunk Guy seemed to take it personally. He bristled. "Why don't you let her decide for *herself*?"

When the man jabbed a finger in Vitale's chest, he

grabbed the finger and twisted with a sickening snap. The man screamed, clutching his broken finger.

The roar in the fighting ring pulsed. On stage, a man wearing blue gym shorts raised his gloved fist in the air, his face splattered with blood. The crowd went nuts. They banged on the ropes separating them from the ring. A scuffle broke out in the stands before men in suits handled it, pulling them apart.

A familiar citrus scent with a touch of sea salt swirled in my nose, and Santino stood beside me. His presence didn't just shift the air. It clenched like a lover's grasp around my throat. His hand slid over my shoulder, gripping it gently. The warmth from his touch settled my frayed nerves.

"He broke it!" bleated Drunk Guy, mistaking Santino for a concerned manager. "He's a fuckin' maniac. He should be locked up. All I did was ask to buy her a drink."

That echoed like a horrible punchline to a poor joke.

Santino glanced at me, glowering, and threads of heat coiled around me. Then he stepped forward, squaring up to Drunk Guy. Santino towered over him. It must've been a territorial thing because the men in my family acted the same, lots of dick-swinging and posturing. I would've rolled my eyes, but too many of Santino's cronies watched me. Undermining him in public wasn't a good look.

Drunk Guy's brow furrowed. "What's your problem?"

"You're hitting on my girl," he growled.

Those words should've suffocated me, but they wrapped around me gently like luxurious silk. Everybody knew me as

Santino's whore. His fuck buddy, his gun moll, whatever. We were *together*, but not in the ride-or-die sense. I was the girl he screwed. That's it. But Santino said it like it meant something.

I had to stop this. It was all my fault.

I hooked onto Santino's arm. "Baby, it's not a big deal."

Santino's eyes locked on mine. They widened slightly, dipped down my halter top dress to the peep toe shoes, up my legs and waist, lingering on my boobs. When his starving gaze crashed into mine, my knees wobbled.

"Santino, he's harmless."

The man snorted. "You think I'm some kinda joke? You're just a little slut who likes the attention. If you weren't such a *tease*, you wouldn't need a bodyguard."

Santino lobbed a punch into the man's gut, who doubled over and groaned. Then he motioned for his guards. They grabbed Drunk Guy, who panicked.

"I'm sorry—"

Santino ignored him. "Take him out back."

Men in suits hauled him away while Drunk Guy screamed. Nobody paid him any mind, but the crowd of onlookers shrank, probably scared they'd be next.

What did *take him out back* mean? Had he killed someone before for being a drunk idiot? I studied the grim line of his jaw, the nostrils that flared when he looked at me.

Two months ago, I walked into Afterlife, seeking the notorious loan shark. I'd done my homework on Santino Costa. Born and raised in Boston. One of six kids. Typical Italian-American family. An old man who owned a deli told me he used to work there as a teenager. He was a good worker but very quiet.

I'd sweet-talked the locals into spilling more details, which wasn't easy because nobody wanted to piss off the Costas. They were the type of people you didn't cross, and Santino gave off touch-me-and-die vibes. He was too intimidating for most women, and darkness clung to him like his fitted Tom Ford suits. The kind of darkness that swallowed everybody around him.

Santino took my hand.

We moved from the chaos into a lonely corridor with many rooms. His grip tightened as he tugged me into a dimly lit office, the heavy door groaning shut behind us. Grimy shelves and posters lined the walls, with a wooden desk in the middle of the room.

Santino turned to face me, eyes smoldering.

I put a hand on my hip. "Are you going to beat up every guy who thinks I'm attractive?"

His nostrils flared. "He called you a slut."

"Why can't you be the bigger man and let it go?" I clasped my fingers around his. "I'm yours. You know that."

He still looked pissed. "Did he touch you?"

"No."

"Are you being honest with me?"

I forced out a laugh. "You're just fishing for an excuse to kill him."

"I don't need one."

His low growl pitted my stomach with sparks. He was crazy. He made the man I'd fled seem reasonable. He was obsessed with me. Dangerously so.

I'd brought this on myself and willingly attached myself to him. This remorseless killer who looked me dead in the eye and discussed murdering a man for being rude to me. Was he doing that on purpose? Trying to warn me?

I swallowed the nerves in my throat. "You're not killing anybody. You're no good to me in jail."

"I'm not worried about jail."

Do I tell him about Ivan?

The man assaulted me in broad daylight, but somehow, involving Santino scared me even more. What choice did I have? If he found out I kept this from him, his feelings for me could flip off just as quickly as they'd turned on, and then he'd no longer look at me the way he did now. Like he'd slaughter a room full of men for me.

His fingers glided under my chin. "What's wrong?"

I bit my lip. "Nothing."

"You seem off."

"Speak for yourself. It's only eight, and you already have a murder under your belt."

He grunted. "I've had a long day."

I rubbed his chest. "Want me to make it better?"

His black eyes collided with mine, and he nodded. His hands were clenched at his sides, and I took one and brought it to my lips, kissing each scarred knuckle. Gradually, his body relaxed, and he opened his palm, allowing me to hold him.

Too many girls assumed men always wanted sex. Sometimes, they needed to be touched and worshipped. I slid a hand through his styled hair. He hated when I messed it up, but I loved how his thick locks slipped through my fingers.

His eyes fluttered shut under my gentle strokes. When they opened again, they were hazy, like a kitten drunk on milk. The aggression dissolved, leaving behind a man whose wild hair and softened features made him almost... tender. I rose on my toes, pressing a soft kiss to his lips.

His tongue flicked my mouth. I opened wider for him, my hand traveling down his abdomen. My fingers trailed the impressive shape tenting his slacks. Already hard. A growl ripped from his throat. Santino's arm roped my waist and dragged me closer, the movement so violent that my right foot stumbled out of a heel. He bent me backward over the desk, scattering papers onto the floor.

I breathed heavily as his hands gripped my waist. Their warmth sparked over my skin, and my heartbeat throttled. Santino stepped in between my legs. He was the devil I chose. The safer bet against the man hunting for me.

My short, pink halter dress shifted up my thighs. He pushed it even further, flipping it over my stomach. Cool air touched my pussy. I'd stopped wearing panties weeks ago. One by one, he took my ankles, his fingers rings of fire as he placed my feet on the desk, spreading me wide for him.

"I can't believe I let you walk around dressed like this."

A shiver ran up my leg. "I only do it because I know who's watching."

His expression hardened, and his hand paused. "Trying to drive every man in my establishment crazy? Or just me?"

"*Both.*"

"Tease," he murmured.

"What's the worst that could happen?"

"Maybe I'll kidnap you and keep you in my house. I could tie you to my bed, legs spread, every inch of you mine to savor whenever I want."

My face burned.

His filthy mouth always made me blush. Sometimes he teased me about that, calling me his sweet *principessa*. Other times, he didn't talk so much. He held me down and fucked me like an enraged beast.

"You're quiet," he said, stroking my clit. "Do you like that idea?"

Sparks erupted low on my belly. "It sounds like a good time."

He purred. "You're too trusting."

"I like dangerous men."

Santino's eyes narrowed. "You're going to get yourself into real trouble one of these days."

"Isn't that what you're for? To protect me?"

His hands disappeared from my pussy as he leaned over, his heavy weight compressing me into the desk. "Delilah, you don't want to be in debt to me forever."

"I don't?"

"No. I'm the trouble you can't escape."

"I'm not looking for an out." I unbuttoned his shirt, my fingers grazing his downy chest hair.

He pulled back. "Careful. I'll assume that's an invitation to take it all."

Anal was a boundary we hadn't crossed yet, and I knew he wanted it. He'd made that clear from the start. I'd never done it before, and offering him that final piece of myself felt like a gamble. I trusted him with my body, but what if he discarded me once he had taken everything?

A predatory grin tiptoed across his face.

I swallowed a lump as he stepped back, turning to face his desk. He grabbed something long and sharp from a drawer—a knife.

My blood froze. "You want to hurt me?"

"No. I want to hold it to your throat while I fuck you."

Good God.

A delicious shiver ran down my body. But then, unwanted memories surged forward—Dimitri's fingers tightening around my neck. My stomach twisted, fear clawing its way to the surface, and I struggled not to let it show.

I lifted my chin, smiling. "You paid for me already. There's no need for posturing."

He raised the knife, its edge catching the light. "This is about trust."

My pulse pounded. "Holding a knife to my throat will make me trust you?"

Santino took a step closer. "It'll make you realize just how deeply I own you."

I shrugged, my heart racing. "Do it then."

The hunger in his eyes grew more intense. "Are you sure?"

"Show me how much you own me."

"You can say no. You don't have to—"

I reached up, pulling him to me and cutting him off with a kiss. A bold move, but that was the rhythm we danced to. His shock melted into fervor, and his hands moved to my waist, gripping me as though I might free myself. A hand slid down, grabbing the back of my thigh while the other held the knife.

The flat of the blade tapped my leg, a cold promise. My thighs parted for him. He broke the kiss, a wicked grin curling his lips as he trailed his tongue over my lip, a tease that left me aching. He gave it a playful lick and tugged at the neckline of my dress, his eyes gleaming. The knife slipped under the strap, the edge grazing my collarbone. A dark thrill shot through me.

Slowly, he sliced through the strap. It snapped, and my dress fell, exposing my breasts. Cool air stung my nipples before his warmth chased it away. He kissed my curves, licking and nipping. The blade followed his scorching mouth.

He descended, each kiss inflaming my skin. When he reached the juncture of my thighs, he looked up.

"You're trembling."

"I'm a little nervous," I whispered. "But I still want you."

"Good. I'm going to make you feel everything."

His mouth covered my pussy. His tongue lashed my slit, and warmth bloomed inside me while electrical shocks jolted me. A hard edge pressed into my thigh as I arched against him, my hands tangling in his hair as I struggled to stay grounded.

I swallowed down a ball of nerves. My heart was a bird, its wings beating against my ribs. All my senses honed in on the knife as he scraped it from side to side, so light it tickled. His mouth made it feel so good, but all I saw was the blade.

I gasped, my body trembling. "Please, I need—"

"What do you need?"

"*You.*"

He made a pleased sound and returned to licking. Wet heat sank inside me, frantic, thrusting. Every hot swirl felt like a lightning strike. The knife charged every sensation, making the pleasure more intense.

It pressed harder, biting into my skin just enough to remind me of its presence. My eyes kept snapping to the mouthwatering view of Santino between my legs, his face buried in me. He suckled on my clit, and I whimpered.

He lifted his head, his attention rapt on my face. Pure greed lit up his face.

"*Santino.*"

He chuckled. "I'm not done with you yet."

With that, he plunged deeper, his mouth working me into a frenzy. I cried out, my body tightening as desire coiled within me like a tight spring.

My thighs tensed, and I shattered, the knife's cold kiss the only thing anchoring me to reality. I trembled with the force of my release and collapsed back, panting, swirls of color dancing in my unfocused vision.

Santino undid his belt, the metallic clink cutting through my heavy breaths. He dropped his slacks to free his hard and throbbing cock.

"Legs up," he ordered.

My calves slid over his thighs, opening for him as he

stroked his cock. He pulled apart my folds, exposing me to his hungry gaze.

Slowly, he entered me. I inhaled sharply as he filled me, inch by inch, until he seated himself with a deep groan. The knife returned to my neck.

"Who do you belong to?" he demanded as he moved inside me.

"You."

He thrust harder. "Who pays to fuck this pussy?"

"*You.*"

His eyes locked onto mine. "I own you. Say it."

"You—you own me."

"Damn right I do," he grunted.

He pounded me harder. The knife stayed at my throat, reminding me of his control over me. How one wrong move could make him fall out of lust with me.

"Say it again, principessa," he said, his voice thick with need.

My body arched into his. "You own me."

"Good fucking girl. You're mine. Always."

The flat of the knife pressed down on me, amplifying the pleasure coursing through my veins. Each thrust pushed me closer to the edge.

Santino's pace quickened, his breathing ragged as he chased his release. I could feel the coiled energy ready to snap. The intensity of his stare held me captive as he deepened his thrusts. He tensed, his hips jerked, and a hot wave jetted my insides.

As the last tremors subsided and he tossed the knife aside, he melted in my arms and stroked my face, whispering an apology as he kissed my forehead. I nodded, but we both knew he wasn't sorry.

We untangled ourselves, Santino handing me a fistful of tissues from a box on his desk. I was a mess. The broken dress strap kept falling down my shoulder, and I tied it off, Santino's gentle gaze unnerving me.

Santino grabbed something from the desk. A metallic ring that jangled as he nudged it toward me. My fingers curled around the cold metal of the keys, the weight of them pulling me down like an anchor.

"What's this?" I blurted.

He stuffed his hands in his pockets. "Keys to my place."

Keys. To his place.

This wasn't part of the plan. We had boundaries. This was business, not...whatever this was becoming. Was this another move to control me? Like the fact he was "not trying" to get me pregnant?

Panic clawed at my heart. "Why?"

"So you can come over whenever you want," he murmured, stroking my back. "I'd like that."

I cleared my throat. "What for?"

"We could hang out."

"We do that all the time."

"At restaurants, bars, and this place." He gestured around the room. "My house would be more private."

"We have my apartment."

He tucked a strand of hair behind my ear. "I want to wake up in my bed. With you beside me."

My chest tightened. "What's so special about that?"

"Being with you in my space. Where it's just us. No interruptions."

"This isn't what we agreed on," I said, my voice tight. "I'm not looking for anything more than what we have. This...this is a big change."

"What are you so afraid of?"

I gritted my teeth. "Nothing, but this sounds like dating."

He cocked his head. "So what if it is?"

"We don't date. I sleep with you for protection and money."

"I'm aware of that."

I fisted the metal ring. "So why are you giving me your keys like we're in a relationship or something?"

"Sometimes a man wants to fuck at home. Don't overthink it."

No, no, no.

I collected my cash, and we went our separate ways. That was the deal. Our sex was always distant. Impersonal. We fucked in stairwells, in his office, in his car. He came over, too, but I had control over how long he stayed.

I avoided challenging him. I gave him what he wanted. It's what made me so addictive. I was a wet dream come to life. Every time I sank to my knees, unzipped his pants, and eased his giant cock into my mouth, I knew that. I'd done everything he'd asked for without putting up a fight, but I couldn't give him this.

Keys meant something. Trust. Commitment. I couldn't handle that. Not after everything I'd been through. Not after what I'd learned about men and their promises. Every relationship I had with men ended with me being used or betrayed. Taking those keys felt like walking into a trap. Once I opened that door, there'd be no going back.

I plastered on a fake smile. "If you want me to come over, all you have to do is call."

"I want you to have keys."

I placed them on the desk, swallowing the lump in my throat. "I'd appreciate it if we kept to our current arrangement. Whatever this is, I'm not into it. I hope that's alright."

Judging by the way his eyes blazed, it was not.

I tutted, rolling his tie around my hand. I tugged, and he came forward. My lips touched his, and tension melted from his muscles. As my tongue glided into his mouth, I reached into his jacket pocket and took out his wallet. He grabbed my wrist and pulled away.

"Trying to bankrupt me?"

I shrugged. "A woman has needs."

He sighed, letting me go. "How much?"

I slipped out the entire wad of cash, tucking it into my purse. The brazenness of it didn't seem to faze Santino. It never did.

He lifted a brow. "That's five thousand dollars. What do you need that kind of money for?"

"Another Birkin bag?"

I needed every dollar to fund Retro Rose Boutique. I'd use it for the first month's rent and to purchase inventory I had my eye on. I stepped toward the door, but his hand shot out, wrapping my arm, and hauled me backward. As I collided with his body, his arm pinned me to his chest while his other hand snaked through my hair and made a fist, bending my head back.

"You'll take the keys and thank me for it."

That dark voice boded no argument.

"But—"

"I make the rules." The hand on my waist drifted too low. "You need a reminder on how to be a good girl. Should I bend you over my knee and spank your pussy?"

My knees turned into jelly. "No, I don't need you to do that."

"You sure?" he snarled. "I'd be more than happy to."

"I know the rules. I'm still not thanking you for what I didn't ask for."

He released his grip on me. "I don't hand my keys out to just anybody."

I straightened. "Give them to someone who cares, then."

"Maybe I fucking will."

I almost flinched. "It's simple. If you'd like me to come over, shoot me a text. Our arrangement is for sex. That's all it is—and all it'll ever be. I'm earning my money. Nothing more. Don't pity me. Don't go easy on me."

He skewered me with a glare. "Believe me, I'm not."

"Good," I shot back.

Santino growled something in Italian. He threw himself in the chair behind the desk and opened his phone. He looked up from it to scowl at me. *Such* a big ego.

He had no problem coming inside me, but if I got pregnant? I'd be on my own. Santino's joke about marrying me rubbed me raw. The keys weren't an offer to upgrade our relationship. They were to keep me close. He wanted me to fluff his pillow at night and suck his cock in the morning.

Men were liars. They promised things and didn't deliver. They cheated. Pretended to care, only to dump you the next day. They ghosted.

Santino spoiled me rotten, but he rarely texted unless it was to arrange a meeting. He wasn't evil like my ex, but he'd use me for as long as I allowed him. Just like everybody else had.

Love didn't exist. Love was for suckers like my stepmom, who'd pined after my cheating father—another man who'd let me down my whole life. He was the reason I accepted Dimitri's proposal and fled Providence to Boston to seek sanctuary, however twisted, in the arms of Santino.

I marched out the door.

Santino said nothing, letting me go with a purse filled with his cash.

ELEVEN
DELILAH

Vitale escorted me out. The air was thick with the promise of rain, and dark clouds rolled in over the city. The wind whipped my hair around my face, and I pulled my coat tighter against the sudden chill. As we stepped outside, the muffled sounds of the fighting ring faded behind us, replaced by the distant rumble of thunder.

The street was deserted, the usual crowd having dispersed now that the main event was over. I kept my head down, trying to process everything that had happened inside, when I walked past a figure slumped against the wall. My stomach dropped when I recognized the man who'd hit on me.

They'd beaten the shit out of him. Blood matted his hair, his eyes swollen shut. His clothes were torn, and his head lolled to the side. A pang twisted in my gut. This was my fault.

I started toward him, but Vitale's hand clamped down on my arm.

"Don't," he warned.

"He's hurt. I can't leave him like this."

Vitale's grip tightened. "Yes, you can."

I gestured at him. "Look at him. He can't even walk!"

"If you help him, you'll only make things worse for him and yourself."

"What do you mean?" I asked.

"You'll just get him killed. And if Santino sees you helping that guy, he'll take it as a betrayal. You can't afford that."

I pulled my arm free. "This is so messed up."

I hesitated, glancing at Drunk Guy. His breathing was shallow, and he looked like he was about to pass out. Another surge of guilt hit me. This was what Santino's world did to people. I'd signed up for this life to survive, but that meant looking the other way.

The door to the ring slammed open, and Santino stormed out. He stalked over, his jaw clenched as his gaze shifted to the man on the ground.

"What'd he do now?" he demanded.

"Nothing. I was trying to see if I could help."

Santino glanced at Vitale, who nodded. "So you think you can play the Good Samaritan?"

I swallowed hard, my throat dry. "He's hurt."

"He's not your problem, principessa."

"Santino, you're being a prick."

He stepped closer until he towered over me, waving Vitale aside. "Go. I'll drive her home."

Vitale turned around and disappeared inside the building.

My heart hammered. The wind picked up, and the first few drops of rain splattered on the pavement.

"He crossed a line," Santino said gently. "He disrespected you, and there are consequences for that. But you're not the one who has to deal with it."

Drunk Guy had collapsed on the ground. Santino followed my gaze, softening. He reached out, gently taking my hand. Rain pelted my head. Santino shrugged off his jacket and draped it over my shoulders. Warmth swirled in my stomach as his scent surrounded me. I felt hot and confused.

He nudged me toward his car.

I pulled the jacket off and handed it to Santino. The rain fell harder, soaking through my clothes, but I didn't care. "I'm not going with you."

"Why?"

"This isn't right. You can't just...do this to people."

His frown deepened. "That's how it works in my world."

"Well, not in mine. You don't get to decide who gets beaten based on some twisted sense of ownership."

"This is how things are."

My mind flashed to the keys he'd given me earlier, the way he'd assumed that I'd fall in line like it was my only option.

"I don't need you to protect me like this. You can't keep treating me like I'm some possession."

Santino's jaw tightened. "I don't see you as a possession. I see you as mine."

"Same difference."

Rain plastered hair to my face. Santino stood there, his shirt turning translucent from the downpour.

This was supposed to be simple. Money, protection, sex—nothing more. But the look in his eyes was anything but transactional. It was possessive, and that scared the hell out of me. He'd already taken control of my body. What would happen if I let him take my heart?

I gritted my teeth. "We agreed to mess around for a few months, not whatever this is becoming."

"And what's that?" he asked, stepping forward.

I stayed silent. I'd built walls for a reason. A nice transactional relationship. No messy emotions. No attachments. No promises that could be broken.

"Tell me. What. This. Is."

My startled gaze crashed into his. "Friends with benefits."

He laughed. "I'm not your *friend*."

"You're my boss."

"I'm not that, either, baby. Try again."

He approached me until I'd backed against the car.

"You're...a lover."

Santino's laugh was low, almost dangerous, as he leaned in closer, his body shielding me from the rain. "Is that what I am? Just some casual fling?"

"That's what it's supposed to be."

"But it's not."

I opened my mouth to protest, to deny it, but the words wouldn't come. I did feel it—the pull between us—even when I should've run the other way. He was right, and we both knew it. This was beyond sex. It had always been consuming. I couldn't want more. That was the deal I'd made with myself. Letting Santino in was more than I could handle. What if he destroyed me?

My hackles rose. "I don't know what's gotten into you lately, but you need to back the hell off."

His black stare stabbed into me.

All I could do was hold my own but judging by his complete lack of giving a fuck, there was no turning back. No escaping the darkness coiling around me.

Santino opened the car door. "Get in."

I stared at him, heart pounding.

"Now," he snapped.

TWELVE
DELILAH

When I got home, I stripped to my underwear and grabbed a robe out of the closet. Then I sat on the black-and-white checkered kitchen floor and drank black Sambuca.

I'd finished half the bottle and still couldn't get Santino out of my mind. His rough hands haunted every drunken thought, pulling at something reckless inside me.

The Shangri-Las spun on my vinyl record player, the same song on repeat. "I Can Never Go Home Anymore." That was the anthem of my life. I blasted it when my father pushed me into an engagement with Dimitri, and it echoed in my head the night I fled Providence.

I pulled my robe around me as I leaned against the cabinets. My thoughts centered on the keys—an offer that felt like a trap. As I swirled the dark liquid in my glass, the herbal scent mingled with the despair pitting my stomach. The keys lay on the table, cutting through the illusion that this was just business.

Why did he give me them?

My heartbeat throttled. He wanted a tighter grip on me. Maybe I should give in. More time with Santino meant more money, not having to pay for anything, and having my physical needs met. Not to mention being able to hang out at his awesome penthouse whenever I wanted. Having access to his stuff. But if I kept showing up at his place, he'd think we were more than a temporary arrangement. He already did.

I felt torn between running from him and longing to give in. I grabbed my phone and unlocked it, scrolling through the contacts list. I hovered over the name *Luca*. My heart pounded.

My thumb slipped, hitting the call button.

It dialed once, and he picked up.

Slowly, I held the phone to my ear. Nothing greeted me but the crackle of static. I licked my lips, trying not to exhale.

"You shouldn't be calling me."

My friend's smooth voice filtered from the speaker.

"I know."

Luca sighed. "Are you okay?"

"I'm alive. How are things on your end?"

"Everybody's looking for you. Dimitri has people searching as far as Seattle. Wherever you are, stay there."

"Staying put isn't an option," I mumbled, swirling my glass. "The man I'm with is crazy. He wants...well, I'm not sure what."

"You're with another guy? Who?"

I bit my lip. "Santino Costa."

"He's in Boston, right?"

"Yeah. How did you know that?"

Luca was silent for a moment. "What's he like?"

"He's nice...scary, sometimes, but he's got a soft spot for his mom. He likes mixed martial arts fighting. He loves taking me out and buying me stuff."

Luca made a noncommittal sound. "Have you met his family?"

"We don't have that kind of relationship. I'm his *comare*."

"Isn't that a girlfriend?"

"No, it means mistress."

"That makes no difference to him. If you're in his life, you're his. Period."

"I see."

"You need to be careful, Delilah. Santino Costa isn't someone to take lightly. Guys like him are in the business of power, not charity."

My blood froze. "I think he wants more. He gave me keys to his place."

"That's good."

"No! I'm freaking out, Luca. He's way more intense than I thought he'd be. You should've seen what he did to this random drunk guy who hit on me. He beat the piss out of him. It was crazy."

"That checks out."

"Also, he keeps not using protection. Why's he doing that?"

"Either he's a fucking idiot, or he's trying to trap you."

I swallowed hard. "What am I supposed to do?"

He laughed. "Don't fuck him without a condom."

Hearing Luca echo my fears made a huge boulder sink in my stomach. Santino dismissed my concerns when I brought them up, but Luca was right.

Santino knew what he was doing. I'd lost count of how many times we had unprotected sex. Every time he agreed to use protection, it felt like him humoring me. I'd never liked how hormonal birth control made me feel, but I needed to look at options and schedule an appointment. Between Santino and planning the boutique, I hadn't had the time.

"I'll figure this out," I whispered. "Thanks for talking to me."

"Watch your back, Delilah. Don't let your guard down for a second."

The line died.

I dropped the phone beside the bottle of Sambuca, the screen going dark. I couldn't deny the truth anymore. Santino was trying to trap me. I had to protect myself. This was my life. That meant untangling myself from him, no matter how much it'd hurt me.

THIRTEEN
SANTINO

My soldier blocked the only exit.

An unnecessary precaution since the man at my feet couldn't walk. Ivan writhed on the concrete floor, moaning, his jeans soaked with piss and blood. Crimson smeared the aluminum baseball bat that I'd cracked over his legs. His arms. His screaming echoed in the warehouse. So loud. I should've gagged him.

Ivan tried to prop himself up but slipped on his blood. Pleas spilled from his split lip. *Stop. Don't do this. I'm sorry.* He'd apologized a hundred times, crawled on his hands, begged.

I'd spent an hour making an example out of him, and my brain still felt like it was on fire. I kept seeing what he'd done to her.

I tossed the bat aside.

One of my soldiers picked it up.

Then I stalked to Ivan and grabbed his hair. I forced

him to his knees and pressed the barrel of the gun against his forehead, feeling his skin twitch under the metal.

I motioned toward Vitale, who handed me my phone. I flipped it open to the surveillance footage. "A civilian recorded you attacking my girlfriend. Right outside their business, two days ago."

Ivans trembled, and his eyes darted away.

Fucking coward. "You hit her, so I thought I'd return the favor."

"I meant no disrespect."

"You attacked my girlfriend."

"I'm sorry. I didn't know she was anything to you." Ivan's voice cracked, the stench of fear as pungent as the piss. "Everybody said she was your whore."

That word flashed through me like lightning.

I pistol whipped his face.

Blood burst over Ivan's eye socket as he rolled on his back. I kicked him, slamming my leather shoes into his ribcage. I seized his hair and put the gun back to his skull.

"I swear, all we did was talk!" he cried, tears mixing with blood. "Dimitri's been on our asses to find her. He told us to check Boston."

I already knew about her ex's frantic search. Hard to miss it, the way Dimitri clawed through the city's underbelly to locate the woman who'd slipped through his fingers.

I leaned in closer, whispering. "Well, now you know. And you're gonna send a message to Dimitri for me. If he even thinks about coming near her, I'll destroy his family.

His sisters. His brothers. Their husbands and wives. Every single one of you Russian pricks."

Ivan nodded frantically. "I will, I promise. Please, just let me go."

"Another question, and I'll set you free."

"Sure," he bleated. "Anything."

I smiled. "Does he know she's with me?"

Ivan's breathing hitched. "No."

Too bad. "You sure?"

"He doesn't know. I swear to Christ."

I lifted the gun, aiming at him.

Ivan sat up, wincing. "Hey—whoa, whoa, *whoa*. I'll do what you asked! W-what about the mess—"

I shot him in the chest.

One, two, three, four—the bangs didn't even make me flinch. I emptied the whole clip, and Ivan fell to the grimy floor with a gurgling sigh. Blood leaked around him. I stood over him, tempted to accompany my soldiers when they dumped his body in Providence. They dragged him over a plastic tarp.

I needed some air.

I walked outside, my head throbbing. Why the hell didn't she tell me a man assaulted her in broad daylight? He yanked her into his car. He could've killed her.

My throat tightened. I'd never let her out of my sight again.

A muscle car rolled into the parking lot. My brother's Dodge. Kill spilled out of the car and strolled toward me.

"Your *comare* is safe."

"You sure?

"Yeah. She's fine. Christian is watching her."

I nodded. "Good."

He frowned. "Sonny, why go through all this for a Romanov?"

"Because she's mine."

His mouth twitched, and a dimple flashed. "You own her? Or is it the other way around?"

"Fuck off."

Kill grinned, crossing his arms. "How much money have you given her?"

I glared at him. "None of your business."

He cocked his head. "Fifty grand?"

I wish.

"Huh," he murmured, his tone growing more amused. "More than fifty?"

"Eighty."

His chest shook with a low chuckle. "I'm impressed. You're usually the one doing the hustling."

"Shut up. I'm not some lovesick fool."

He held up his hands. "I'm just breaking your balls a little."

I couldn't blame him.

This woman bled me dry. My bank account could take it but not my pride. She spent cash like someone desperate to get rid of it. She was a gold digger through and through.

"I let her think she's hustling me. She's part of a bigger plan."

Kill leaned against his car, smirking. "Last I checked, you don't keep pawns in your bed."

I shrugged and turned away, staring out at the darkening sky. The lingering traces of sunset had slipped below the horizon. This fixation on Delilah was problematic. Dating led to feelings, and feelings led to love.

And love?

Well, it made people do stupid things.

My old man, a degenerate gambler and a drunk, hammered that lesson into me early. We grew up dirt poor because he couldn't keep his hands off the cards. He'd stagger home after losing everything at the track, reeking of booze and ready to pick a fight. I hated him. We all did except for Julia, the baby of the family, and Mom. She clung to him like a life raft, believing he'd change. He never did. Her loyalty brought us nothing but misery.

Love had chained her to a man who hurt her repeatedly. I swore I'd never fall into that trap. So I chased quick flings and one-night stands, girls who didn't mean a damn thing to me. Delilah was supposed to be a distraction.

Two months in, still hooked.

This girl was different. *Felt different*. Fucking her wasn't enough of a release. Around her, I acted like a drug addict, hitting my dealer for a fix. I needed more, but the closer I tried to get, the more she danced out of reach. It made me want her even more.

Delilah *only* wanted my money.

I was turning into the type of guy I preyed on. The sad, delusional men lining up at stripper bars, throwing cash to women who'd never reciprocate their feelings. I thought I was better than them. That it could never happen to me.

Bullshit.

Delilah had "borrowed" an obscene amount of money,

and I kept giving her more. I'd lost my damned mind. Nothing she did stopped me from imagining things I had no business imagining.

I had no clue where this obsession came from or why it had chosen Delilah Romanov, but it was real. Like a beast living under my skin, gnawing at my rib cage, inflaming my brain with jealousy. She had to be mine. It ate away at me and consumed my thoughts, every waking moment filled with her image, her voice, her taste.

I'd given her my keys. She'd handed them back like I'd offered her loose change. I'd thought we were beyond this transactional bullshit. She didn't want for anything. I'd given her more than enough to make sure she didn't have to worry. Maybe that was the problem. In her mind, this was still an arrangement. No strings attached.

I *needed* more.

I'd given her everything, and she'd taken it all. Money, protection, a lavish lifestyle. But the keys? Too much for her. Giving them back to me proved she wasn't ready.

Maybe she didn't want anything deeper.

No. I couldn't accept that.

Kill raised an eyebrow, still skeptical. "The closer you keep her, the more attention you draw. The Romanovs won't let her go."

"They'll never take her from me."

His gaze drifted to the door behind me. "And what about her ex? What if he finds her first?"

"He won't. I'm keeping tabs on him."

He'd come for her. Who wouldn't?

And when he did, I'd kill him.

FOURTEEN
DELILAH

Men.

Just when you needed them the most, they disappeared. I hadn't heard from Santino in days. I expected him to get bored eventually, but with Ivan accosting me in broad daylight, hinting that Dimitri was closing in, it was bad timing. I needed to be close to Santino when my ex found me.

And he *would* find me.

I still hadn't told Santino about Ivan, even though I should have. Santino had this way of making everything feel... manageable. He was turning into the one steady thing in all this chaos. But did that make him less of a threat? Maybe not to my body, but definitely to my heart.

Santino wasn't Dimitri. He didn't control me, didn't hit me, didn't treat me like garbage. He listened to me, and he made me feel safe. But what if that safety was just the bait?

The keys still messed with my head. He obviously wanted more. A stupid part of me didn't hate the idea. But guys like him never gave without expecting something back. The keys were just another way to own me. I couldn't let that happen again.

He acted like he didn't care about getting me knocked up. In what world was that normal? If I got pregnant, he'd take this obsession to another level. Thankfully, I'd taken a test, and it was negative. That didn't rule out a pregnancy completely, but I'd messaged my doctor and had her rush a delivery of birth control pills. Uncertainty gnawed at me. I paced the living room, back and forth past the packed boxes of inventory. My pride faltered, and I sat down on the sofa and texted him.

> When am I seeing you again?

His reply came a minute later.

> SANTINO
> You told me to back off.
> If you want to see me, ask.

I pursed my lips.

Great. He was probably still pissed about the other day. Maybe he was busy. After all, he ran half of Boston's underworld. Or maybe he was with someone else. That gnawed at me.

I forced myself to stand again, knees wobbling. I needed to think. I had to stay calm and figure out my next move. Taking a deep breath, I tried to steady the whirlwind of emotions inside me.

The phone rang.

I answered with a grin. "Hey, Santino."

"Santino?" my ex's voice growled from the speaker.

My fingers clenched around the phone. "How did you get this number?"

"Who the fuck is Santino?" Dimitri snarled.

"He's a good friend."

I couldn't hear anything, not even his breathing, but he was there. Seething. Connecting the dots. Silence used to be his favorite weapon. He'd come home sometimes, fists balled, his steel gaze sweeping over me. We'd pass a whole dinner in silence before I'd beg him to tell me what I did wrong.

Dimitri let out a low laugh. "You're baiting me."

"Nope. It's the truth."

"Where have you been, Delilah?"

I swallowed the bile in my throat. "I don't owe you the answer to that question."

"You stood me up at our wedding."

"Yeah, I guess you're right. That does merit an explanation." I blew out a breath. "How long did it take before you figured out I'd left?"

He laughed again. "I'll have to see if you're this funny in person."

My head throbbed. "Where are you?"

"Here."

"What does *here* mean?"

"I'm around. That's all you need to know." Dimitri's oily tone hinted at impatience, not rage. "It's good to hear your voice."

"I wish I could say the same."

He clicked his tongue. "That's not a nice thing to say to a fiancé you haven't seen in two months. You should be more grateful for me. There aren't many guys who'd put up with you."

"Poor thing," I mocked. "How many black eyes did *you* have to cover up with makeup?"

He paused on the other end of the line. I could picture him, jaw clenched, that one crazy vein in his neck pulsating. "You always had a sharp tongue. I'll have to remind you what happens when you use it."

"You'll never see me again."

"I wouldn't be so sure about that, *kotyonok*. Maybe I'm waiting outside your door right now. Or maybe I'm giving you a chance to come to your senses. To be the good girl I know you can be." An erotic tone entered his voice, flooding me with nausea. "Come to me now, and I'll go easy on you. I'll let you pick your punishment."

"Go to hell."

"Mhm. I'm at the Hilton in Back Bay in case you change your mind."

He's in Boston.

My spine went rigid. "Stay away from me."

He chuckled. "Still afraid of me, huh?"

The taunt jabbed at me. Our engagement had only lasted a few weeks, but he'd controlled me since the day my father introduced us. Months before we became official. My father hadn't warned me in the slightest about Dimitri. He'd tossed me to a wolf without a second's hesitation.

"I'm done with you, Dimitri."

"We both know you can't run forever."

"I'll die before I go back to you."

A long pause. Then he laughed. "You always were dramatic. You love the thrill of the chase. That's why you ran, to see if I'd follow."

My pulse quickened. "I ran because you're a monster."

"I might be, but I still own you—"

I ended the call, throwing the phone onto the bed like it burned my hand. He was too close. I could feel it. If I stayed, he'd find me.

I had to leave.

I grabbed a bag, my mind racing. In went my Fred Perry polos, skirts, and dresses that Dimitri complained were too low-cut. I carefully packed the most valuable vintage pieces and essential documents. Each item stowed away was a piece of the future I was determined to salvage. It killed me to leave behind my vinyl, but I couldn't fit everything in the bag.

Then I took a taxi to a hotel where Santino had a standing reservation. I raided the minibar as soon as I checked in. Santino would notice it on the bill, but I didn't care. I needed to steady myself. Once the headache throbbing in my temples disappeared, I dialed Santino.

He picked up on the second ring. "Hey."

His smoky voice rolled over my ears, calming me instantly.

"Where are you?"

"At an event right now," he said, the noise in the background dimming. "Boring work thing."

"Oh, I see."

Static crackled.

"What's wrong?" he asked.

I bit my lip. "Why does something have to be wrong?"

"I hear it in your voice."

My heart pounded as Dimitri's words replayed in my head. *Still afraid of me, huh?* The bastard was so smug. Like terrorizing women made him such a big man. I didn't want to run to Santino. I wanted to handle Dimitri myself.

And I knew exactly what to do.

Sighing, I carefully gathered my thoughts. "I don't like how we left things at the ring. I want to see you."

Santino paused. "I can be there in twenty minutes."

Relief hit me hard. Santino wasn't the type to leave me hanging. He'd show up, and just knowing that made my chest feel lighter.

"I'm at the hotel right now. I needed a change of scenery."

"I'll meet you there and bring you to the event."

"Where am I going?"

"A charity gala for the Boston Hope Initiative. It's at a museum on the wharf. Get dressed and meet me downstairs."

"Alright."

Santino didn't say anything for a while. "And if anybody's bothering you, tell me. I need to know."

It was easy to fall for Santino's gestures—the way he protected me, took care of me, made me feel wanted. It was intoxicating. But wasn't that how it always started? A few whispered promises, and suddenly, I was back in a cage.

How long until the man I relied on became another monster?

I wanted to trust Santino, but the more I believed it, the more that voice in my head insisted that I was setting myself up for heartbreak.

I twisted a strand of hair around my finger. "I'm fine."

He sighed. "See you soon."

Guilt nagged at me as I hung up.

But then I kept replaying the words of that smug asshole. Dimitri was so sure I'd run back to him. That I hadn't moved on with another man. I could've told him, but the ultimate revenge would be showing him.

I texted the number Dimitri called me from.

> I won't come to you, but I'm willing to meet.

UNKNOWN
> Where?

I forwarded the address for the museum.

I would survive. I would find a way to live my life free of Dimitri's shadow. No matter what it took, I'd never let him control me again.

FIFTEEN
DELILAH

I'd set the bait for Dimitri.

Hopefully, he'd fall into my trap.

I had too many monsters after me. Time to take them out—starting with my ex. It was risky, but it was the only way to confront the bastard. And I wanted to rub Santino in his face.

I stood next to him in the dimly lit museum. I'd dressed to kill: a crimson vintage dress from my private collection, fuck-me pumps, my hair swept up, and jewelry Santino had gifted to me sparkled on my ears and wrists. He hadn't let go of me since we entered the venue.

"You're going to give every old man who looks at you a stroke. Always finding ways to make my life harder, aren't you?"

The heat from his gaze warmed my skin. "Only because you make it so easy."

"Don't think I haven't noticed how much you enjoy dressing up in things I buy for you." His teasing voice dipped into something darker. "You love that I can't take my eyes off you."

Who wouldn't love that?

I shrugged. "Yeah. It's nice."

His hand tightened around my waist, pulling me closer.

My pulse quickened. Teasing was fun, but it was harder to hide the truth when he looked at me like this.

"You act like I'm some kind of trophy."

"You are." His hand loosened, his thumb tracing a slow circle on my back. "And I like the way you challenge me."

My heart stuttered. "Challenge you?"

"You don't give me what I want. You make me work for it."

I swallowed hard. "What can I say? I'm not an easy prize."

"Yeah, I figured that out quick."

"You're reading too much into this. You give me what I need, and I give you what you want. That's all it is."

Santino's grip tightened just enough for me to feel the heat of his frustration, but his voice was smooth as ever. "Look, I know you're with me for the money. It doesn't bother me. I'm not delusional about what this is, but I need more."

My throat tightened. God, I wanted to say yes. That I felt everything he did, but I couldn't. I'd been here before, trusting a man, thinking he'd be different. It always ended the same: disappointment.

"Santino, I've never been with anyone like I've been with you." My voice wavered, but I kept going. "This is closer than I've ever been to a relationship, and I admire you. The way you take control and protect me. I've never had anyone like that in my life."

His eyes flickered with something—hope?

A waiter approached us with a tray of drinks.

I took a glass of bubbling golden liquid. "Thank you."

The waiter smiled. "Of course. Hit me up if there's anything else I can do for you."

Santino glared at him until he'd strolled away. "Everyone's a bit too friendly tonight."

I leaned into him. "Don't be jealous."

"How can I be when you're wearing all my gifts?"

His hand sailed up to trace the necklace he'd given me on our third meeting. His lips brushed the juncture of my neck and shoulder, heat stirring in my uneasy heart. Each caress dragged me into a sea of feelings I wasn't ready to drown in. My eyes fluttered as another kiss touched my cheek. Warmth melted over my body as he held me. His hold tightened as we stood amidst the soft clinks of glasses and the low hum of conversation.

"You're distracted. Something you're not telling me?"

I forced a smile. "Just enjoying the evening."

"Delilah, I know when you're off. Talk to me."

"There's nothing to say."

He sighed. "Why are you hiding from me?"

"I'm not your possession, Santino. I don't owe you every piece of my mind."

He hooked a finger around the platinum chain on my neck. "Says the woman wearing everything I bought her."

"Gifts won't buy me. Only my obedience."

"They should at least earn me honesty."

I leaned back into his body. "Maybe I like keeping things mysterious."

"Is that what we're calling secrets?"

I turned within his embrace, facing him. "It keeps it exciting between us."

He studied my face for a moment, his touch lingering as he traced the diamond drop earrings. "Not when it feels like you're slipping through my fingers."

"I'm not going anywhere."

He snorted. "You freaked out when I gave you keys."

Could he tell how much he messed me up inside? When he used that possessive tone, a spark lit up all the crazy feelings I tried so hard to hide. How much longer could I pretend I only cared about money when every second with him pulled me deeper into something that terrified me?

I looked away. "I'm still escaping my ex. I'm not trading one master for another."

"Master, huh? Does that make you my slave?"

I slapped his chest. "Stop it."

"Hey, I'm just trying to understand the rules. Last I checked, slaves didn't negotiate terms."

"Don't mock me. You control everything around you."

"I control situations that require it."

I huffed. "Now I'm a situation? Are you going to fix me?"

He tugged on my waist. "I'm here to protect you. I won't apologize for keeping you close."

"Santino, I'm not the type you can keep."

Santino said nothing, staring at me with the calm determination I'd seen many times before his cock slammed inside me. His eyes sparkled like I'd given him a challenge.

"Prove it."

I frowned. "What?"

"Prove that I can't keep you."

I laughed. "How am I supposed to do that?"

"Door's right there. Leave."

I lifted my head. "Maybe I will."

Santino's voice dropped. "Go on, then."

"You think I won't?"

He smiled. "I think you're stalling."

Smug prick.

He knew damned well I couldn't leave. Not with my ex haunting my footsteps. I wanted to prove him wrong, but I couldn't. Not yet.

"This doesn't mean you've won," I growled.

He rubbed my back, grinning.

A bell toned to signal the start of the charity auction. Santino hooked my waist and led me from the noise into a smaller area with catered food. He approached a group sitting at a table.

A small boy with dark, wavy hair slipped off his chair, and a petite woman in a spangled dress and loose, blonde curls dragged him back. The boy ripped free of her grip, crashing into Santino's legs.

Santino helped him up, adjusting his little tie. "Where are you running off to, huh?"

The boy's eyes widened.

Santino's lip curled. "What, no *hello* for your favorite uncle?"

The boy looked at Santino like he was a god. "Hi."

Santino crouched beside his nephew. "When are you going to visit me?"

The boy shrugged. "When will you buy me another present?"

The blonde woman nearby flushed a deep red. "Oh, Jack. You did not just say that."

Santino chuckled. "My apologies, boss. Didn't realize I was behind on your payment schedule. How about I bring you something nice next week?"

"A big present!" Jack burst.

Santino rumpled his hair. Then he dug into his pocket and fished out a wrapped piece of chocolate. "Here you go, kid."

Jack tore into the candy and shoved it into his mouth. "Who is that?"

Santino claimed my waist again. "My girlfriend."

I shot him a look, irritated, but I couldn't say anything in front of the kid. Jack gawked at me, eating his chocolate.

"Your *girlfriend*?"

Santino kissed my head. "Yup. Isn't she beautiful?"

The boy nodded.

The blonde woman hovering nearby approached us, her expression a mix of curiosity and politeness. She gave me a warm, welcoming smile, though there was a slight edge to it. Turning to me with a smile, Santino straightened. "Delilah, meet my sister-in-law, Violet."

Violet shook my hand. "So you're the one keeping this man smilin'. It's lovely to meet you."

"It's nice to meet you, too."

Santino watched our exchange, his arm casually draped over my shoulder.

Violet's eyes flicked to Santino. "So, looks like you found yourself someone to keep you in line, huh?"

Santino looked down at me, smirking. "I don't know about that."

Violet's laugh was light, her tone tinged with sharpness. "I remember when Achille used to be all tough. Took him a while to admit he needed me. Seems like you're still workin' on that part."

His jaw tightened. "Delilah's got me rethinking a few of my rules."

Violet's eyes twinkled. "Delilah, you must be quite the charmer to have him all twisted up like this."

I enjoyed the subtle tug-of-war between Violet's playful jabs and Santino's attempt to maintain control. Despite her bubbly demeanor, Violet wasn't one to let Santino get too comfortable.

A flush crept up my neck. His fingers brushed my arm, stirring the turmoil inside me. Was I more to him, or was this another ploy to trap me? The affection, the closeness felt genuine, but how could it be real when every moment was paid for? The thought gnawed at me.

Kill approached our group, his posture relaxed yet imposing. Violet leaned into him with a sigh.

"Good to see you out of the ring. Sonny doesn't bring around just anyone."

"We're not—"

Santino squeezed my side. "We've been seeing each other for a while. I kept it on the down low. You know how

Mom gets. As soon as I tell her I have a girlfriend, she'll be planning the wedding."

My face flushed.

What the hell was he doing?

Kill smirked. "You might as well give her what she wants, bro."

The playful banter wrapped around me like chains. How could he introduce me as a girlfriend to his family? Every touch was accounted for in his ledger.

"If you two ever make it official, we have the best chapel in Tennessee." Violet beamed, nudging Kill. "Ain't that right, baby?"

He kissed Violet's forehead.

A pang struck me. I excused myself, murmuring about needing a moment. Santino's hand lingered on my back, his touch burning through the fabric of my dress. The way he touched me, how he included me in his family—it felt too real.

I headed toward the restrooms. The less crowded space was a relief, but it did little to calm me. Santino kept pushing my boundaries. He came inside me like getting me pregnant was his job. Then he'd given me *keys*.

Now *this*?

I'd come so far from the scared girl Dimitri had controlled, but Santino was making me question everything. Why was it so hard to keep my guard up around him? Nothing between us was real. Was it?

My hands gripped the edge of the sink, the cool porcelain grounding me. I could hear the faint murmur of the gala outside—laughter and music that felt worlds away.

I left the bathroom and escaped to the bar, ordering a double shot of vodka on the rocks. I drained it, and my pulse steadied. I could *not* let Santino into my head. This was a man whose brother killed people for a living. A man from the same world I'd run from. A world that forced women to marry monsters and bear their children.

Never again.

Santino was just a means to an end—Dimitri's end.

I set the glass down as the crowd parted slightly at the venue's entrance, framing a man in a suit with an unruly wave of black hair who just walked in. A cold knot formed in my stomach.

Dimitri.

SIXTEEN
DELILAH

Dimitri spotted me almost immediately.

His eyes narrowed as he took in my figure-hugging red dress. Dimitri wasn't a fan of me showing off skin, so for this event, I chose a halter dress with a plunging neckline. A final fuck-you to the man who'd been a controlling bastard.

The day we announced our engagement, he marched into my bedroom and went through every article of clothing. He hated anything that showed cleavage, didn't like the color blue on me, and claimed that crossbody purses made my breasts too prominent. Scarves, long sleeves, and muted colors became my wardrobe. Most of my vintage clothes went into clear bins shoved in my closet.

I put up with it for a while. I was always told I wasn't worth a damn, so why not give up everything for my only shot at marriage? Nobody else would ever love me. Maybe it'd make my father proud. He'd treat me like I existed, and I wouldn't feel like a worthless human being.

Dimitri was probably the worst partner Dad could've picked for me. Any self-esteem I had before, and I didn't have much, was ground into rubble. Dimitri screamed at me for looking at men. Talking to men. Simply meeting their gaze was off-limits. I couldn't talk to Luca anymore, even though he'd only been a friend, and Dimitri made me quit my gym. The last straw was him canceling an appointment behind my back because he objected to a male doctor touching me.

When I snuck into Afterlife, it was the first time in months I'd let myself wear whatever I wanted. It felt incredible, like I'd been stuffed in corsets and could finally breathe. Reclaiming myself didn't happen overnight. Asking Santino for help had felt like jumping from one fire into another. But he was different from Dimitri. Despite his reputation, Santino treated me with respect. Dimitri controlled everything about me—how I dressed, who I talked to, what I did. Santino gave me space.

I felt safe around him. He never ordered me to dress down, and he gifted me things that suited my style, nothing that changed me. It felt like he was celebrating me, unlike Dimitri, who treated me like a decorative piece to complement his image.

Dimitri had been unable to resist the bait. He glowered as he weaved through the crowd.

I lifted my chin as he approached.

Dimitri sat down next to me at the bar, leering. "So this is how you taunt me? Dressing up like a *shlyukha* and asking me to meet you in public?"

The bartender glanced at us, wiping a glass.

I smiled at him and turned to Dimitri. "I dress for myself now."

He sneered. "You look desperate."

"Funny you mention that because I've seen the men you've been sending after me. Seems like you're the one who can't let go."

He slung his arm over my chair, baring his teeth. "Don't flatter yourself. You're a loose end that needs *tying up*."

"I feel the same way about you."

Dimitri's gaze stabbed into me. His fingers traced my neck, an icy touch that made my skin crawl. "You're still mine. No one will want you once they know the real you. That's why you ran, isn't it? Because there's no escape."

"I left you to be with someone else." Pausing, I let the suspense build, relishing in the tightening of Dimitri's jaw. "His name is Santino Costa. You might have heard of him?"

His grip on his glass tightened, the knuckles turning white. "You whored yourself out to the Italians?"

"He bought this dress I'm in, the earrings, the necklace. Pretty much everything I'm wearing."

"You're baiting me," said Dimitri in a ragged voice.

"Nope. Just being honest."

He rubbed his flushing face, clenching and unclenching his hands.

"I did what I had to do to survive." I drank the rest of my cocktail, savoring his rage. "No regrets."

"You think you're smart, running to Costa? He's just another cage. You'll see. Once he's bored, he'll hand you over, broken and used. And I'll be waiting."

I tensed. "If I were you, I'd forget I existed, turn

around, and walk out that door. Before he sees you talking to me and rips out your throat."

He laughed. "I've had enough of your bullshit."

Dimitri gripped my arm and hauled me off the stool.

I grabbed the empty glass, smashing it on his head.

The crowd gasped as Dimitri staggered, clutching his bleeding forehead. He looked up at me, fury and humiliation screwing up his features.

A dark figure stepped in, blocking his path. Relief washed over me as Santino's hand shot out and gripped Dimitri by the neck. Dimitri lunged at Santino. Santino dodged, Dimitri's knuckles grazing his cheek, then buried his fist into Dimitri's gut, driving air from his lungs with a satisfying grunt.

My heart pounded as Dimitri came at Santino with a wild right hook. Santino caught his wrist midair, twisting it, but not before Dimitri's other hand clutched Santino's shirt. They crashed into a table, sending glasses flying, before Santino slammed Dimitri against the counter. Bottles rattled as Dimitri struggled to regain his footing. Santino punched Dimitri's jaw.

Dimitri roared in pain, head-butting Santino. Shaking it off, Santino seized Dimitri's collar. Dimitri tripped over a chair, and they both went down. Straddling Dimitri, Santino hammered his face, cheek, and nose. Crimson spurted from Dimitri's lip.

Santino got to his feet, towering over him. "Get up. We're not done."

Dimitri spat blood, pushing himself up with a grimace. "She's mine. I'll bury you both before I let her go."

Santino laughed. "You think you can keep her, you pathetic piece of shit? You couldn't even keep a grip on your balls."

The crowd around us buzzed with a mix of shock and morbid curiosity. People whispered to each other, their eyes glued to the scene. Some seemed uncomfortable, while others smirked.

Santino's taunt had struck a nerve. Dimitri flushed a deep, angry red. It was a public dismantling of his ego, and everyone in the room could see it. The way Santino treated him like a joke only added fuel to the fire.

Dimitri's fists clenched, his breathing ragged. "You stole her from me."

"Poor baby," Santino taunted, grinning.

"I'll kill you—"

Santino kicked Dimitri's leg out, sending him crashing to the floor. Dimitri struggled to rise, but Santino pinned him down with a leather shoe on his chest. "You belong here. Stay there before I decide to really fuck up your night."

A surge of satisfaction welled up inside me as Dimitri lost his shit, screaming a tirade of Russian insults. This was going much better than I'd imagined. Santino kicked Dimitri's ribs until he shut up. Then Santino's men appeared out of nowhere, dragging Dimitri's limp body away.

Santino turned to me. "Did he hit you?"

I shook my head, reaching up to smooth his lapels and straighten his tie. Santino scooped my trembling hand in his and brought it to his lips. His knuckles were red and looked like they hurt.

Santino didn't let it show. *Of course.* The men I grew up with would rather die than utter the smallest whimper. My heart ached as his swollen fingers linked with mine. He walked me toward the exit.

"I'm sorry, Santino."

Santino texted someone on his phone. "For?"

My throat tightened. "It's my fault you got into a fight."

"Nah. That was gonna happen no matter what."

"No. You don't understand. He called and threatened me. He said he was in town." I fidgeted under Santino's intense glare. "I know. I should've told you."

He put the phone away. "And you shouldn't have talked to him alone."

"I had to stand up for myself. I needed to prove to Dimitri I wasn't the same girl he tried to control. And a stupid, selfish part of me wanted him to see us together. I'm sorry. You deserve better than that."

Streetlights cast shadows across his face.

"We'll talk about this later." A car pulled up to the curb, and Santino opened the door for me. "Vitale will take you home."

I stepped in.

Santino closed the door behind me and leaned in through the open window. "I want you to stay at my place."

I caught his hand before he pulled away. "Are you mad at me?"

He tensed, confirming my suspicions. "I have something to deal with, but I'll see you soon."

"Are you in trouble because of me?" I whispered.

He slipped out of my grip. "Don't worry about it."

He tapped the roof and backed away. As the car drove off, I watched him through the rear window, a heavy feeling settling in my stomach.

What had I done?

Santino had fought for me, and I'd lied and set him up. I stared at my reflection in the window, the city lights blurring past. I couldn't shake the image of Santino's raw knuckles. He'd defended me, but at what cost? I fidgeted with my phone, desperate to make sure he was okay. But what could I say? Sorry I dragged you into my mess? The words felt hollow.

The knot in my throat tightened.

The car stopped in front of Santino's building, and I stepped out, my legs shaky. I rode the elevator to his apartment and used the key he'd given me. Once inside, I locked the door and leaned against it, closing my eyes.

SEVENTEEN
SANTINO

I gagged Dimitri and tied him up. I'd soaked a cloth in gasoline before stuffing it in his mouth. Then we transported him to a secure spot.

Dimitri kneeled in the dirt beside a small red tank. His eyes widened as he watched me flip the lighter through my fingers. Burning him alive seemed like a fitting end for a Romanov thug.

After what they did, it'd make us square.

"Don't do it, Sonny," Romeo warned.

Romeo elbowed through the angry mob to stand beside me. He hadn't played the big brother role in a long time. But he was doing a good impression of it. Hands on his hips. Stern voice, his narrowed gaze full of disapproval.

"What do you think you're doing?"

"Taking care of a problem."

He glanced at Dimitri. "You'll start a war with the Russians."

"They're savages, Rome. They deserve worse."

He hardened. "And what'll the boss say when he finds out you made this decision without clearing it with him first?"

I glared at him. "He doesn't give a shit about protocol when it comes to the Romanovs."

Romeo's jaw tightened. "Torching him without Vinn's approval is a death wish."

I didn't want to hear this. "He's a loose end."

"Killing him will bring more heat on us. We need to do this right."

"What's your plan then?"

"We take him to Vinn," Romeo said firmly. "Let him decide Dimitri's fate. He'll still die, just in a way that doesn't make us look like impulsive idiots."

The flame flickered in my hand, and I stared at it, rage simmering beneath the surface.

I snapped the lighter shut, signaling to the men to grab Dimitri. "Let's go."

Once, when I was little, I took the long way home from school to walk past my cousin's place. Vinn used to work outside on vintage cars and always had a pretty girl dangling on his arm. He was the height of cool. He never lost his temper.

Until a couple of guys in leather cuts stopped me and tried to get me to sell cigarettes for them. I ran the rest of the way to Vinn's, and he ushered me into his garage. As soon as I told him about the men, he grabbed a baseball bat and climbed into his car. He told me to get in, and we drove the streets until I spotted them. He stopped, got out with the bat, and beat the shit out of them. He left them on the sidewalk, moaning, and hopped back into the driver's seat. Then he bought me ice cream.

He became my hero that day. He taught me that when someone crossed you, you didn't just settle the score—you sent a message.

And now, years later, standing in front of him again, I saw the same cold determination that made him untouchable.

"We're gonna use this as an opportunity." Vinn stood from his stoop on the porch.

I exchanged a glance with Romeo. "For what?"

"I'll set up a meeting. Sonny, you'll be there. Dimitri, too. We'll let him go and make 'em think we made a mistake, that we want *peace*." Vinn's stony gaze drilled into me. "But it's just to draw out Mikhail. If he believes we're bending, Mikhail will stick out his neck. Maybe far enough for me to chop it off."

My fingers twitched. "And Dimitri?"

Vinn waved me off. "After I've dealt with Mikhail, do whatever you want with Dimitri."

My stomach hardened. I had no love for Delilah's father, but killing her dad might not score me any points with her.

"Not a fucking word of this goes beyond this circle until everything's lined up." Vinn's hostile glare drifted to me. "This is about avenging what happened fourteen years ago."

I nodded, but a lead weight sank in my gut.

Vinn's hand shot out and grabbed my jacket, dragging me close. Close enough to glimpse details I didn't usually notice—the slightly red eyes and the purplish shadow growing underneath them. I saw the flames dancing in Vinn's black pupils, crawling up the house, destroying, *smothering—*

"What they did to Luca has to be repaid with blood." Vinn loosened his grip, his stare drilling into me. "You get what I'm saying?"

"Yes."

He released me, nodding. "Then get to work."

EIGHTEEN
DELILAH

My stomach twisted as I stared at the phone's screen, my heart pounding. Santino had been so calm when he left, but his silence hadn't been reassuring. It had screamed disappointment. With every passing second, I was spiraling.

I sent him a message.

> When are you coming back?

His reply came a minute later.

SANTINO
> Meeting ran late. What's going on?

I stared at the message, trembling. What was I supposed to say? Guilt gnawed at me.

> Nothing.

Santino had every right to be pissed. I'd put him in danger by not telling him sooner. I'd let Dimitri corner me, and Santino had to clean up the mess I'd made.

> **SANTINO**
> I'll be there soon.

I stared at his response, panicking. He was mad. I knew it. I tossed the phone onto the couch. I'd spent the last few hours since the fight with Dimitri at Santino's bachelor pad, a swanky spot in the middle of downtown. As soon as I stepped through the door, I headed straight for his liquor cabinet. I grabbed the bottle of vodka from the table. My hand shook as I poured another glass, the clear liquid splashing the sides. I raised it to my lips and took a burning gulp.

> **SANTINO**
> Are you taking care of yourself?
>
> I might be indulging just a little.
>
> **SANTINO**
> Drinking?
>
> Toasting survival.

I could imagine him rubbing the bridge of his nose.

> **SANTINO**
> I don't like you drinking alone.
>
> Come keep me company then.

I smirked, the edges of my vision slightly blurred.

SANTINO
We need to talk.

I set the phone aside, the last message floating through the ether like a leaf on the wind. As the room spun around me, I drank more. *We need to talk.* Everybody knew what that meant.

I swallowed the last mouthful of alcohol, my eyes burning. A slideshow of our *relationship* swept through my head in vibrant pictures. Our first dinner together. That date a few weeks ago, when we grabbed brunch at Paramount and went shopping on Charles Street on Beacon Hill. He'd dropped several grand on dresses for me. His teasing, soft voice when he called me *principessa*. Vodka couldn't drown out the warmth of those memories.

My lip quivered and my hands shook.

I stumbled into his bedroom and stripped, slipping into one of his long-sleeved shirts. He always insisted I wear his clothes. His way of marking me as his, even when he wasn't there to do it himself. Then I rolled up the sleeves and finger-combed my hair. The mirror reflected a vision of calculated beauty as I dabbed makeup on my cheeks. I had to look like I didn't give a fuck, but I knew when he walked through the door, he'd see right through it. Just like when he sent me a single white rose with a note that said, *You can't hide from me.*

I *didn't* care. We weren't supposed to stay together anyway. If he wanted to leave, *fine*, but not before I rubbed it in that he'd never have me again.

The latch on the door turned, and my heart dropped.

I dashed out of his bedroom and waited for him in the kitchen. His shoes clipped the flawless floor as he stepped in, his dark eyes narrowing as he saw me. I was the picture of nonchalance as I leaned over the porcelain kitchen island in his shirt, a glass in my hand.

"What are you doing?" he growled.

I swirled the liquid in my glass with a flick of my wrist. "Wanna join me?"

His fingers brushed mine as he gently removed the glass from my hand and set it on the island with a decisive clink. His gaze landed on the empty vodka bottle I'd forgotten to hide. He didn't even try to conceal his disappointment, his gaze scanning my face as though searching for me beneath the flush of alcohol.

"Principessa," he chided. "The whole bottle?"

A pang twinged through me.

"How often do you drink like this?" he asked.

I shrugged. "I like to indulge. So what?"

He frowned. "An entire bottle though? You should be in the hospital."

"I'm Russian. Drinking is in my blood."

He raised an eyebrow. "Yeah? Maybe we should test that theory with something stronger."

"Like moonshine?"

"Paint thinner."

I hitched a grin. "Only if you join me."

Santino leaned against the kitchen counter, no longer smiling. "How long has this been going on?"

I'd been drinking since I was twelve. It started small, sneaking out of school with friends and raiding

Dad's liquor cabinet, huddling with Luca outside family events, passing the bottle back and forth, and daytime drinking at bars. Pool halls. Slamming back shots.

"Principessa?"

The warmth I saw in his eyes scared me more than the need clawing at my brain. I reached for the glass, but he grabbed my wrist. He dragged me to the sink and seized a cup from the drying rack. Then he filled it with water and shoved it in my hands.

"Drink."

I sighed. "I'm not thirsty."

"Do it, or I'll pour it down your throat."

I huffed. Then I gulped down a mouthful. And another. When I'd finished, he refilled it. I pushed his hand aside, but my aim was a little off, and I ended up swatting the air.

Santino's frown deepened.

I waved him off. "I don't need a babysitter. I'm fine."

He gripped my shoulders. "You've had a bottle of vodka. In two hours."

"My body can handle it."

The room spun, and his hands were the only thing grounding me. I tried to shrug him off, but he held fast.

"I just need some air."

"Delilah, have you ever been to rehab?"

Been there. Done that.

Everybody thought rehab was a magical solution. That you emerged from it transformed. Fixed. Healed. It didn't. It was the first step in a very long journey. Every time I went, it made me feel used up, tired, and sick. Maybe I couldn't pull off sober living.

My cheeks flushed. "I won't go to rehab."

"I won't let you destroy yourself."

"And what if I want to be destroyed?"

"That's not funny."

"It wasn't meant to be," I shot back.

I looked at him, my insides splintering. Santino couldn't understand what I'd been through. My asshole ex was right. Santino lusted after the image I'd spent months perfecting, not the mess in front of him. He'd probably lost all attraction to me. He was disgusted.

He had already decided to break up with me. He just hadn't said it yet. Maybe he wanted his dick sucked one more time, or he was searching for words that wouldn't shatter me. Because even though he broke a dozen laws daily, he'd always been kind to me.

Do not fucking cry. Just rip off the Band-Aid.

"I think we should break up," I blurted, my throat tightening. "This relationship has run its course."

Santino looked like I'd tossed a match into a barrel of gasoline. "You don't get to decide that."

"But we were never going to work."

"You're not getting rid of me that easily, principessa. I'm not some fling you can throw away."

That sank in, mingling with the alcohol in my veins. Part of me wanted to dissolve into him. To feel the safety I'd been craving.

He leaned in, his expression filled with a yearning that swelled inside me. His lips pressed against mine, and his erection dug into my hip. He gripped my waist, pulling me closer as if he could fuse us together.

The nerves in my body ignited. I had to free myself from his grip around my heart, but every fierce stroke of his mouth let me taste the passion beneath the dominance. His tongue coaxed me to give in. My hands glided to his chest, fingers curling into his shirt as I kissed him back.

He pulled away. "Don't ever mention breaking up again."

"But I'm not what you want," I stammered, my lips tingling. "You want a living doll you get to fuck, but I'm... I'm a mess. I'm not the fantasy you have in your head."

"Good. I want the real thing."

My heart hammered. "You say that now."

"You think I don't know what it's like to struggle?"

"*I'm toxic*. I'll ruin you."

He smirked. "You're giving yourself too much credit. I've seen ruin. You're not it. Besides, you owe me."

My insides twisted. "For what?"

"All the cash you borrowed," he said smoothly.

"*Borrowed?*"

"Yeah. What, you thought that was *free*? After you took enough for a down payment on a house?"

He laughed, and panic threaded through my dread. I fought the urge to show him the boutique's website and prove I wasn't wasting his money.

I gritted my teeth. "Those were gifts."

"Cash gifts are for wives and serious girlfriends. You've made it clear you want to be neither." He shrugged, his mouth twitching. "If you don't want to be more to me, I'll have to treat you like you're not."

"But I wasn't *aware* they were loans," I choked out.

"Delilah, I'm a loan shark."

Irritation clawed at my skin. "You never mentioned there were any strings other than sex attached to the money."

"I have every dollar accounted for in my ledger. You've been at two points. That's two percent of the principal. It adds up fast."

I bristled. "So how much do I owe?"

"You're just shy of a hundred grand."

I glared at him, hands on my hips. "There was never an asterisk next to the jewelry you gave me, so why would there be one on the money?"

"There's always an asterisk, baby. You chose not to see it."

I took a step back. "You can't just spring this on me!"

He shrugged. "I warned you. You didn't listen."

"The hell you did! I don't remember *that* conversation."

"I did, at the fighting ring. I told you to have a plan. You said, and I quote, 'I'm not looking for an escape.'"

"I was flirting with you!"

His lip twitched. "Everything has a price."

My stomach knotted. "I thought we were...I thought..."

Santino's black eyes bored into mine. "You have to pay your dues, principessa. That's how this world works."

"I can't believe I trusted you."

"Me neither," he drawled. "But you did, and there's no going back."

I'd been naive to think the thousands I lifted from Santino's wallet were gifts. The carefree spending, the luxurious lifestyle—it all had a price tag.

I shook my head. "I've been so stupid."

"You're not. You just didn't understand the rules."

I looked up at him, my vision blurring. "Are you blackmailing me into being your girlfriend?"

"I'm reminding you of the terms. If you want to keep pretending this is just a fling, I can make it feel that way. But we both know it isn't."

I wanted to push him away, but watching him beat the crap out of Dimitri knocked something loose inside me. What if he'd gotten hurt? The balled-up tissues on Santino's coffee table proved that he meant something to me, and that scared me.

"I never asked for this. I just wanted to be safe."

He shrugged. "I never asked for this either. But here we are."

My heart fluttered and tears stung my eyes, but I fought them back. I didn't trust men. I couldn't afford to, but Santino wasn't like Dimitri. He'd never hurt me. Not the way I'd been hurt before.

"Delilah, you can twist yourself into a pretzel about how you'll pay me back. Or you can be honest with me."

"What are you talking about?"

He didn't flinch. "I want more."

"What does that even mean? I don't understand what you want—"

"Tell me something real, not something to stroke my ego."

I scoffed. "Like what?"

"What makes you feel safe? How can I give that to you?"

I blinked, stunned by the softness in his voice. "I want to be free! Don't you get that? You think you're different, but you're not. You're just like all the other men who want to own me, use me, and throw me away when they're done!"

His jaw clenched. He just stood there, watching me unravel.

"You're trying to trap me! You keep me close, give me things, and then hold it over my head when it suits you. But I'm not like the women you're used to. I'm not someone you can control."

Santino's face darkened. "You think I don't know that?"

I stared at him. "Why are you demanding this from me?"

"You're the only thing in my life that I can't buy with money. I'm trying to figure this out, just like you are."

"I thought this was just business for you."

"It started that way, but it stopped being that the second I realized I actually gave a damn about you."

My heart pounded. "But you don't—how could you even—?"

"You're the first person who's ever made me feel like this. I don't know what the hell this is between us, but it's real. And you're trying to run from it."

"I'm not running!" I screamed, my throat raw. "You're asking for things I can't give. You want me to open up, to believe that you're different from every other man who's ever used me, and I can't do it! I *can't* trust you like that!"

"I don't want to use you. I want you to feel like you belong with me."

I shook my head. "You want to get me pregnant. Just admit it. You don't have feelings for me. This is just another form of control."

"No, baby. I understand my feelings. You're the one who doesn't understand what this could be."

My heart pounded, torn between the deep fear that he was lying and the desperate hope that maybe he wasn't.

His expression softened. "Delilah, I'm not perfect. I'll probably screw up. But the difference between me and the others is that I'm not going anywhere."

I give up.

The fight drained out of me as I sank onto a chair. I had no energy to push him away. Santino grabbed my hand, the sight of his raw knuckles twisting something inside me.

"I want us to go away somewhere."

I glanced at him. "Like on a trip?"

"Yeah, for a few weeks."

I couldn't leave. The shop was just coming together.

My breathing hitched. "Where?"

Santino only kissed my forehead. "Pack your bags."

NINETEEN

DELILAH

Santino hauled our luggage up the steps of a private jet. I followed, gripping the railing as we disappeared from the humid, damp tarmac and entered a luxury airplane.

The flight attendant smiled. "Welcome, Ms. Romanov. What would you like to drink?"

A vodka on the rocks with lime, please.

I caught Santino's eye and cleared my throat. "A Coke. Thanks."

Santino grabbed a window seat and buckled himself in. "I'll have the same." The flight attendant whisked away as I slid into the seat beside him, still fuming. The plush leather seemed to mock me, a reminder of the luxurious trap I'd stepped into.

"You still haven't told me where we're going."

"Where's your sense of adventure?" he quipped.

"I've had enough of that, thanks. Are you planning on giving me a hint, or do I have to guess?"

He leaned in his seat, looking annoyingly relaxed. "You'll find out soon. Sit back and enjoy the ride."

The flight attendant returned with our drinks, and I sipped my Coke. "At least tell me why we had to leave in such a hurry."

His expression darkened. "Things are heating up, and I don't want you getting caught in the crossfire."

The plane taxied down the runway.

My throat tightened. "What happened?"

"Don't worry about it."

"Santino, you can't keep me in the dark forever."

"Neither can you," he said coolly, sipping his drink. "Confronting Dimitri at the gala was dangerous. You could've gotten yourself killed because you're too proud to ask me for help."

"I'm used to handling things on my own. I've been taking care of myself for a long time."

He raised a brow. "You're a Pakhan's daughter."

"You think that meant I had everything I ever wanted? I had nothing. Dad was too busy with his job, and my stepmom was checked out." I looked out the window, watching the clouds roll by. "I started drinking when I was twelve. There was always vodka lying around. My father's men would bring in cases of expensive liquor, and nobody noticed when a few bottles went missing. I'd drink to numb the loneliness. No one ever stopped me.

"By fourteen, I was sneaking out to parties, doing whatever I could to feel something. Boys liked the idea of being with the Pakhan's daughter, but none of them saw me. I was just a conquest. I'd come home drunk, and Dad wouldn't even notice. Or maybe he did, and he didn't care. I was invisible."

The flight attendant came by to check on us, but Santino waved her off.

I swallowed hard, the pain of those years still fresh. "I tried to find solace in school, but even there, I was an outsider. The other kids knew who I was. They either wanted to befriend me for protection or avoid me out of fear. I was always alone."

His thumb traced circles on my hand. "What changed?"

I sighed. "When I turned sixteen, I realized I couldn't keep going like that. I had to do something to get out. So I started saving money, hiding it away, but the drinking didn't stop. It got worse. It was the only way I coped. Things were really bad when I turned eighteen. I was out of control. My father finally noticed, but not because he was concerned about me. No, he was worried about his reputation."

Santino listened intently, his eyes never leaving mine. I continued, my voice trembling. "When I was twenty, I went to a party. I don't remember what happened, but I caused a scene. The police were called, and it made the local news. Dad was furious. Not because I was hurting myself but because I embarrassed him. A Pakhan's daughter was making headlines for all the wrong reasons."

I paused, the pain still fresh. "He forced me into rehab. Said it was to heal me, but it was to save face. He needed me out of sight until the scandal blew over. I spent months in that place, more alone than ever.

"When they released me, I did everything I could to stay clean. I was pretty good for a few years. And then my father arranged for me to marry Dimitri. 'A strategic alliance to strengthen ties between the families.' I barely knew Dimitri, but I accepted it. I needed to prove I could be a good daughter."

Santino's eyes darkened. "What did he do to you?"

I looked away. "He was controlling. He wanted to mold me into his idea of the perfect wife. I felt trapped. I began drinking again. I hid it at first, but it became harder to keep it a secret. I got so drunk I passed out at a family dinner. Dimitri was livid. He dragged me out in front of everyone, calling me every name you can think of, and sent me back to rehab, but it didn't work. I was too far gone by then. I knew I couldn't marry Dimitri. That's when I made a plan to visit you."

A muscle twitched in Santino's jaw. "You should have told me all this sooner."

"It's not like we talk when we're together."

"We'll fix that."

"And if I tell you everything, you'll still want me?"

He smirked. "I guess you could say I have a type. Girls who need saving and then try to hustle me out of eighty-five grand."

"Well, you're doing a terrible job if you let me rob you blind."

Santino's smile faded. "Delilah, I'm not some fool you can manipulate."

"I know you're not," I whispered, swallowing hard. "I've never seen you like that."

"What do you see in me?"

Raw, male beauty. Fierce loyalty. Strength. Unexpected kindness. Like how he'd adjust the blankets around me and kiss my forehead.

"Someone who's strong. You're loyal to the people you care about, even when it costs you. You... you look out for your family...for me. You've shown me kindness in ways I wasn't expecting. You're not the monster I thought you were when we first met, and that scares me."

I see a man I'm falling for.

The way he looked at me made it hard to breathe. It was as if he'd heard that thought, loud and clear.

He clasped my face in his hands. Then he kissed me, his lips crushing mine. I softened like butter, pouring all my longing into the kiss. He gripped my waist, pulling me closer, deepening the kiss until I was breathless. The smooth glide of his tongue made warmth bloom on my chest. I melted into the seat.

We broke apart. He leaned over, pulling a blanket from the side compartment and draping it across our laps. Then he tugged me over until I leaned against him.

Slowly, I allowed myself to relax into his embrace. As the cabin lights dimmed, Santino reached for the remote and picked a film. A romantic comedy played on the small screen. With his arm around me, holding me close, I started to feel things. Warmth. I teased my fingers across his thigh, and he inhaled a tight breath.

I nipped at his earlobe.

His body tensed. Then he caught my hand and brought it to his lips.

"I just want this. You, me, and a movie."

I blinked at him. "Really?"

He shrugged. "It's nice to be with you."

Santino's hand found mine under the blanket and threaded our fingers together. I closed my eyes, savoring the sensation.

The movie ended too soon. As the credits rolled, Santino stretched and gave me a mischievous smile.

"Not bad."

"I never thought I'd see the day when Santino Costa would snuggle under a blanket, watching a romcom with me."

"That's where you're wrong. I've always had a soft spot for happy endings, but I like the ones we make more."

"Believe me, I know." I leaned in closer, our noses nearly touching. "I guess I can stick around for a few more."

His full mouth molded to mine like silk. A slow burn spread all over my body. I pressed my lips against his, my nerves buzzing with need. It felt so right. My heart exploded with yearning. I couldn't stop myself from wanting this.

He groaned, pulling away from me. There was a moment where he looked like he'd kiss me again, but he steeled himself and faced the screen. A dark flush claimed his cheeks.

Maybe I could trust him. With him, things could be different. I wouldn't end up broken. I dropped my head against his shoulder, his breathing lulling me to sleep, and I didn't want to be anywhere else.

TWENTY
DELILAH

The warmth of the Italian sun embraced me as I stepped out of the car. We'd landed an hour ago in Florence. The only time I'd been abroad was a brief trip to St. Petersburg when I was a toddler. Our drive was quiet, filled with the lush, rolling hills and sprawling vineyards of Tuscany.

The villa was gorgeous with its ivy-covered walls and terracotta roof. The housekeeper, a middle-aged woman with kind eyes and a warm smile, greeted us outside.

"Welcome, Miss Delilah, Mr. Costa," she said, her accent thick and melodious. "We have everything prepared for you."

The interior was just as breathtaking. High ceilings with exposed wooden beams, large windows flooding the rooms with sunlight, and a mix of antique and modern furnishings gave it a timeless charm.

Santino watched me as though eager for my approval. "This was my grandmother's home."

"Beautiful." I gaped at the rows of grapes in the backyard. "I'm going to get sober in a vineyard?"

"We don't make wine. We sell the grapes."

"I see."

He squeezed my hand. "Don't worry, principessa. You won't find a drop of alcohol anywhere on this property."

"Okay, but you still haven't told me why we're here."

"There's too much drama in Boston right now."

"You're being cryptic. What are we running from?"

He paused, his gaze sweeping over the vineyard before settling on me. "I did something against my boss's orders. He's not happy with me. We had to leave before things got complicated."

"What did you do?"

"Don't worry about it."

"I hate being kept in the dark."

He smiled. "It's not something you need to concern yourself with. I'm handling it."

"But I'm involved, aren't I? I left everything behind. I have to know what's happening."

"And you will. I promise. But I need you to focus on your health."

I tried to shake off the nagging feeling that his secrets were more dangerous than the truths he shared, but I wanted to believe in the man who'd swept me away to Italy.

He transferred his grip to my hand. "There's somebody I want you to meet in town. He's a doctor. He's going to help you."

The sterile smell of antiseptic clung to the air as I sat on the edge of the examination table. The room was cold, and the paper sheet beneath me crinkled with every movement. Santino stood beside me, his arms crossed over his chest, watching me with an intensity that sent shivers down my spine.

"Relax," he ordered.

"Easy for you to say," I muttered, fiddling with the hem of my sweater. "You're not the one being poked and prodded."

"It's for your own good. I want you healthy."

The door opened, and Dr. Moretti entered, clipboard in hand. He greeted us with a polite nod.

"Delilah," he began, glancing at the notes. "I've reviewed your bloodwork and some of the preliminary tests."

My stomach twisted. "And?"

Dr. Moretti looked at me, then at Santino, before settling his gaze back on me. "Your liver enzymes are elevated, which is typical for someone who's been drinking heavily. There's no immediate damage, but it's a warning sign. Your body's under a lot of stress, and we must address this before it becomes a serious issue."

The doctor's expression darkened. "Detoxing can be dangerous. We need to manage it to avoid withdrawal symptoms. We'll gradually reduce your intake over the next few days. It's safer than stopping abruptly, which can cause seizures."

A shiver ran through me at the thought.

"We'll monitor you closely," he assured me. "I'll prescribe medications to help."

Santino's hand found mine, his grip warm.

"Hydration will be key. Drink plenty of water, and avoid caffeine and sugar, which can make the withdrawal worse. Eat balanced meals. Your body will need the nutrients to recover."

I nodded. I'd gone through this before. "And what about... when I feel like I need a drink?"

The doctor's gaze was sympathetic. "That's a normal part of recovery. When cravings hit, find something to distract yourself. Go for a walk, call someone, engage in an activity that keeps your mind off it."

Santino squeezed my hand. "I'll help you through this."

Dr. Moretti gave him an approving nod. "Support is crucial."

I'd never had someone like Santino in my corner. Maybe I could get through it without falling apart.

Dr. Moretti smiled gently. "You're taking the first step towards a healthier life. It's not easy, but it's worth it. If you have any questions, don't hesitate to reach out."

After a few more instructions and a prescription for medication, Dr. Moretti left the room, leaving Santino and me alone.

I looked down, my fingers twisting in my lap. "I've tried to quit before. It never sticks."

He reached out, lifting my chin so I met his gaze. His eyes were a storm of emotion. "This time will be different."

"What makes you so sure?"

His thumb brushed over my lower lip, sending a thrill through me. "Because you have me."

My heart pounded. "But why do you care so much?"

"I need you healthy. Not just for you. For us."

"Us?"

"Yes. I've got plans for us, and they don't include you drowning in a bottle."

"A future together?" I asked.

He smiled. "One step at a time. First, you need to take care of yourself."

My breathing hitched, imagining the future he envisioned. One filled with stability, commitment, and...a baby. My pulse raced. I'd never let anyone get close enough to want that with me, but Santino was different. He made me feel things I didn't know I was capable of feeling.

I swallowed hard. "I don't know if I can."

His grip on my waist tightened. "You're stronger than you think."

I leaned into him, his steady heartbeat lulling me into peace. Santino held me tight as if he could shield me from the world. Maybe he could. Maybe everything would be okay.

But deep down, I knew the truth.

Nothing about us was safe.

TWENTY-ONE

DELILAH

The first few days of detox were hell. Dr. Moretti and his nurse, Maria, made frequent house calls. They were both kind and professional, but there was no escaping the torture of withdrawal. Nausea, sweating, shaking...my body rebelled against the absence of alcohol with a ferocity that exhausted me.

Santino never left my side. He was there through every agonizing moment, holding my hand, helping me shower, whispering words of encouragement as he wiped vomit from my chin, and reminding me why I was doing this.

Each night, as the sun set over the vineyards and the pain clawed at my insides, Santino carried me onto the balcony. He'd hold me close, his words weaving a tapestry of hope that felt too good to be true.

"Imagine a life where the hardest part of your day is choosing which vineyard to stroll through."

He painted a vivid picture of a dream so beautiful,

making it seem within reach—stability, safety, and maybe love. I clung to it through the tremors and tears.

After the fourth day, cravings gnawed at me with jagged teeth. I'd catch myself staring at the phone, considering calling a local bar or, worse, trying to find a hidden stash Santino had overlooked.

But I never did. Because Santino was there. He'd notice the slight tremor in my hands and be there with a distraction—a book, a game, a walk among the grapes, or simply his presence. Other than kissing, we didn't do anything sexual. He wanted me to focus on healing.

By the end of the first week, the worst of the withdrawal had passed. My body, though still weak, found a new equilibrium. The cravings lurked in the background, but I felt like myself again.

"I'm proud of you," Santino said as we sat on the terrace, the Tuscan sun bathing us in its golden warmth. "You did it."

I glanced at him. "I couldn't have done it without you."

"You could have, but I'm glad I helped."

"You kept me going. You believed in me when I didn't."

I was falling for him.

The realization crept up on me slowly, like sunlight spreading over my face. I couldn't deny it anymore. I didn't want to. Somewhere between the chaos of Boston and the quiet of this Tuscan countryside, he'd gotten under my skin, and I couldn't shake him.

I'd started to lean on him, not just as a savior from my old life but as a pillar in my new one. It was terrifying. The more I depended on him, the scarier losing this became.

"You've been patient with me, and it's been so nice here. Thank you for doing this."

He brushed hair from my face, making my heart ache. "We're in this together. For better or worse."

"I—what do you mean by that?"

Santino slid his hand across my back. "You belong to me, and that's never changing."

Never? "That's quite the leap of faith."

"It's more than that, principessa. It's a fact."

I chuckled, my cheeks flushing. "Okay. Take it easy."

He smiled. "You still don't get it."

My face flushed. "Get what?"

"There's nothing I won't do to own you completely."

The warning in his tone set me on edge. He'd tamped down on his possessiveness in the weeks we'd been in Italy, but now that I'd recovered, the monster was out to play.

"You're the only man in my life, Santino."

"That's not what I'm talking about."

My body stiffened as he splayed a hand on my knee, the contact burning through my summer dress. Santino's smile stayed light, but darkness rumbled through his words.

"Have you taken a pregnancy test yet?"

The question hung in the air like a thundercloud. I stared at Santino, my mind reeling.

"Um, not in a while."

Santino dropped a thin package onto the armrest of the lounge chaise, his expression heavy. "Take it."

"Now?"

"Yes."

I swallowed hard. "Why?"

"Because if you're not, we need to keep trying."

I blinked at him, shock rippling through me. "Trying to improve my Italian?"

Santino's lips twitched, but his gaze remained firm. "We can't go home until you're pregnant."

I shook my head. Fear, confusion, and an inexplicable flicker of hope tangled together, leaving me breathless. "What the hell are you talking about?"

He smiled as I gaped at him. "The threat in Boston isn't going anywhere, but if you're pregnant, you'll be safe. I'll have leverage to negotiate something with my boss."

"What does your boss have to do with it?"

"My boss wants you dead."

My throat tightened. "What did I do to him?"

"Nothing. Vinn wants retribution for an old feud."

"What feud?"

"It's a long story. Happened years ago." Santino stared at the vineyards, his posture rigid. "He wanted me to lure your father to a meeting, kill him, and then kill you. I couldn't let anything happen to you, so I brought you to Italy."

I sank back into the chair. "You took me to Italy...to get me pregnant?"

"To protect you," he corrected. "My boss won't come after you if we're having a baby."

"That's your *solution*?"

"It's the only way to keep you safe."

I glanced down at the pregnancy test on the armrest. "So all those nights you've been coming inside me without a condom. Was this your plan all along?"

"I did what I had to do, Delilah. If you're pregnant, Vinn can't touch you. You'll be the mother of my child, and that gives you protection."

A dark suspicion entered my head.

For weeks, I hadn't taken my birth control pills. The moment we landed in Italy, I looked for them to take my next dose. I swore I'd packed them, but they weren't in my zipped clutch or my makeup bag. I'd brought it up to Santino, but he patted my hand and told me to focus on getting better. We didn't have sex during my recovery, so it slipped from my mind.

Did he throw them out?

It was as though the ground had slipped beneath my feet. The world tilted, and I couldn't breathe.

My heart pounded. "So...so all of this, bringing me here, helping me through detox. It was all to keep me alive long enough to *knock me up?*"

Santino smiled. "You can't get pregnant if your drinking is out of control."

"You're fucking crazy."

I tried to push myself up, to get away from him, but my legs wobbled. Santino caught me, his arm around my waist, and helped me stand.

His grip on me tightened. Then he slowly picked up the pregnancy test from the armrest, as though giving me a chance to react. But I couldn't. I was frozen, torn between reality and the impossible hope that this wasn't real.

"Let's go inside," he said, rubbing my back. "You need to take this."

I opened my mouth to protest, but nothing came out. I

let him guide me back in, his hand warm against my back as he led me toward the bedroom.

When we reached the bedroom, Santino paused at the door. Softness lingered in his predatory gaze, making this whole situation even more surreal.

"You came inside me our first night together."

He smirked. "I just liked the idea of defiling a Romanov bride."

"So you wanted to humiliate me."

"It was never about hurting you, principessa. I thought I'd play with you for a while, and then...I don't know. Maybe I caught feelings right away. I'm not sure."

That wrapped around me like velvet shackles. The warmth of his hands soothed the chill settling in my heart. All the alcohol I drank in the past must've damaged my brain. Why else wasn't I fighting him tooth and nail?

He pushed me inside the room.

Like a helpless child, I let him guide me. A lump lodged in my throat at the sight of the bed. A deranged excitement zipped through my limbs as he looped an arm around my waist. I gripped his wrist, intending to fling it off me.

"*Stop*," I whimpered.

"Delilah, you knew coming to me was a risk."

"You were supposed to have your fun and move on!"

"So you can drink yourself into an early grave? I don't think so, principessa. You are too valuable to throw your life away." He closed the door to the bedroom.

"Bringing a child into our mess isn't the answer."

"It's the only way to keep you safe."

"Why didn't you tell me?" I asked, my voice trembling. "Why wait until now?"

"You had to focus on getting clean. I didn't want to add more pressure on you."

I barked out a laugh. "Always so concerned for my well-being."

"You couldn't even handle keys to my place. You'd pitch a fit if I brought up trying for a baby."

"This is insane," I hissed.

"Plenty of guys have kids with their mistresses, and I intend to make you my wife. So. If you don't mind. Take the test." He nudged me into the bathroom, flipped the lights, and set the pink box on the counter.

Kids. Marriage.

He'd lost his ever-loving mind.

I needed to escape, to find some space to breathe, but Santino blocked the exit. "You're a scheming prick!"

"Let's not pretend I'm the only manipulator in this room."

"I won't take the damned test," I snarled.

"I'm not moving until you do."

Asshole.

I ripped open the box, hating him, and slammed the door shut. I leaned against it, breathing hard. I did my business in the bathroom and took the test, my hands shaking so much it was difficult to hold it steady. Then I set it down on the counter and waited, my heart pounding.

Minutes dragged on, each one stretching into an eternity. I stared at the plastic window as a thin line appeared.

Negative.

A strange mix of relief and disappointment washed over me. I wasn't tied to Santino in the way he wanted, but the threat still loomed behind the door.

I opened it.

Santino's hopeful gaze locked onto mine. "Well?"

I handed him the test.

He looked down, frowning. "Negative."

I nodded, biting my lip. "What now?"

"We try again," he said.

"Santino—"

He closed the distance between us, grabbing my neck. His lips crashed into mine, stealing the breath from my lungs. The kiss was raw, filled with all the pent-up lust from not being able to touch me the past few weeks.

Despite the whirlwind of rage inside me, my body responded. I kissed him back, pouring all my confusion into the moment. His hand anchored me to him as if he feared I might slip away.

The kiss deepened. His lips were demanding, almost punishing, but I welcomed the roughness, how it made everything fade into the background. There was no threat of Dimitri, no looming ultimatum. *Just us.*

Santino's grip tightened as he pulled back slightly. His eyes held me captive. "I need you. It's been too long."

TWENTY-TWO
DELILAH

Santino kissed me again, his lips exploring mine with a tenderness that made my chest ache.

He guided me backward, his hands steady on my waist, never breaking the seal of our mouths as we moved. My back hit the bedpost, and I gasped into his mouth, the sensation sending a thrill down my spine. It knocked me out of his spell.

I pulled away from him, ducking out of his arms and moving to the other side of the bed. "Why are you doing this?"

His gentle smile made my heart flip. "This is how you stay safe from your enemies."

"By locking me up? Trapping me with a baby?"

Santino chuckled. "Let's not be melodramatic, principessa. It's not trapping when you're walking into it with your eyes wide open."

"You're a manipulative asshole."

"You manipulated me first, babe."

"I never did *anything* like this."

"So Dimitri just happened to show up at the gala at the same time you did? You didn't want me to kill him for you? What about every time you got on your knees, sucked my cock, and took my money? You did everything in your power to get me addicted to your pussy, and then you have the gall to act surprised when it worked." He shook his head, smiling. "You could coach a masterclass in manipulation."

"I didn't want a baby out of it!"

"No, you wanted to use me. I just played the game better."

"I swear to God, I didn't."

He laughed. "You wanted me to kill your ex-fiancé. That's why you lured him to the gala. Then you were going to drop me without so much as a kiss goodbye. Am I right?"

"Let's not pretend you would've been brokenhearted."

"You don't know that," he said, stunning me. "You never ask about my feelings. You're too afraid of what I'll say."

"Th-that's not true."

"Just ask, Delilah. What's the worst that can happen?"

I gritted my teeth. "Your feelings are none of my business."

He stalked closer, walking around the bed. "You are so afraid of wanting more, and you shouldn't be. It makes me angry. I want to kill everybody who made you feel this way. Starting with your piece of shit father."

I backed away, but he grabbed my arm, pulling me

closer. His grip was firm but not painful. "Santino, you don't understand."

"I understand more than you think. You've been hurt, used, and discarded. But I'm not like them. I'm not going to let you go."

"You can't just claim me like a possession."

He tilted his head, a dangerous glint in his eyes. "Can't I?"

"You're insane if you think I'd just accept being bred like some kind of—of *broodmare* for your empire!"

Santino's smile didn't waver, but his eyes hardened. "You and me are inevitable. You'll see that in time."

"And if I don't?"

He stroked my hip, his voice a velvet threat. "Then I'll spend every day convincing you."

"Don't you see how fucked up that is? We're two screwed-up people, and this baby is going to come out *wrong*."

"Our baby will be just fine."

I shook my head. "I'm not pregnant. I don't want to be, so don't even think of trying!"

"But we've already been trying."

"No," I growled. "I asked if you were trying to knock me up, and you said no!"

"I lied to you."

"What the fuck is wrong with you?" I shouted.

"I could ask you the same. You'd rather be treated like a slut than someone important to me."

I pulled back from him again, trembling. "I never asked

you to swoop in and...fix me. I just wanted to have some semblance of control."

"All I've ever done is try to take care of you."

"Trapping me isn't taking care of me."

"Call it what you want," he said with a shrug. "But it's the only way to keep you safe. I've already picked out our house. As soon as you're pregnant, we'll move into a place next to my brother so our kids can play together."

A cold shiver ran down my spine. "There's something seriously wrong with you."

"What's wrong is that you're too scared to admit you want this, too." His hands found my waist, dragging me against him.

I tried to push him away, but he held firm, his grip strong. "You're a monster."

"And you love it. Don't you? You love how I fuck you. How I make you feel safe."

I turned away, but he gripped my chin. "Look at me. Tell me you don't want this."

His words were sweet poison. A shameful flush of heat spiraled low on my belly.

"Santino, please..."

He kissed me again, harder this time. His closeness disoriented me, and his sea salt and citrus scent enveloped me.

"Santino, I—"

His lips met mine again, this time with a ferocity that melted my defenses. His kiss was demanding. His tongue traced my lips before delving deeper, coaxing a moan I couldn't hold back.

My hands found their way around his neck, pulling him closer. The kiss deepened, and I lost myself in the rush that drowned out fear. He groaned, and our lips separated.

"Take off your dress."

I didn't move. This flimsy bit of fabric was all that protected me from him and my insane urge to give in to his demands.

"You'll have to force me," I hissed.

His eyes flashed, and then he threw me on the bed.

My body bent over the bed, his hands shoving up my dress. He ripped it off my head, and then his palm cracked over my butt. Once. Twice. I jerked from the rough impact.

I gasped, my heart pounding as the sting of his hand on my skin sent shockwaves through my body. Anger and something darker twisted inside me.

"Santino!" I tried to sound furious, but it came out desperate.

Another slap on my ass made me yelp.

He leaned over me, his breath hot against my ear. "I'm going to fill you up, over and over, until there's no doubt who you belong to."

"You think this will make me stay?"

He chuckled darkly, his fingers sliding to where I was already wet. "You're not going anywhere."

Each stroke made it harder to resist the pull he had over me. I hated him for it and myself even more for wanting it.

"You don't have to do this," I gasped.

"How else will I give you a baby?"

"You're sick," I whispered. "You should be locked up."

"You can pretend all you want, but we both know you're never leaving."

I hated how right he was. Every logical part of me screamed to run, to fight, but Santino had a hold over me I couldn't shake. I had no idea what was more terrifying: the fear of being trapped or the fear of wanting it.

He nipped my ear. "By the time I'm done with you, you'll beg for everything I'm offering."

I gasped as his fingers found my clit.

"You don't own me," I managed to spit out.

He paused, his fingers stilling. His grip on me softened, and hope flickered in my chest. But then his hand tightened, and he turned me to face him, his eyes burning.

"You belong to me, and I'll make sure you never forget it." His lips crashed down on mine as his rough hands roamed my body, cupping my womb. "I'm putting my baby inside you. Right here."

My breathing hitched. "No, you're not."

"I am. And you'll get big with our baby, and I'll spoil the fuck out of you, and you'll love it."

"*No.*"

His lips curved into a wicked smile, his hands sliding down to my hips, pinning me in place. I bit back a moan. His strength was becoming a twisted sanctuary.

I'm sick in the head.

Broken.

"I shouldn't want this," I whined.

"But you do. You're wet for me, even now. And when you're carrying my baby, you'll know it's where you always needed to be."

His hands left my hips as he backed up slightly. His belt jingled as he ripped it from his slacks. The sound of the zipper cut through my scattered thoughts, and then his naked thighs pressed into mine. His palms slid up the backs of my legs, squeezing my ass, and then he pumped his fingers inside me. I arched against his touch, gasping.

"*Please.*"

Was I asking for more or begging for him to stop?

"No more running, principessa," he said, lining up his cock to my aching pussy. "This is your life now."

His cock stabbed inside me.

My traitorous pussy welcomed it.

His hard thrusts jarred my body. Getting fucked by him hurt. It hurt so good, joining the pleasure jangling my nerves. This was supposed to be temporary, but every sweet name he'd ever called me hinted at deeper feelings. He couldn't say no to me. He'd never been able to deny me a single thing.

I had a power over him. It was intoxicating, the way he melted when I touched him, how his eyes softened when I let down my guard. Like he craved my approval as much as I craved his comfort.

I didn't want him to stop.

I wanted more. I wanted to drown in the intensity of what we had.

"Santino, please."

He chuckled darkly. "Please, what? Please fuck you harder? Please fill you up?"

I whimpered. "Harder."

He pulled out, then slammed into me, making me cry out.

Shame and arousal combined into a potent cocktail that left me dizzy. His finger rubbed my clit. His touch sent shockwaves through my body, the pleasure unbearable. I was on the brink, teetering on the edge of a cliff with no way to stop the fall.

"Come for me," he demanded. "Show me who you belong to."

The orgasm crashed over me, my body convulsing as wave after wave of pleasure ripped through me. I screamed, my nails digging into the sheets as I lost myself in the ecstasy he forced on me.

He didn't stop, thrusting into me. "That's it. Take it all."

As the pleasure ebbed, I collapsed onto the bed, panting. He stayed inside me, his cock still hard. He started moving again.

He flipped me onto my back, moving my legs over his chest. Santino worked his body into a frenzy, his face screwed up in the utmost concentration. His forehead sparkled with sweat as he thrust into me like a machine.

My scattered gaze locked onto his black eyes. So black. His pupils had almost swallowed his irises as he watched my face. Unblinking, like a creep. Like he actually cared about what I felt. Other men looked at me like an object.

Santino stared into my fucking soul.

I tangled my fingers in his hair, yanking him closer. My legs locked around his waist, the heels digging into his back. He groaned.

"Oh fuck, Delilah."

I wanted him. I didn't care how fucked up he was or how he'd basically tricked me into this position. I had a broken brain. That wasn't news. My nails scratched him as I held onto his back, gouging his flesh as he fucked me so hard my body slid up the bed. I kissed his panting mouth and sucked on his lip, biting down hard.

He came, clutching me closer as he emptied inside me. He stayed there, his eyes shut, breathing hard. Eventually, his dazed eyes opened.

"I can go again in a few minutes," he said.

"You're insane, you know that?"

His mouth pulled into a beautiful smile.

I traced his lips. "Santino, why do you want a baby with *me*?"

"Why do you think?"

"I don't know. I think you're crazy."

"You've driven me to this point," he whispered harshly as he slowly thrust his cock inside my tender pussy. "You made me crave you in ways I never thought I wanted."

This was such a bad idea.

And yet, my hips lifted to meet his, and I moaned when he sucked on my nipple. He bit my breast like a beast claiming his mate. Every moan from my lips was a surrender I hadn't agreed to give. Escape wasn't an option anymore.

TWENTY-THREE
SANTINO

Delilah was pissed.

She was curled up on the couch, her mouth drawn tight as she stared at the TV. She'd left the bedroom in the middle of the night. I'd followed, keeping my distance. She needed her space.

After last night, she needed to readjust her expectations of this relationship. She hadn't realized how serious I'd been despite the heavy hints I kept throwing at her. Delilah was a little delusional sometimes. That was alright.

I watched her from the kitchen island as she flicked through the local Italian channels. She settled on a baking show featuring a model-thin brunette who looked like she'd never eaten a cornetto in her life. Did Delilah like pastries? She hadn't eaten much since she got here. Just some pastina mixed with broth. Withdrawal had hit her hard, and it made me feel like shit for not noticing sooner.

I'd had no idea about her drinking problem. Two months of hanging out, sex, and fun. I thought she could handle her booze. She was good at hiding it, but when I saw her at my apartment...? That's when it clicked. When I realized this, I researched alcoholism on the internet. It'd been so long since my old man died, and I couldn't remember much about the disease. All the literature said that withdrawal from alcohol was dangerous. She could've died without a medical team closely monitoring her, so I contacted a few uncles who still lived in Italy, and they helped me find doctors. She'd be okay. The worst was over. Maybe the TV show she chose meant her appetite was coming back.

I texted Anna, the housekeeper, to bring fresh pastries in the morning. The leather couch creaked as Delilah turned around, scowling.

"Are you going to stand there and stare?"

I put my phone away. "I'm trying to give you space."

She glared at me. "Just come here."

I walked to the couch and took a seat beside her, far enough so that she didn't feel crowded. Her head turned back to the screen as a baker applied a glossy layer of chocolate to a cake.

"You ever watch shows like these?"

I shook my head. "I'm more of a news and sports guy."

She fell silent again, pushing the strap of her nightdress up her shoulder. Hard to believe that hours ago, I'd been balls deep inside her tight pussy.

My cock swelled as I replayed last night. She'd been angry, for sure, with the way she gripped my back. And her nails dug into my scalp as she held me to her body, her tongue in my mouth, her hips in sync with mine.

She was perfect.

It felt good to have that final layer of secrecy ripped away. She rode my cock just like I knew she would, holding me tight with her thighs, taking every drop of my cum like a good girl. Holding it inside her for ages. I researched it, and experts recommended twenty minutes to an hour. So I just kept fucking her. She'd loved it. She cried out my name and came over and over again. And when she was too sleepy to continue, I cradled her in my arms, her face buried in my neck, and she held me back. Finally, she treated me like I belonged to her.

Now she was sullen again.

I broke the silence, trying to keep things light. "What's the show about?"

"Baking," she said curtly.

"Yeah, I got that. Do you like baking?"

She shrugged. "It's fine. I just like watching people make pretty things."

"Maybe we could try it together."

She glanced at me, her expression softening. "You bake?"

"Not really, but I can follow instructions."

We watched the show in comfortable silence for a while. The model-thin brunette tasted the tiniest piece of a cake with intricate flowers and talked to a girl wearing an apron.

Delilah sighed, her eyes still on the screen. "I used to bake with my stepmom. Before she turned bitter from my father's affairs. Every year, she went all out with pastries for

Christmas. Trying to impress my dad, I guess." She pulled the blanket tighter around her.

"And your mom?"

Delilah shook her head, her gaze fixed on the flickering images on the screen. "Died when I was little."

"I'm sorry. That's a kind of loss you don't just get over."

I reached over, tucking a loose strand of her hair behind her ear. She leaned into my touch, then pulled back, her walls back up again. Delilah turned to the TV, her body tense.

The show moved on to judging, and the contestants awaited the verdict with bated breath. We watched in silence, the only sounds the judges' critiques and the occasional laugh track.

"What about your family?" she asked.

"My old man was a gambler and a drunk. My mom did her best to protect us, but it wasn't easy. He'd blow in like a hurricane, mess everything up, then leave again like nothing happened."

Delilah's eyes softened. "Sounds familiar."

"Not all parents are what they should be."

"And your siblings? You mentioned them before."

"They're a mixed bag. We look out for each other the best we can. Family's family, right? Even when they drive you nuts." I paused, memories surfacing like ghosts from the past. "After a fire killed my cousin, everything fell apart."

"A fire?"

"A house fire. My aunt and uncle never stood a chance.

Luca, who was ten at the time, didn't either. The entire family was wiped out."

Her eyes widened. "That's awful."

"It's haunted me ever since. That night changed everything. My dad started drinking even more. My mom lost her fucking mind. Me and Rome had to pick up the slack and work for the Family. For a few years, we had to fend for ourselves."

She turned around fully to face me. "That's really messed up."

"Yeah."

"Is that why you started working for them?"

I nodded. "Somebody had to help put food on the table. Six kids. Two parents."

She tensed. "Why are you telling me all this?"

"I know your deep, dark secret. I figured I should tell you mine."

She raised a brow. "Having a rough childhood isn't a secret."

"Maybe not, but the idea of going back to that keeps me up at night. Being powerless again. It drives everything I do. It's why I can't be weak."

"Is that why you threw out my birth control?"

A pack of pills was all that stood between me and keeping her forever. If I told her that, would she get pissed? I wanted her to keep talking to me, to stop looking so wounded when I walked into the room. Sighing, I raked a hand through my hair.

"It was the only way to get what I wanted."

She fumed. "You didn't even try to find another way."

"No. I can't say I did."

Telling her about my feelings hadn't worked. Neither did giving her the keys. Delilah's stubborn streak would have ruined a perfectly good relationship, and I couldn't have that.

Delilah turned her attention to the TV, frowning. The show continued, and she settled into her blanket and pillows, her foot almost touching my thigh.

She glanced at me.

I pretended to watch a baker frosting a cake as Delilah checked me out. Her eyes lingered on my dick, which hardened. I couldn't help it.

I watched her bite her lip. The room was drenched in soft light that caused shadows to dance across her face.

Gradually, I edged closer. When she didn't shift away, I reached out, my fingers brushing her foot. She didn't jerk back. I began massaging, working the tension from her arch. A soft sigh slipped from her. Her expression melted into something more pliable. I kept my eyes locked on hers, watching every subtle surrender. My hands slid up her calves.

Her eyes fluttered.

I pulled on her legs, dragging her over my lap. I wrapped my arms underneath her and stood. She clung to my neck as I carried her out of the living room.

"I don't know why I let you do this to me," she sighed.

She could pretend to be bewildered by her desire for me. If that got her in my bed without a fuss, it suited me just fine.

I carried her over the threshold of the bedroom, just like

a newly married couple. A flashback to our first night together burned in my head. Her in that wedding dress. The stolen Romanov bride I'd been determined to defile. She showed up to my hotel room, the most beautiful thing I'd ever seen. So pretty. I should've married her right there.

I gently laid her on the bed.

Climbing onto the bed, I moved between her spread legs, my hands rough as I pushed her silk dress up to her waist. She sucked in a sharp breath, her skin covered in goosebumps in the cool air. Her panties were soaked, and I ripped them down her legs.

Her hips lifted, inviting me in. I smirked, lowering my head between her thighs. My tongue darted out, teasing her clit, and she gasped, hands gripping the sheets. The taste of her was addictive, driving me to lap at her with a fierce hunger. My tongue flicked her most sensitive spot. Her moans filled the room.

Her body trembled, and I knew she was close. I wrapped my lips around her clit, sucking hard, and she shattered, her orgasm ripping through her like a storm. She cried out my name, her hands fisting in my hair.

I didn't stop until she was a quivering mess beneath me. Her body bucked, her nails dragging painful trails along my scalp as she came apart.

I came up, wiping my mouth with the back of my hand. I moved closer to her, positioning my cock at her needy pussy. Then I leaned forward, my cock nudging her. "I'm gonna fill you up, baby."

I thrust into her, hard and deep. She gasped, a sound that made my balls ache. I set a brutal pace, each thrust meant to claim. Her sounds, her scent, and the feel of her wrapped tightly around me drove me closer to the edge.

She met my every thrust, her cries filling the room, telling me she was close again. That was all I needed. With a few more deep, punishing strokes, I let go, coming hard.

I collapsed on top of her, breathing heavily, the sweat from my brow dripping onto her flushed skin. We lay there entwined, the only sounds our ragged breathing. I rolled off, lying on my back, feeling her shift beside me to rest her head on my chest. The silence stretched between us, a thick blanket that neither of us seemed ready to lift. But then, Delilah's voice cut through, low and more steady than I expected.

"You're not forgiven just because I let you come inside me."

I kissed her stubborn jaw. "I know."

"You can't fuck me into submission," she mumbled, staying nestled against me.

I stroked her hair. "It's a start."

She snorted. "That's not how it works, Santino."

"Yes, it is. When you claim something with everything you got, it's yours."

She was quiet for a long moment, her breath warm against my skin. "You need therapy. Fuck, so do I."

I shrugged.

Delilah lifted her head, glowering. "It'll take more than good sex to win me over."

"Go to sleep, principessa."

TWENTY-FOUR
DELILAH

The villa's sprawling vineyards stretched out before me, a sea of green under the warm Italian sun. I wandered down the rows, marveling at the vibrant, lush vines heavy with grapes. The beauty and serenity of the place felt surreal, like stepping into another world. I reached and plucked a grape from the vine, popping it into my mouth. I grimaced.

Definitely not ripe.

I continued my exploration, enjoying the solitude and the sound of the breeze rustling through the leaves. It was a rare moment of peace, away from the chaos that had defined my life lately.

"Enjoying the view?"

I jumped, my heart racing. Santino stood a few feet away.

"Damn it, Santino."

He smiled, stepping closer. "You scare easily."

"Maybe that's because you kidnapped me and are trying to knock me up like I'm a prized mare."

He paused, inches away. "Is it so wrong to want something permanent with you?"

Was it?

I wasn't sure how to feel. Part of me longed for stability, someone who cared enough to fight for me, but I hadn't entered this agreement with Santino expecting a real relationship. There was also the fact that men lied. All the time. Santino had done it several times.

I crossed my arms. "I'm supposed to believe you suddenly care about me? Where were your warm, tender feelings when I begged you for help?"

"I didn't feel for you then the way I do now."

"You act like your intentions are pure when they've been anything but."

"I never said they were. I said that they changed."

My cheeks burned. "How?"

He shrugged, taking another step closer. "People change their minds. It's nothing to be scared about."

"How did they change? We don't do anything together. We barely talk. All we do is have sex."

"I'll take you out more. I promise."

I sighed. "Why do you think we'd be good together?"

"I don't know," he murmured. "I haven't put a lot of thought into why. It feels right. That's enough for me."

"It feels right?"

"Yeah. That's what I said."

"How do you know that?"

He seemed annoyed with the questions. "I bought a ring two weeks ago."

My heart pounded. "You're kidding."

He reached into his jacket pocket. Slowly, he produced a small, black box and opened it with his thumb. A ring with the biggest diamond I'd ever seen winked inside. I barely glimpsed it before he snapped the lid shut, stuffing it back inside his jacket.

He bought a ring. For me.

I kept glancing at where the ring had disappeared, certain I'd imagined it.

"Delilah, I'm not the type to kneel. I'm also not one for big speeches, but I want you. That's all I've known for the past two months. I always want you."

His words stirred something deep within me, a flicker of hope I smothered. Just because he bought a ring didn't mean he was in *love* with me.

He shrugged, the corner of his mouth twitching. "It's not just about what I want, though. You need stability. I can provide that."

His words engulfed me in frigid water. I frowned, the idyllic setting of the vineyard suddenly less enchanting. "You make it sound like a transaction."

"It can be both. You get the support you need, and I—well, I get to keep you."

It wasn't the declaration of love I'd dreamed about as a girl when I still clung to fantasies. It sounded like a strategy.

"And if I say no?"

He studied me, his gaze unwavering. "I'll convince you."

His confidence shook me. He predicted us getting married as though he'd already seen me walking down the aisle to him. That would've been sweet if it weren't for his delivery. *I'll convince you.* My heart sank. It wasn't the plea of a lover but the strategy of a tactician.

"You're assuming a lot," I murmured.

"No, I'm betting on us."

My cheeks flushed. "You make it sound so clinical."

"Isn't a strategy to keep you by my side better than me going down on one knee?"

No, I wanted to scream. I wanted to tell him that his practicality stripped the beauty from the gesture. But instead, a deep, weary sadness echoed inside me. He was offering permanence, yes, but it was tethered to necessity. Not love.

Santino offered me his arm. "Come with me."

I took it, the sadness thick in my throat. "Where are we going?"

"You'll see," he said.

We walked in silence, our feet crunching gravel. We reached a small clearing where a dilapidated gazebo stood, its paint peeling and vines creeping up its sides. It looked out of place amidst the well-maintained vineyard.

"This place belonged to my grandparents," Santino said, his tone unusually somber. "After they died, nobody was around to take care of the property. It fell into disrepair like so many of the farms scattered all over Italy. Until I started renovations, slowly making it like it used to be."

"Do you want to live here someday?"

"I like the idea of growing old here with a family. Away from all the bullshit in Boston. But I'm probably not cut out for life out here."

I studied him, trying to reconcile the ruthless man I knew with this version of him who dreamed of a simpler life. It was hard to imagine Santino living a quiet life in a vineyard.

"Why tell me all this?"

"Because I want you to see that there's more to me than illegal fighting rings and collecting debts. A part of me craves something normal."

"Is that even possible for you? You'll have a target on your back for the rest of your life. So will your children."

His expression darkened, and I knew he was remembering the fire that took his cousin's life. Every time it crossed my mind, horror pitted my stomach. He took my hand, and we strolled out of the farm onto a gravel road.

We headed down the winding stone road into a small outdoor market. Hunched over old women dressed in all black filed into a small church. The doors opened, and I glimpsed a priest in white robes waving incense over the pews. A funeral. My skin prickled as Santino brought me to a cafe.

We settled at a small table outside, the smell of freshly baked bread and brewing coffee wafting through the air. Santino ordered for us in rapid Italian, and the waitress blushed. Irritation heated my chest as she fluttered away.

"Is this your way of showing me you'll be a good father?"

"I think you know that already, principessa. I took care of you, didn't I? Everybody who hurts you has to deal with me. Dimitri. Ivan. Anybody who looks at you the wrong way."

How did he know about Ivan?

I froze.

"I helped you get clean for the first time in years. I held your hair when you vomited, washed you when you could barely stand, cooked you food."

Everything he said made me feel worse.

"I don't know why you want anything to do with me. Your dad was an alcoholic. Aren't you afraid I'll be just as much of a mess?"

Santino's expression softened. "My father gave in to his demons. But you're fighting them. That makes you strong."

I pulled away. "That doesn't change what I am."

"We all have our issues. The question is whether we let them control us."

I stared into my coffee, the swirling darkness reflecting my tumultuous thoughts. I allowed myself to imagine it—a real fresh start with Santino.

As we walked back to the villa, the sun was setting, casting long shadows over the vineyards. It was a beautiful, almost haunting sight—a reminder of the fleeting nature of peace.

When we reached the house, men in suits were gathered around a black car, their expressions tense. Santino's demeanor shifted, the mask of the mafioso slipping back into place.

"Stay here."

TWENTY-FIVE
SANTINO

The Romanovs had found us.

Costa soldiers stationed at the villa informed me that several men had been spotted in the village. I had no intention of letting them get any closer. The villa was a place of refuge for Delilah, and I would not allow it to be tainted by violence. We packed into a car and headed straight for the cafe I'd just left with Delilah.

I spotted them as soon as we arrived—five Russians seated casually. We exited the car, not bothering to conceal our weapons.

Locals scattered as we approached. The men glanced at us, their expressions shifting. Then, the first shot rang out, a deafening crack. A woman screamed.

I raised my gun. Fired. The first Russian went down, the bullet zipping through his skull, his blood splattering the pavement. The cafe erupted into chaos. Patrons scrambled for cover, tables overturning in the frenzy.

One of the Russians, a kid in a badly fitted suit, tried to draw his weapon. I slammed the butt of my gun into his face. He staggered back, blood gushing from his broken nose. I followed up with a swift kick to his knee, bringing him to the ground.

I aimed a gun at his head. Another shot rang out, grazing my side. Pain flared, but I pushed it aside, focusing on the fight.

My men moved in, relentless and efficient. Two Russians bolted, trying to escape into the village. I gestured after them, clutching my bleeding side. Marco and the others chased them down. I turned my attention back to the kid, who couldn't have been more than nineteen. I didn't give a fuck.

He was a threat to the woman I'd sworn to protect. I did not see anything else. My fists pounded into his face and ribs. He cried out. Blood coated my knuckles, and still, I didn't stop. He deserved to suffer.

My men caught up with the fleeing Russians. They didn't grant them the mercy of a quick death. They beat them to death. Bones cracked. Flesh tore. Grown men screamed for their mom.

One of them fought back, but Marco grabbed him by the hair, smashing his head into the cobblestone until he stopped moving. Another of my soldiers kicked a man in the gut, sending him sprawling before stomping on his chest repeatedly, each impact driving the breath from his lungs.

Beneath me, the kid lay on the ground, barely

conscious, blood pooling around him. I stood over him, breathing hard, my knuckles stinging, and raised my gun. His eyes widened, and I pulled the trigger. The gunshot echoed through the street.

My side throbbed. I pressed my hand against the wound, the blood warm and slick under my fingers. Delilah couldn't see me like this, not after I'd tried to show her there was more to me than just the violence. How many people had we killed?

Five? Seven?

"Marco," I called out.

He rushed over, concern etched on his face. "*Sei ferito.*"

"Just a scratch. Make sure the area is secure."

He nodded, but his eyes lingered on my wound. "*Dobbiamo farti medicare, capo.*"

"Get the doctor. Tell him to meet me outside the house."

The drive back to the villa was a blur of pain and adrenaline. Delilah had enough on her plate without adding my injuries to it. But when we reached the courtyard, she was there, waiting.

"Oh my God. What the hell happened?"

She gasped as I exited the car, and I glanced down. Blood had soaked through my shirt. I straightened, pain slicing into me. "It looks a lot worse than it is."

She dragged me to the lounge chair outside. A servant brought a bowl of water, bandages, and a needle and thread. They'd probably stocked up before I flew into town.

Delilah's mouth thinned as she ripped my shirt,

studying the gash on my side. "Looks like you got grazed. You lucky idiot."

I smiled. She could call me every name in the book. Watching her work, focused and capable, stirred something in me. She had a way about her that demanded attention. Her hair fell in waves, framing her face like a Renaissance painting.

"You're a natural at this," I muttered.

She looked up. "Grew up in a household where you learned to patch up or shut up. No room for the squeamish."

Her matter-of-fact tone cut through the air. I grunted from the sting of the needle. We weren't so different, her and I—both forged in chaos.

"I like that about you," I said, watching her carefully thread the needle. "You're not some damsel. You've got grit."

Delilah snorted. "Grit won't keep you from bleeding out."

"But it'll keep you fighting, won't it?"

She paused, frowning. "Someone's got to keep you alive. You're hell-bent on getting yourself killed."

Careful, principessa. I'll think you care.

She kept on working on my wound, her hands steady. Something about Delilah anchored me, but I wasn't about to lay all that on her. Guys like me didn't spill our guts even if someone sliced us open. Words were cheap, and in my line of work, they could be too revealing. Actions mattered.

"Delilah, you know I'm not one for many words."

She paused and met my gaze. "I've noticed."

"But you've got a solid hand. I appreciate it."

Her smirk softened, and she returned to her task. "Just keeping you in one piece."

"Thanks for taking care of me."

The smirk returned to her face. "With a wound like this, you'll probably have to put baby-making plans on hold."

I raised an eyebrow. "You think this is gonna slow me down?"

"Silly me. I guess it'll take more than a bullet graze to keep Santino Costa on the sidelines."

"Damn right," I grunted, the pain sharpening as I shifted.

Delilah's face sobered, and she placed a gentle hand on my shoulder. "Just try to keep the heroics to a minimum, okay?"

The comment was light, but the underlying concern was clear. She cared more than I expected, and it tugged at something inside me.

She finished bandaging the wound and sat back. "There. You'll live. Just keep it clean and try not to get shot again anytime soon."

"I'll do my best."

Moments like this gave me hope. Maybe not for a peaceful life, but one with her by my side. She could fall for someone like me. She was in this just as deep as I was. That was something worth fighting for, even if I had to bleed to make it happen.

Delilah was out cold, her body sprawled across the bed.

I sat in a chair beside the door, my hand on my gun. The weight of our situation settled on my shoulders. Staying hidden forever wasn't an option. Dimitri would keep coming back.

Part of me wanted to stay in this bubble where it was just me and her, away from all the shit, but that was a fantasy. Reality had already knocked on my door. The phone buzzed in my pocket, Kill's name flashing on the screen. I answered, keeping my voice low.

"Yeah?"

My brother loosed a sigh. "You're alive. Good."

"So far."

"Vinn wants you back in Boston," Kill grunted.

"Tell him I'm on vacation."

"I'm not telling him that." He paused. "You weren't supposed to leave with the girl."

I smiled. "He didn't tell me not to."

"Vinn's not a fan of improvisation. You know that. You need to come back and face the music."

My jaw clenched. "What if I don't?"

"The men guarding that villa are Costa soldiers. They're loyal to the Family, and they've been reporting everything back to Vinn. He told me to tell you that," Kill said, unease creeping into his tone. "He also wants you to know that if you don't come back, he's ordered his soldiers to take you both out."

"That's extreme."

"You disobeyed a direct order."

"I'm a fucking captain. I don't get some leeway?"

He heaved another heavy sigh. "Look, I'm sure you can smooth this over with him. Calm down, board a plane, and get your ass back to Boston."

TWENTY-SIX
DELILAH

"Dad, I can't believe you did this," I hissed into the phone. "You sent men to kill Santino? Have you completely lost your mind? How could you?"

I paused, my breath hitching as I struggled to find the words. "He's the only person who's ever protected me. And you...you tried to take that away. I don't know how you found us, but I swear to *God*, if you ever come near us again, if you so much as breathe in our direction, I'll make sure you regret it. I'm not your little girl anymore, and I won't let you control my life. Stay the hell away from us. I mean it, Dad. This is the last time you'll ever try to hurt someone I care about."

I ended the call, my chest heaving. The voicemail was a small victory—a desperate attempt to draw a line between my father's madness and my relationship with Santino. But as I stood there, phone clutched in my trembling hand, I knew it wouldn't be enough to stop him.

"Didn't know you had it in you, principessa."

I spun around. Santino leaned against the doorway, smirking. The bandage peeking from his shirt reminded me of how close I'd come to losing him, but he acted like he hadn't just taken a bullet two days ago.

"I never thought I'd see you get riled up on my behalf."

"Really?" I snapped back, still fuming. "Because I can dial him up again if you want more of a show."

He chuckled as he walked over to me. He looked different. My gaze flicked down to a pair of Converse shoes. His jeans were rolled up at the bottom, and he wore a white, tucked-in T-shirt. He'd even styled his hair into messy waves.

"What the heck are you wearing?" I asked.

Santino brushed his shirt. "Found some things in my bag that I thought might catch your eye."

"How'd you do your hair?"

"Online tutorial."

My heart stumbled. "You did that...for me?"

He nodded and shrugged.

I blinked. "Well, you look amazing."

"Glad you approve."

I more than approved. My heart swelled. Santino had gone through all this trouble just to make me smile. It was surreal, this blend of ruthless mafioso and a man who watched hairstyle tutorials to impress me. He didn't have to do any of this, but he had. For me.

It was almost too much to process. As soon as he stood in front of me, I traced the muscles beneath his shirt.

His mouth hovered close as I curled my fingers into his shirt. His scent swirled in my nostrils as his lips fell on mine, hot and insistent. A tumultuous feeling threatened to upset my balance as I clung to him, tasting every stroke of his tongue. Heat pooled in my core as I kissed him back, surrendering to the craving that followed me every waking moment. My hand slipped under his shirt and teased the tanned skin.

Santino groaned, gently disengaging himself. "Not now, baby. I'm taking you out on a date."

"Is that a good idea?"

"Yes. We've been cooped up in this damn villa for too long. It's time we go out."

The idea seemed ridiculous. He'd just been shot, but the hard edge in his eyes softened just for me and made it impossible to say no. I folded my hand in his, smiling.

"Where are we going?"

His smirk widened. "Somewhere that'll remind you why you're with me. But first, a quick stop at a cafe."

Holding my hand, he led me out of the room.

We went outside and strolled to the village down the road, the street bustling with people. We entered the same cafe of the other day. Santino chose a secluded table at the back and sat against the wall.

Unease began to creep back in, gnawing at the edges of my happiness. I'd been here before—caught in the warmth of someone's affection, only to be burned when I let my guard down.

But Santino was different. He wasn't trying to charm me with empty words. He'd seen the worst of me, and still, he stayed. The thought made my chest ache. He made me believe in us.

After our coffee, we walked down the cobblestone streets, the vibrant energy of the village wrapping around us like a comforting blanket. Santino led us to a record shop, its exterior plastered with old posters.

Inside, the air was filled with the musty scent of old vinyl covers. Classic rock played on a turntable in the corner, and Santino watched me with an amused smile as I darted from bin to bin, my fingers dancing over the records.

"How did you know I like this stuff?"

He gave me a sly smile, shrugging. "You mentioned it once."

I couldn't remember. It must've been an offhand comment that he'd stowed away. My heart fluttered. Santino paid attention to me. How much of his time had he spent thinking about me? Creating lists of what I liked and didn't like?

We spent the next hour flipping through records, sharing stories about our favorite bands. Santino surprised me with his knowledge of ragtime music. As we walked back to the villa, the sun setting behind us, I felt deliriously happy. Even with all the chaos surrounding us, this felt right. But that sense of peace shattered the moment I checked my phone.

An urgent email flashed on the screen:

Subject: Urgent: Retro Rose Boutique

Delilah, we have a major issue with the zoning permits.

They're threatening to revoke them unless we provide additional documentation by the end of the week. We need you back here ASAP to sort this out. Please respond immediately.

My heart sank.

"Everything okay?" Santino asked.

I forced a smile. "Yeah."

He studied me for a moment, then nodded.

I couldn't shake the dread settling in my stomach. I needed to get back to Boston, but how could I explain that without revealing everything to Santino?

As we had dinner on the terrace, my mind raced. I had to figure out how to fix the situation with the boutique without tipping him off. Miraculously, Santino himself solved the problem. As the sun dipped below the horizon, he turned to me, frowning.

"We have to go back to Boston. There's something I need to deal with back home. I wish it could wait, but it can't."

Perfect.

As much as I loved the rolling hills of Tuscany, I needed to get back to Boston, too. I had a mountain of other work to address besides the zoning permit.

"That's fine with me," I said.

"And from now on, you're staying with me. I'm moving you into my house."

I blinked, taken aback. "Santino, *no.*"

"It's not up for discussion."

"I can't just move in with you."

"You have to," he growled. "My boss is still a threat to you."

I grabbed the glass of sparkling cider, wishing it was alcohol. "I don't understand why he'd go after me. I have nothing to do with whatever my father did."

"You're related to him. That's enough." His eyes darkened. "And your ex is still hunting for you. You think you can handle all that on your own?"

"I'm not," I said, sliding my hand over his. "I have you looking after me."

"I can't be everywhere all the time."

"So put some guys outside my door. I don't mind a few bodyguards."

Santino's gaze fractured. "Or you could move in with me."

His words twisted something inside me. I wanted to be with him. I craved the security he offered, but the thought of losing my independence terrified me.

"I'm not doing that."

Santino raked his hair with his fingers. "You living in a completely different place makes it harder to keep you safe."

I swallowed hard. "But not impossible."

"I'm not letting you stay in that apartment."

"But moving in with you changes everything!"

"That's the idea, principessa. I told you this arrangement wasn't enough for me anymore. And remember," he added, tapping his forefinger on the table, "there's a financial incentive if we make this official. Marry me, get pregnant, and it's all yours."

Money. Always with the money.

I'd dug that grave by treating him like an ATM. I should've been thrilled. Marriage was the goal of most gold-digging women. The idea of being his wife dangled in front of me like a golden ticket. I'd never really been able to afford what I wanted, thanks to my dad's stinginess. The possibility of wearing Santino's ring hovered in the air like a shining soap bubble.

His earnest plea broke through my defenses. He looked so sincere, his black eyes starved for me. Maybe he did feel something for me. If all he wanted was a trophy wife, he could've married one with far less effort. Santino never let me doubt that he wanted me, not for a second. Whenever I looked at him, I saw his need for me.

He reached into his jacket pocket, pulling out the small box. He popped open the lid. Such a beautiful ring. Tears flooded my eyes. I wanted it so badly. The rational part of my brain screamed to keep my distance, but my heart had already made its decision.

His haunted black eyes watched me. "Say yes, Delilah."

"Santino."

"Trust me."

I shook my head, trying to ward off his velvety purr that seeped into my head. His voice was like a sinful cocktail, snaring through my bloodstream, making me too warm.

"Let me take care of you."

I breathed fast, suddenly lightheaded. I wanted to say yes. Everything inside me ached to say yes.

Santino grasped my hand and squeezed. "Take it, baby."

The question I couldn't ask burned in my mind: *Do you even love me?*

It shattered the gorgeous illusion of this perfect scene, the Tuscan vineyard bathed in golden light, which made everything it touched appear softer. This was the perfect proposal. Santino looked incredible. His hair, clothes, and even that look in his eyes matched the fantasy of undying devotion.

"You say this is what's best for me, but what's best for you? What do you really want from me, Santino? Because I don't know if I can give you everything you're asking for without losing myself."

"I want you with me, Delilah. Whatever it takes."

I reached out, hand hovering over the box, and shut the lid. "I need more time. I'm not saying no."

Santino frowned, like he'd expected it but was still disappointed. He stuffed the box in his jacket and shrugged. His smile was resigned, almost sad. His willingness to give me space twisted something inside me.

"We're not ready for this, Santino."

"You're not. I am."

I stood, my hands trembling. "I'm not pushing you away. I need to be sure I'm doing this for the right reasons."

"This has always been about money. You've been taking what I give you since the beginning. Cash, protection, anything you needed. So why stop now?" He stepped closer, his gaze hard. "You want security. I'm giving you that."

"You can't buy me with money."

Santino watched me calmly. "Yes, I can."

Chills ran down my spine, his words echoing in the empty space between us like a threat. I backed away, my resolve hardening.

He smiled. "Whether you say yes now or later, you're mine."

TWENTY-SEVEN
SANTINO

Delilah's hands were clasped tightly in her lap. She sat next to me in the car, looking out the window. During the flight back, she'd barely talked to me.

Stonewalled.

All because I'd asked her to marry me. She stole glances when she thought I wasn't looking. Sneaking peeks under her hair. She wasn't happy with me.

I wasn't too thrilled with her, either. Rejection didn't sit well with me. I shouldn't have to beg a woman to marry me. What about me wasn't good enough? I had all the money in the world. A good family. I worked out constantly. I gave her everything, and she still said no.

Why was I not enough?

Trees whipped by the window as I drove outside of Boston. Delilah finally abandoned her pretense of ignoring me and whipped her head toward me.

"You missed the turn."

My fingers tightened on the steering wheel. "We're not going to my house."

"Where, then?"

I kept my mouth shut. If she *only* wanted to be my girlfriend, then she wasn't entitled to every little detail.

"Santino," she pressed, louder this time. "Where are we going?"

"Sit back and relax. We'll be there soon."

Delilah's petulant sigh made me want to swerve onto the shoulder, get out, and bend her over the car hood.

An hour later, a cabin popped out of the horizon, a black triangle silhouetted by dark blue. Gravel crunched under the tires as we turned down the tree-lined driveway.

We got out of the car. The cabin looked the same—rustic, a bit run-down, but solid. A piece of the past that had seen many grisly ends. I glanced at the shed in the distance. My brother used to kill people in there. He'd drag them into that small shed, and they'd come out in pieces, which he buried around the property.

I strode inside, Delilah following me. I flipped on a switch, and the bulbs flickered to life, casting a warm glow. The sharp pine scent triggered even more memories.

I grabbed old newspapers and kindling, arranging them under the logs I'd placed in the fireplace. I struck a match and lit the newspaper. It turned black and curled, the flames eating up the paper.

Delilah came out of the room, her long hair brushed in shiny, loose waves. She wore one of my shirts and a pair of socks. Nothing else. I could see her tits bouncing freely, the areolae dark circles peeking through the translucent white cotton. My cock twitched.

Back to her old games.

Irritation heated my chest like a rash. She flashed her pussy to get what she wanted from me, and it worked. Every single time. She'd done her job too well. She'd turned me into a junkie addicted to her taste. Would there ever be a time when I wouldn't get hard just thinking about it?

Delilah kneeled beside me, her floral scent drugging me.

An orange glow began to fill the room. Light flickered in Delilah's eyes as she rubbed her fingers together. The cabin was freezing. The only heat came from the fireplace.

I grabbed her hands, rubbing warmth into them. "Better?"

Delilah's mouth softened. "Yeah."

The fire caught, the small flames licking eagerly at the wood. Delilah jumped a little when a log popped.

"Is this where you had your family vacations?" she asked.

"Not exactly. This was more like a training ground. My Nonno on my mother's side believed in preparing us for the real world."

His version of it, anyway.

"Training for what?"

"Survival. Power. Control."

She slipped out of my hands, and I sat back on my heels, watching the flames.

"Nonno was from the old country. He came over as a young man, scarred by poverty and war. Italy wasn't kind to him, and he didn't know if America would be either. So he made sure we were tougher than the rest."

"Sounds like he was a hard man."

"He had to be. He'd lost too much before he even stepped foot in America. When he finally made it here, he was determined not to let the world break us."

She frowned. "Did you ever resent that?"

I leaned forward, resting my elbows on my knees. "Nah. He just wanted us to be prepared."

"Is that what you want for your kids?"

Good question. "They'll be prepared, but they'll know they're loved."

She frowned. "How do you know you'll be a good dad?"

"You've met my brother Kill. You're familiar with his reputation, right?" I watched her nod, remembering how she'd tense whenever he came into the room. "If he can be a good dad, so can I."

"You're sure about that?"

"Yeah."

"I'm nothing like him or Violet. My childhood was...awful."

I laughed hollowly. "And mine was so much better? We slept four to a bed in a rat-infested apartment. My father was a bitter old man who drank and gambled every cent we earned."

"Still, it'd be so much easier to find someone without my issues."

"I don't want easy. I want interesting and complicated."

Her laughter, light yet tinged with sadness, filled the

cabin. "Are you sure that's really what you want? Because that's all I can give you."

"You gave me a reason to care about more than just surviving."

Her eyes glistened. "I'm a magnet for trouble."

"I want something that burns hot, even if it's a little dangerous."

"You're so crazy," she whispered.

I squeezed her hand. "We're in this together, no matter how dark it gets. I want the good and the bad."

She smirked. "So, everything, then."

"Yeah," I agreed, a small laugh escaping me. "If you're going to want something, you might as well take it all."

Her gaze dropped to the floor. "I told you, I'm not good at being kept."

Well aware of that, principessa.

I needed to get her pregnant.

Reaching over her, I grabbed her phone from the table. I turned it on and held it to her face, unlocking it.

She frowned. "What are you doing?"

"My sisters have apps to track their cycles. You probably do, too."

I thumbed through them, stabbing on a pink icon. It opened to today's date, a giant magenta circle highlighting the words: *You're fertile!*

My smirk grew. "Perfect timing, Delilah."

"Hey, you can't just look through my stuff!"

I put the phone aside, sliding my arm over her shoulder and dragging her onto my lap. I kissed that gorgeous dent at the base of her throat, my lips trailing up her smooth skin.

She shivered. "Are you serious?"

"I want this," I whispered in between kisses. "I won't stop until your tits get swollen and your belly grows."

Her skin flushed, but she let me fondle her over the shirt. I kissed her nipples, the dark circles standing at attention. I nipped her, and she dug her nails into my scalp. I sucked her through the fabric, playing with the stiffening peaks.

"Santino, this is crazy."

"It's what we both need."

I set her on the couch and ripped off her panties, sliding to the floor to kneel between her legs. Her pussy was spread wide, glistening. She was ready for me before I'd touched her. What a perfect girl.

"You are irresistible," I growled.

My hands glided over the tender skin of her inner thighs, teasing her. Delilah's grip tightened in my hair, pulling me in.

I chuckled. "Can't wait, huh?"

But I was done teasing her, too. My mouth closed over her, my tongue lashing out to taste. Delilah's back arched off the couch, a sharp gasp slicing through the air as my mouth moved with precision.

"You taste so damn good," I muttered, muffled by her wetness. I held her hips, pulling her closer. My other hand traveled up to circle her clit, pressing just right to send shocks of pleasure through her trembling body. I built up the pace slowly, alternating between quick movements and slow licks that made her writhe.

Delilah's fingers tightened in my hair, her breaths

coming in short, sharp gasps. Her mumbled words broke off into a whimper as I increased the pressure, my tongue and fingers moving in a relentless rhythm that pushed her closer to the edge.

I could feel her body tensing, the signs of her impending climax clear in the way her legs trembled and her breathing became erratic. I looked up at her, our eyes locking as I brought her over the brink.

With a loud cry, Delilah's body bowed, her climax washing over her in waves. I didn't relent, my tongue thrusting inside her, drawing it out until she was gasping for breath. A flush spread across her cheeks and chest.

As her tremors subsided, I kissed my way up her body, my lips tracing the path of her quivering muscles until I reached her lips. I kissed her deeply, unbuckling my pants.

I stood, pulling her up with me. Her eyes were hazy, her body still trembling from her orgasm. I turned her around and bent her over the arm of the couch, her ass raised, presenting her perfectly for me.

I entered her in one thrust. Delilah's fingers dug into the cushions. I set a demanding rhythm, punching my hips forward. The sounds of my cock slamming into her wet pussy filled the room, highlighted by Delilah's moans. She was so tight, clenching me in all the right ways.

Mine. All fucking mine.

Delilah's body tensed, her climax building again. I could feel it in the way she tightened around me. She pushed back with her hips, meeting my thrusts. She groaned.

"Come for me again," I commanded, my voice rough. "Let me feel you."

Delilah convulsed around me, crying out. I thrust into her harder, my own release barreling through me. My balls tightened, and hot jets shot into her pussy. I kept fucking her in short jerks, riding out each wave.

We collapsed onto the couch, panting. I pulled her into my arms, holding her close. I grinned, still wading in euphoria. My hand brushed her lower belly.

"One day, this is going to grow our baby."

Delilah's brow furrowed, but I kissed it away.

I needed to get her ready for the next round.

She had a really good chance of being pregnant. I still had three more days before the fertility window closed, and then it'd be another few weeks of waiting.

Delilah had passed out around eleven p.m. I couldn't sleep, so I scrolled my phone for hours. Then I called her father. I sat at the rickety kitchen table as it rang once before being picked up.

"I'm surprised to hear from you," said Mikhail.

Asshole. "I bet you are."

"I don't know what you're talking about."

"Delilah is the only reason you're still breathing."

"Is that so?" he mocked. "You have no idea who you're dealing with."

"You're a snake. You sent your soldiers to Italy and risked your daughter's life just for the chance to kill me. And for what? Because I stole her away from Dimitri?"

"Santino?"

I turned toward her.

Delilah stood at the doorway, wearing my button-up shirt. The firelight softened her figure, and she wore her hair in a messy bun, tendrils framing her face. She stepped closer, hesitating, before sitting next to me.

"Is everything okay?" she asked.

The line crackled with his heavy breathing. I ended the call and put the phone down, hitching a smile.

"Yeah, babe. It's fine."

Delilah glanced at the phone. "Who was that?"

"Nobody important."

She grabbed my wrist, squeezing hard. "I heard you say Mikhail."

"Go back to bed."

She fumed. "You talk about wanting more with me, but you don't tell me anything real. You feed me scraps, not the whole truth."

I toyed with a strand of her hair. "I don't want you to worry about anything, principessa."

"Well, I do. So, can we skip to the part where you tell me what's going on?"

Men in my line of work didn't confide in their women. I took out my wallet from my back pocket.

"Do some shopping. That'll take your mind off things."

She glowered at me. "I don't want your money."

"My bank account begs to differ."

Delilah flushed down to her neck, that gorgeous pink

shade spreading everywhere. Her eyes widened as she tried to come up with an excuse, but I didn't need to hear one.

"I don't care that you only want money from me," I ground out, the lie heating my chest. "As long as you're with me."

"Being used for money doesn't bother you?"

Of course it does.

I kept my voice even. "You get what you want, and so do I."

"It hardly seems worth the money."

"I disagree. I have the most beautiful woman in the city right where I want her. And soon, we'll have a family. You think I'd let that go just because it costs me?"

"Maybe I'll start charging interest."

"With the rates you'll probably charge, I'll be bankrupt before the wedding."

She lifted a brow. "Assuming there will be a wedding."

"There will."

"I don't know. I don't exactly have a stellar track record when it comes to following through on those."

My lips curved. "You'll want to marry me."

I said it like a certainty, but I wasn't sure of anything. The nagging feeling that she would leave twisted in my gut.

"Oh yeah? How come?"

"Because I'll deposit a quarter of a million dollars into your bank account once you're pregnant. And you'll get more once we're married. Plus, jewelry and clothes. Whatever you want."

Her eyes lit up. "Seriously?"

"I'll write it in the prenup."

I grew up poor. I understood the appeal of wealth better than anyone. Who wouldn't want complete freedom? I'd fantasized about being rich. Not just comfortable but *rich*. Extravagant vacations. Custom-built houses. Luxury cars.

Delilah had grown up with a silver spoon in her mouth. She had a taste for expensive things. Few men could afford to keep Delilah. Marrying me should have been a no-brainer. Yet she seemed conflicted.

I needed her with me. Money wasn't enough, but it was the only leverage I had. That was all I was to her. A walking bank account. A means to an end. The second she got what she wanted, she'd walk away.

"I can't agree to marry you for money," she muttered.

"What do you want, stock options?"

She glared at me, then got off the chair and parked her ass on my lap. She twined her arms around my neck. "I'm not *only* interested in your money, you know."

Sure, babe. "I was starting to think you need an itemized invoice to remind you why you're with me."

She huffed. "Stop it."

I smirked. "What about a detailed expense report?"

Delilah rolled her eyes, but the corners of her mouth twitched. "I should start sending you bills for all the therapy I'll need after being kidnapped. Again."

I slipped a finger in between the buttons of her shirt, grazing her stomach. "You look good in my clothes."

Delilah's fingers stilled, and her eyes closed. When they opened again, she looked like the lost girl that had stumbled into my club. All the fierceness left her.

I kissed her cheek. "Listen, I need to go somewhere."

She dug her nails into my shirt. "In the middle of the night?"

"Don't worry about it. You're safe."

She still looked freaked out.

I sighed, taking out my Glock. "Safety's on. It's loaded with one in the chamber."

She gaped at me as I set it on the table.

I lifted her off my lap and headed to the coat rack. "You know how to use a gun, right?"

She grimaced.

I stood, heading to the door. "I'll have to take you to the range."

Deep inside Franklin Park, through a trimmed path and up lichen-covered stone steps, sat a group of giant, rusted enclosures. The old bear dens of a zoo. They'd been abandoned decades ago, left to rot to their skeletal remains. Early morning sunlight poked through the branches, illuminating the stone carving of two bears standing on hind legs.

I checked my watch.

As I glanced up, movement caught my attention. A strong silhouette moved out from a tree, flanked by two others. Vinn and his bodyguards.

I nodded at him.

Vinn's eyes were like two tar pits. "You finally show your fucking face after taking off to Italy."

"I couldn't do what you wanted me to do."

He crossed his arms. "Why?"

"She's pregnant."

Vinn exhaled roughly. "Knocking up the Romanov girl puts a kink in my plan to wipe them off the face of the earth."

"Then set it aside. We're not ready for an all-out conflict with the Russians. We're still fighting for territory in Chelsea. We have the 12th Street gang and the Animals growing in Dorchester and Beacon Hill. Another war will break us."

"Sonny, you brought this conflict to *my* door."

A foot scraped the path, and cold metal kissed the back of my neck. I didn't move. I wasn't too worried. If the boss wanted me dead, I'd be gone already. He had a reason for dragging me all the way out here.

"Look, I get that you're pissed. But the Romanovs are dying. Mikhail has no heirs except Delilah. This marriage will let us dip our hands in Providence, which no Costa boss has ever been able to do."

Vinn's glare didn't waver, but interest flickered in his eyes. "Those bastards turned our cousin into a human torch."

"We need to think about securing our future."

He smiled wryly. "*Your* future, you mean."

"The docks in Providence are a gold mine, not to mention the smuggling routes through New York. We could expand beyond Boston. Isn't that better than a war that leaves us weakened? This kid could bridge the gap between our families. It's peace or leverage, depending on how we play it."

"Mikhail's not going to sit back and let his daughter marry into the family that's been trying to kill him."

"We have his daughter. We'll make a deal with Mikhail. Offer him stability under our management. We've done it before with the MCs."

"Can you get him to agree?"

I met his gaze steadily. "I think so. He's getting old. He knows Delilah's the only future he's got."

Vinn nodded. "Alright."

"It'll work," I assured him. "We handle this carefully, and we'll come out stronger."

Vinn motioned to his men, and they backed off, giving me space. "If you fuck up, it'll be on you."

I nodded.

I didn't need a reminder of the stakes.

TWENTY-EIGHT
DELILAH

A zipping noise startled me awake.

I blinked, pushing the sheets back. I'd been in the middle of a strange dream, so it took a moment for my eyes to adjust. The rustling came from the other side of the bed. I rolled over, watching Santino bent over his suitcase. He stuffed it with clothes, packing as though his life depended on it.

"Are you wearing jeans?" I asked.

He shoved my bra into his suitcase. "I need you to get dressed."

"What's the matter?"

He glanced at me. "Nothing."

"You're making a lot of noise for nothing."

"We're going home," he said, cramming my toiletries bag into the suitcase.

Home?

A brief flash of Providence entered my head, but that

hadn't been home in a long time. Maybe once when I was too young to understand neglect. No, Boston was home. It was where I'd turned my dreams into reality.

Santino patted my knee through the sheets. "Get up, baby. I wanna get out of here."

"What's the rush?"

"I'm starving, and there's a good diner down the road."

He squeezed my leg, the touch reminding me of last night. He must have finished inside me four times. Every time I suggested we take a break, Santino urged me on all fours or flipped me on my stomach and ate my pussy until I *needed* him inside me.

Men like Santino didn't stop until they got what they wanted. I would get pregnant. Once that happened, his family would never leave me alone. I'd been at a few of his family gatherings, and Italians went nuts for babies.

Having his baby didn't *feel* like an option. It felt like an absurd fantasy. No matter how many times Santino insisted differently, people like us couldn't have a nice house in the suburbs and kids.

Grudgingly, I ripped the coverlet off my legs and got dressed. Santino hovered as I went through my skincare routine, his black gaze throbbing with impatience. He ushered me into the car. We zipped to a fifties-style restaurant by the highway, Santino drumming his fingers on the Formica table until the waitress took our orders.

His breakfast came on several platters—pancakes, eggs, bacon. A sugar, fat, and carb overload. I dug into my egg whites and oatmeal. For all her faults, my stepmother had been a good cook. Borscht with a dollop of sour cream, pelmeni, pirozhki, and the sweet, delicate layers of medovik cake. Russian cuisine was nothing like Italian.

Santino cut into the pancakes, stabbed a stack with his fork, and shoved them in his mouth. He devoured them with a single-minded intensity, ignoring everything around him. We'd been out to dinner before, but there was always an air of keeping up appearances. Both of us would be dressed to the nines. Santino shoveling down pancakes was almost endearing. Maybe with five other siblings, he had to learn to eat fast.

Santino frowned. "What?"

I smiled. "You really like your food."

He continued eating, gesturing at my plate with his fork. "You should eat something more filling than that."

I rolled my eyes but felt a warm flutter in my stomach. "Maybe watching you eat is enough for both of us."

He grunted.

I propped my chin on my hand. "So where did you go last night?"

He hesitated. "Did you sleep well?"

"Nice dodge." I winked at him. "Yeah, I slept fine."

"Good."

"I tried to stay awake until you got back, but I passed out." I'd spent two hours staring at the phone, waiting for him. "Is everything okay?"

He nodded. "Yup."

"Can you elaborate?"

Once again, he took forever before answering.

"My boss needed assurances, but we're good now."

I sipped my coffee. "So, he doesn't want to kill me anymore?"

"If you stay with me, you're safe."

I sat back in the chair.

All I had to do was keep my legs open, and my face wouldn't end up on the evening news. How nice. Dimitri was still out there, too, biding his time.

"We're meeting my brother at his place for dinner later."

"What should I expect?" I asked.

"Nothing fancy, just dinner."

I sighed. "Alright."

Santino took out his wallet. "Relax. It'll be fine."

Ribeyes sizzled on the grill. Santino and Kill drank beer, discussing the latest roster on his fighting ring, while Jack, Santino's nephew, shrieked as he ran through a sprinkler. Santino caught my eye and winked.

I smiled, my stomach twisting in knots.

Violet exited the house carrying two drinks. She made a beeline for me, sliding the tall green drink into my hands. "Made you a virgin cocktail."

"Thanks. That's so nice of you."

My cheeks flushed as I took it from her. Santino must've warned them ahead of time about me, but I appreciated that they didn't give me a hard time.

"Thought I'd come by and check on you," said Violet as she sank into the chair next to me. "How you holdin' up?"

"I'm not sure what you mean."

She smiled knowingly. "This family can be an adjustment. It took a few months before my mother-in-law warmed up. I just want to make sure you feel welcome."

I clutched the drink. "Thanks, Violet. It's a lot to take in, but everyone's been really welcoming."

She nodded. "It's like walkin' into a dance where everyone already knows the steps but you."

I laughed. "Exactly. I was raised Russian. We're very different."

Violet's nod was full of sympathy. "Oh, honey, I know that feeling. I'm from Tennessee, born and bred. You can probably tell from my accent. I stuck out like a sore thumb when I first got here. But being an outsider ain't always a disadvantage. Gives you a way to see things others might overlook."

"How did you manage to fit in?"

She sipped her drink, a thoughtful smile playing on her lips. "By not tryin' too hard. I brought a little bit of the South up here with me. Santino and the rest, they came around. There ain't nothin' quite like Southern hospitality."

Her chuckle was infectious, and I couldn't help but join in. "Maybe I should start bringing a little bit of Russia into the mix, then?"

"Absolutely. This family is like a quilt. Every piece adds color. You'll find your place, just you wait."

Violet was just as much an outsider, yet essential to this

family's dynamic. "It's about finding balance, isn't it? Between where we come from and where we're headed."

"That's right. And remember, if you ever feel out of place, just come find me. Us *outsiders* gotta stick together."

"I'll hold you to that."

Violet winked. "Between you and me, it's not all bad. Just wait until the holiday parties. They're somethin' else."

"I'll take your word for it."

"I'm glad you're getting along with Santino. He's a decent man, just a bit intense. He's had a tough life. They all have." Violet paused as though deciding how much more to say. "When you've been through what they have, trust doesn't come easily. You're always waitin' for the other shoe to drop."

"I guess that makes two of us then."

She reached out, touching my hand lightly. "Just give it time. He's got his demons, sure, but he's also got a good heart."

The sound of laughter pulled us back to the present. Santino smirked at something his brother said, but he looked over again. His gaze found mine across the distance, and his smile broadened.

"Come on." Violet stood, pulling me gently by the arm. "No use broodin' over things out of our control, right?"

"Right."

I allowed myself to be led while my mind raced.

Santino slid his arm around my waist. He kissed my cheek and frowned. "Everything okay?"

"Yeah." I smiled, sharing a look with Violet. "We were discussing how difficult Costa men can be."

"And what's the verdict?"

"She said patience is key, but I think I might need a little more than that."

"You have everything you need to handle me, principessa."

"Princess?" Violet burst, clinging to her husband. "That's the cutest pet name. So much cuter than *Bumpkin*."

His brother grinned. "It's softer than what we're used to hearing around here."

"Oh, come on, baby." Violet pouted. "It's sweet. Makes a nice change from all the tough guy talk."

Kill smiled. "You wanna trade it for something fancier? Maybe duchess?"

Violet rolled her eyes.

Santino dragged me away from them, his voice dropping. "Is that really what you were talking about?"

"Yeah, why?"

"You seem rattled."

"I'm just nervous. Your family is different from mine." I licked my lips as his eyes bored into mine. "They're very nice."

"You'll fit in."

I raised an eyebrow. "You seem pretty confident about that."

"That comes with knowing what you want."

"Which is what?" I whispered.

He smirked, his hand moving to my belly.

My heart pounded. "You really have a one-track mind, don't you?"

"My little brother's already got a leg up on me with a four-year-old and another on the way."

"So it's a competition?"

His grip on me tightened. "I want my own with you."

"Are you that eager to start a family?"

"Damn right, I am. I'm always thinking about filling you up."

My face flushed. "Jesus, Santino. Say that a bit louder."

"I don't care what anyone thinks."

I pulled back slightly, trying to gauge if he was serious or caught up in the moment. I didn't know what to do with him anymore. He had me constantly questioning my own sanity. Fighting him felt pointless. I couldn't win against this maniac. All I could do was keep my eyes on the future. Build my business.

Santino's arms trapped me in a cage of heat. Over his shoulder, I glimpsed Violet staring at us. She smiled and exchanged looks with her husband. We'd never be like her and Kill.

It bothered me.

I couldn't build a life with a man who threw dollar bills in my face. Something deep inside me craved more. I *deserved* a man who loved me. Could I find that with Santino? Could I trust him to see me as more than a transaction? The fear of being used gnawed at me.

He didn't trust me enough to tell me the truth. How could we ever raise a child? He threw out my birth control pills. And I was still fighting off the urge to drown myself in alcohol.

"I need a drink," I muttered.

"It's normal to have cravings."

"I know, but what if I just had one?"

"You won't stop at one. You know that." Santino pulled back from our embrace, cupping my face. "Remember what the doctor said?"

"He said a lot of things."

Warmth sparkled in his eyes. "You just have to make one decision—not to have that first drink. After that, it's out of your control. It's like handing your car keys to a lunatic."

He was right. I just needed to hear it again.

I sighed, trying to steady my nerves. "Sometimes it's hard to remember that when everything feels so overwhelming."

"That's why I'm here, principessa."

I nodded, feeling a bit more at ease.

We spent the rest of the evening enjoying the food and company. Santino and his brother shared stories from their childhood, and I found myself laughing more than I had in a long time.

As the sun set, casting a warm glow over the yard, we gathered around the table for dessert. Violet served homemade apple pie, its sweet aroma wafting through the air. We were all relaxed and content, and it felt like a real family gathering.

Just as we were finishing up, my phone buzzed. I pulled it out and saw a voicemail notification from an unknown number. My stomach twisted as I excused myself and walked a few steps away to listen.

Santino followed. "What's wrong?"

"I think he sent me a message."

His face darkened. "Play it."

I hit the button, and Dimitri's snarl erupted from the speaker.

"You're a fucking idiot if you don't come back to me. I will hunt you down, and when I get my hands on you, you'll beg for death. This isn't over, bitch."

TWENTY-NINE
SANTINO

Stay away from Delilah.

I thought I'd driven that point home with a mock execution, a brutal beat-down, and thoroughly humiliating him before I dumped his ass on Mikhail's doorstep. The dumb fuck couldn't take a hint. She walked out on him on his wedding day, and he still wouldn't leave her alone.

It pissed me off.

I'd been willing to let him live. But now, I was going to decapitate him and punt his head into the harbor. The next day, I drove past his house in Providence, a Sig in my lap, but he wasn't there. Delilah had given me the names of some businesses he owned. No dice. So I made a detour to my future father-in-law's house.

One didn't simply walk into a Pakhan's home without getting shot by bodyguards, so I called Mikhail. Told him I was in the area and wanted to talk.

The gates opened after a thorough inspection of my car

and a pat-down. Mikhail's estate was a fortress. More cameras than a celebrity rehab center.

Guards led me through a manicured garden where Mikhail waited for me on the veranda, looking like the dictator of a small, corrupt country. He wore a black satin robe, his expression wooden.

Mikhail nodded. "Costa."

"Thanks for meeting me."

One of his men opened the door to his house, and he waddled inside. I followed, feeling naked without my piece. The house reeked of cigar smoke and old money. Heavy velvet drapes cast a dim pallor over everything, and the walls were lined with dark wood paneling.

Mikhail led me to a study. He gestured for me to sit, and I took the chair across the desk. Mikhail took his time, slowly making his way around, the desk chair groaning as he sat down. He made a show of arranging papers and stacking them before he finally looked me in the eye.

"I never thought my daughter would be involved with one of you."

I sat down. "An Italian?"

"A Costa," he spat.

"Maybe you should've taken better care of her."

He stabbed his finger in my direction. "*Watch your mouth.* You're in *my* house. If you want to leave in one piece, you'll speak to me with respect."

Who did this guy think he was?

The tough guy act didn't work when you ruined your reputation by allowing a psychopath to abuse your daughter.

I smiled, knowing it would incense him. "Your daughter came to me."

"You defiled my little girl. Stole another man's bride."

Yes, I did. "She needed my protection from the man *you* sold her to."

He made a dismissive hand gesture. "I should have never raised her in this country. It filled her head with nonsense. Dimitri is a good man."

Debatable.

"You took advantage of my girl." Mikhail pointed at me, his finger trembling. "You *forced* her."

"There wasn't any coercion."

Mikhail's eyes blazed. "She was engaged."

I shrugged. "She ran away from the wedding."

"I don't believe it. You must have tricked her."

I wanted to laugh. "Isn't there footage of her fleeing the church?"

A rhetorical question, considering I'd watched it weeks ago when the video had made the rounds through the criminal underbelly.

Mikhail shook his head. "My daughter would never disobey me."

This guy was delusional.

"Look," I said, keeping my voice even. "Delilah made her choice. She's with me now."

"You're either very brave or very stupid."

My patience was wearing thin. I leaned forward, resting my elbows on the desk. "She'll just run back to me every time you force her into Dimitri's arms."

"Not if I kill you *right now*."

I drummed my fingers on the desk. "Mikhail, I didn't come here without backup. If you hurt me, they'll make what you did to my cousin seem like a mercy killing."

Mikhail's face turned a deep shade of red. "Why are you here?"

"I came here to negotiate a truce. I plan on marrying your daughter. There's no need for more bloodshed. Let's focus on our businesses and keep our families out of it."

His eyes narrowed. "What's in it for me?"

"Peace. Stability."

Mikhail shifted in his seat, the leather creaking under him. "And the terms?"

"I want Dimitri gone."

Mikhail's eyes flickered. "Why would I kill a man who's been loyal to me?"

"It's good business. Delilah will never go back to him willingly. If he tries anything against her, it'll just escalate things. Plus, I'm prepared to offer you a payment in good faith to show I'm serious." I paused, letting the weight of my words sink in. "Half a million dollars. Your businesses will continue without any interference from us, and I'll pull back any operations encroaching on your territory."

He studied me for a long moment. "Half a million for my daughter?"

"I'll do two hundred now and the rest when Dimitri is in a hole in the ground."

He mulled over this, the silence stretching between us. Finally, Mikhail nodded slowly. "We have a deal."

He extended his hand.

I hesitated before taking it. "When will it be done?"

"It might take a few days, but I'll contact you."

Delilah's father waved me out. I stood, my stomach churning. He didn't even flinch before serving up one of his men. I caught the gaze of the guard, who ushered me out of the house. I wonder how his guys felt about that.

Walking out of that house was a relief.

Never in my wildest dreams did I imagine shaking hands with a Romanov. Making a deal with her dad went against every sane instinct, and Delilah thought I'd trapped her?

Such a fucking lie.

She was mine. And I was all hers.

I told Vinn about the deal with Romanov.

He said he'd be speaking with Mikhail to iron out a few more details. There would be weeks of negotiations, but it looked like the alliance was moving forward.

Costas and Romanovs.

Working together for the first time in decades. I had my doubts. Mikhail wasn't known for his honor. I didn't trust him, but I didn't have to. I had something he wanted. As long as we held each other's balls in a vise, nobody could move.

When I got home, Delilah was perched on the couch, her legs crossed. She wore a black dress with a plunging neckline, the fabric hugging her figure. Loose brown waves cascaded over her shoulders, her lips painted deep red. She looked gorgeous, like an actress from a noir film.

She glanced up at me, smiling. "How did it go?"

Something flipped in my chest. Her smile always fucked me up. I crossed the room and stood in front of her.

"The deal's moving forward."

She arched a brow. "And you trust my father?"

"Nope."

Delilah took my hand, gently pulling until I sat beside her. "Did he ask about me?"

"I told him I was taking care of you."

She gave me a sad smile. "So he just handed me over? Again?"

"He tried to get you back, but I'm a good negotiator." I leaned over, kissing her cheek. "With everybody except you."

She put her hand on my chest, showering my skin with sparks. Any lingering sadness on her face vanished as she straddled my waist. Her fingers traced the line of my jaw.

"Speaking of, I need more money."

My gaze drifted down her neck. "So that's why you're dolled up, huh?"

"You know me so well," she purred.

My principessa had no concept of money. How did she already blow through what I gave her?

I stroked her hair, inhaling the scent of her flowery shampoo. Delilah kissed the base of my throat. She didn't need to fuck me for money anymore. All she had to do was ask. Should I remind her? I couldn't think while her lips teased me.

I groaned as warmth flicked my skin. She nipped at me. My thumb traced her mouth, and she let it slip inside. Her lips formed a tight seal around me. Then she sucked. Her tongue swirled around me, and my cock hardened.

"How much do you want, baby?" I whispered.

"Eight."

Eight *thousand*? "For what?"

"There's a vintage Dolce dress on an auction website that's exactly my size. I want it."

Didn't she give me that excuse already?

The questions faded as she slipped down between my thighs. She kneeled at my feet, hands on my thighs, and began unbuckling my belt. She ripped it off and tugged my pants. I lifted my hips, and she dragged my slacks and briefs down to my ankles.

Delilah wrapped her hand around my cock. She squeezed around the head, and precum slipped down my shaft. She leaned forward and licked. She didn't take me in all the way, but her tongue swirled, caressing the underside of my cock.

My thigh muscles twitched.

The first time she'd wrapped her lips around me, it'd been at the hotel. I'd dragged her mouth to my cock sometime during the night, enjoying the sight of the Russian princess at my feet, giving me a hand job with her engagement ring still on.

Then she took me in her mouth. I remembered feeling out of my depth. That I'd planned to own her, but...the way she made me feel? She owned me. It began my obsession with her. I'd pay every last dollar in my bank account to keep her.

Delilah buried her face between my thighs. Her little mouth could barely fit me, but her throat opened up nicely. I kept my hands at my sides for as long as I could before I grabbed her hair. My hips rocked slightly as I guided her mouth up and down my shaft. She hummed around me, and my balls tightened. It felt too good. I pulled her off my spit-slicked cock, hauling her up my body.

She crawled over my lap, and my cock slipped into her soaked pussy. She braced herself on my shoulders and rode me, giving it her all. I sat back, watching her. Her eyes fluttered. The shoulder strap of her dress slipped. I tugged it down further, exposing her tits. My arm wrapped around her, pulling her toward me. She lost her balance, catching herself on the back of the couch. I grabbed her breast. Sucked it into my mouth. My tongue played with her nipple, and my cock twitched inside her. She moaned, her hands sliding to my hair and tightening.

Bossy girl.

Her tit slipped out of my mouth with a pop. I lifted her off me, my hands grabbing her ass. Holding her, I stood up and stumbled for the bedroom. She slipped down my arms, but I caught her before her toes hit the ground. She slammed her lips into mine. She *really* wanted that money.

I fisted her hair, pulling her head back. "For eight grand, you need to give me more than your mouth and pussy."

Her mouth twitched. "You want to fuck my ass?"

Blood pounded in my ears. "*Yes.*"

"Take it, then."

When she offered herself up like that, I couldn't resist. I positioned her over the bed, grabbing cuffs from a drawer and tying her ankle to the ropes attached to the footboard. Then I hiked up her other leg, tying that one, too. When I finished, she was bent over, perfectly exposed to me. I grabbed a bottle of lube before I slid inside her soaking pussy and squirted a dollop onto her. I grabbed her ass, my thumb following the trail of lube and slipping inside her.

So fucking tight.

Delilah moaned as my thumb worked her. I applied more lube, slowly opening her up with another finger. Then I tossed the lube aside. My cock twitched inside her as I watched her squirm. She was a sight—tied up, exposed, and ready for me. I kept slamming into her, my balls tight and aching. Fuck. She felt too good. I buried myself deep as I came.

I caught my breath and pulled out slowly, not wanting to leave the warmth of her pussy.

Panting, she turned her head to the side. "Oh my God, Santino."

I leaned over her, my chest pressing against her back. "More, principessa?"

"Yes. Yes, please."

My cock throbbed. I pulled all the way out of her, covered in our combined cum. I grabbed the lube, slicking it over her and myself, prepping her for the next round. I lined up myself at her asshole. The tip of my cock pressed against the puckered hole. Slowly, I pushed in. Her body tensed, but she made the effort to relax and push back against me. Inch by inch, I worked my way inside, and she gasped.

Once I was fully seated, I paused, giving her time to adjust. She clenched around me, her body trembling. I pulled back slightly and then thrust in again, harder.

"Fuck," she groaned.

She was tight. It took every bit of control not to just pound into her. I started moving, building a slow rhythm. She screwed her eyes shut, meeting my thrusts. Her gasps turned into keening wails.

My hand slid around her waist, finding her clit. I rubbed it in time with my thrusts, her body convulsing with each touch. Her moans were different this time, deeper, more primal. She was close.

"Come for me, Delilah."

She screamed, her body locking up as she came hard, her muscles squeezing me like a vise. I kept thrusting, riding out her orgasm until I felt my own release building. With a final, deep thrust, I came inside her again, filling her up completely.

We stayed like that for a moment, both of us catching our breath. I slowly pulled out, watching my cum drip from her. She looked thoroughly fucked, her body spent and quivering.

I untied her, lifting her into my arms and carrying her to the bed. I laid her down gently, brushing her hair from her face.

"You did good," I murmured, kissing her forehead. "I'll get you that money."

She smiled weakly, her eyes fluttering shut.

As she drifted off, my heart pounded. That post-nut clarity hit like a freight train. Delilah had been burning through cash faster than a forest fire. Vintage dresses and shit—sure, she liked them—but this was starting to feel off.

I slipped out of the bed, my gaze catching her laptop left carelessly open on the dresser. A move so unlike Delilah, who was always covering her tracks. Curiosity gnawed at me. Maybe it was the trust issues talking, but I needed to know.

I crossed the room quietly, opening her laptop. It hummed to life under my fingers, the screen lighting up to show her email logged in and open. My eyes darted to her bank notifications—too many recent transactions not to raise a flag.

I clicked it. Bank statements lined up like a breadcrumb trail of deceit. I went through the tabs, scanning the transactions. My jaw clenched as the pieces started falling into place. Large sums of money were disappearing into accounts I didn't recognize. Dresses, my ass. She'd been lying to me.

Every transaction was a jab to my gut. Payments to suppliers, rent, design fees—she'd built something big behind my back. Every dollar I gave her was being funneled into her secret life.

I'd known from the beginning what this was. She wanted my money and protection. I'd agreed to it. Hell, I'd even liked it at first. But now it fucking wore on me. The more she took, the more I felt like nothing I gave her would ever be enough.

I turned back to the bed. The woman I called

principessa stirred on the bed, murmuring something in her sleep. A storm brewed inside me. Mikhail and Dimitri were still threats, and now I had Delilah's secret stacked on top.

I needed to confront her, but not tonight.

I closed the laptop with a snap.

THIRTY
DELILAH

The next day, I headed to the shop.

I told Santino I needed to stop at my apartment to pick up some items, but I made a detour on the way back to his place. I'd fixed the issue with the zoning permit and needed to unlock the door for the artist I'd hired to paint a mural on the white brick interior.

I unlocked the door and stepped inside, flipping on the lights. The empty space felt like a blank canvas, waiting for the artist's touch to bring it to life. I busied myself with some paperwork at the counter, losing track of time as I reviewed invoices.

The door opened.

I looked up, my heart dropping when Santino strolled inside. "What are you doing here?"

He stepped inside, closing the door behind him. "I could ask you the same thing, principessa."

I swallowed hard, my mind racing.

His eyes scanned the room, taking in the empty racks and boxes of merchandise. "What's Retro Rose Boutique?"

I met his gaze steadily. "A store I'm opening."

"For what?" he asked.

"Vintage clothing," I whispered, relieved that he didn't seem angry. "I wanted to make them more accessible. It's a passion of mine. I thought...I hoped I could become more independent if I started my own business."

Santino leaned against the counter, his gaze roving over the buckets of paint sitting next to the wall. "You let me believe you were a gold digger."

"It's not far off the mark."

"It is when you're signing leases, contracting painters, hiring designers, and buying inventory for your fucking store. That's different from using my cash to go on a shopping spree."

"I know."

He sighed heavily, hands stuffed in his pockets. "So you're setting up a fallback plan? Like you're getting ready to bail?"

I shifted on my feet. "No, I just...it was easier that way. If you thought I was after your money, you wouldn't ask questions."

"Why did you keep this a secret?"

"I didn't have a choice. I had to protect myself."

His eyes searched mine. "From me?"

"Yes. Dimitri told me he'd help with the store, and then he screwed me over. I couldn't let that happen again."

"I'm not the same as that piece of shit."

I chewed my lip, pained by his stony expression. "I was scared of losing what little freedom I had."

"Delilah, I've given you everything you asked for." He circled the counter, his voice darkening. "You know why I do that, don't you?"

I sucked in a tight breath, shaking my head.

His fingers glided under my chin, forcing me to meet his intense stare. "Because of *you*. Because you got me hooked. Every time you walked away with my money, all I could think about was getting you back in my bed. But I want more. I want kids. I want to put a lock on that pretty pussy."

My cheeks flamed. "So romantic."

A wry smile tipped his mouth. "You don't want romance."

"Yes, I do. I want more than an arrangement where it's all about what you give me, and I take. I want a real relationship."

He blinked, his fingers stilling under my chin. "What does that even mean to you?"

"It means you don't just throw cash at me whenever you think I need something."

"You *insisted* on the cash."

"And now I'm telling you it's not enough. I don't want to be part of your empire. I want a real relationship. I want to laugh with you, talk about stupid things that aren't life and death. I want to be more than a woman you bought."

He stared at me, his jaw tight. Slowly, the tension in his face eased and his lips quirked into a half-smile. "You mean that?"

"Yes."

He stepped closer. Butterflies soared in my chest as Santino cradled my face in his hands before he lifted me onto the counter. He kissed me firmly, making my heart pound, and I kissed him back.

When our lips parted, I leaned back slightly. "I should have told you about the store. I'm sorry for keeping it a secret."

"I get it. You've been trying to protect yourself."

A knot in my chest loosened. "So you're not mad?"

"No, baby. I understand why you did it." He paused, his hand still resting on my face. "You've been burned before. But listen, I'm not another guy you need to protect yourself from."

"I'm starting to realize that."

He stroked my hair. "I just want to keep you."

How did this man make me feel so cherished? Warmth spread through me, filling the spaces that had been so empty for so long. I'd been so used to the push and pull between us, but this was different. There was something raw in the way he looked at me.

Something warm and overwhelming bloomed inside me. I couldn't say it out loud yet, but I...I loved him. He fought for me. He gave me space even when he wanted to keep me close.

"You make me happy, Delilah."

I smiled. "You make me happy, too."

I didn't add what my heart was screaming—that I'd fallen for him.

He grinned. "I know."

His hands rested on my hips as my fingers traced his jaw. The pull between us was stronger than it had ever been. He wasn't just someone I wanted in my life. I couldn't imagine my life without him.

He stepped back and looked around. "So, what's the next step in getting this place up and running?"

I slid off the counter. "The mural. I hired an artist to paint it, and she should be coming in soon. Then there's the inventory, marketing, and a million other things."

The artist popped through the door a moment later and got to work painting. In the meantime, I brought Santino up to speed about everything the boutique needed. After we wrapped things up at the store, we went home to Santino's penthouse.

He disappeared into his gym, and I drifted into the kitchen. As weights clinked, I looked in the fridge.

I pulled out ingredients for spaghetti carbonara—Santino's go-to comfort food. A peace offering. I set the water to boil and chopped garlic and pancetta, sizzling it in the pan.

He came into the kitchen, wiping sweat from his brow with a towel draped around his neck. "Smells good."

"It's your favorite, right?"

He nodded, a hint of a smile on his lips. He disappeared into the bathroom to take a shower, leaving me to finish up the meal. I set the table, plating the pasta with a sprinkle of fresh parsley. The aroma filled the kitchen, making my stomach rumble.

A few minutes later, Santino returned, his hair damp and a clean shirt clinging to his muscular frame. He sat down at the table, his expression full of anticipation.

I set a plate in front of him. He waited, fork poised, as I sat down with my own plate. Then Santino dug in, shoveling the carbonara into his mouth. He moaned with the first bite. He finished his plate by the time I was halfway through mine, his fork scraping the last bits of egg and cheese.

Santino set his fork down and wiped his mouth. "So good."

"You're welcome."

He patted his lap. I slid off my chair and moved over, settling onto his lap. His hands found my hips and pulled me close.

"Making me dinner, sitting pretty on my lap. What are you up to?"

I leaned against him, playing with his T-shirt. Something lingered in the back of my mind that I'd been too afraid to bring up before. Maybe it was the softness of the evening or the way Santino had opened up to me lately, but I felt like I could ask him.

"The fire," I began, my fingers stilling on his chest. "The one that...killed your cousin. You've never really talked about it."

His entire body tensed. "What do you want to know?"

"What happened?"

He exhaled a rough breath. "I was just a kid. Twelve years old. My aunt and uncle were like second parents to me. My aunt, uncle, and cousin. Gone in one night. I watched the whole thing."

"That must have been horrible."

"It was," he admitted, his voice rough. "My cousin was

only ten. We'd been playing together earlier that day. And then he was gone."

"What happened?"

His jaw tightened. "Arson."

"Did the police ever catch the person responsible?"

He shook his head, glowering.

"What was your cousin like?"

"Luca? He was a tough little bastard. Fiercer than most men I know now. Once, cops caught us stealing bikes. Luca swore we'd be riding again by sunset. He wasn't wrong. My uncle pulled some strings, and hours later, we pedaled down the street like nothing happened."

I tried to smile, but it felt more like a grimace. "He sounds a lot like you."

Santino shrugged, his gaze drifting to the window. "We never got to find out, did we?"

"No, I guess not."

He grabbed his wallet out of his pocket and pulled out a worn photograph. "This is him."

He handed it to me. A young boy with a mischievous grin beamed at the camera.

I took the photo, my heart stopping.

"What is it?" Santino asked.

I stared at the photograph. "He looks like you."

"Yeah, kind of."

My fingers lingered on the photo, tracing the outline of Luca's face. "It's strange to think about how different your lives could have been."

As I looked at the boy in the photograph, my hands

shook. I knew that face. I had seen it before, many times. My breath caught as the pieces clicked into place.

This boy...Luca...was alive.

I'd grown up with him. He worked for the Providence Bratva, and judging by the blank look on his face, Santino had no idea.

THIRTY-ONE
DELILAH

He's alive.

I couldn't believe it.

The boy Santino mourned was the same boy I grew up with in Providence. Luca—my childhood friend—had *somehow* been raised in the Bratva. I recognized him immediately in Santino's photo.

It *had* to be him.

An Italian in a Russian family stuck out, especially with dark hair and permanently tanned skin. No one on Dad's side had those features. They all had the stereotypical Slavic look—blonde or light brown hair and pale skin. I'd inherited my brunette waves from my mother. It was implied Luca had been adopted. I'd never asked for an explanation, and nobody had offered one.

I stopped asking questions about anything that happened in my house after third grade. Two of my uncles dragged a man I'd never seen—who was covered in blood—into the formal dining room and laid him over the table.

They shut the doors, and I heard strange noises all afternoon. I stopped my dad outside the dining room and asked what they were doing to him. He told me to keep my mouth shut and never ask questions. When I defied him by asking again, he introduced my face to the back of his hand.

So I didn't think twice when Dad introduced me to Luca when I was ten. It was during one of his many attempts to smooth over the fractured lines of our family with displays of wealth. Throughout the years, Luca kept to himself, lurking in the shadows at gatherings, much like I did.

One winter, we sat on the icy steps outside my father's mansion during Christmas and passed a stolen bottle of vodka back and forth, the alcohol burning our throats as we chased away the loneliness. Luca, even then, wrestled with demons I didn't understand, and he never spoke of his family.

Why not?

Every Sunday was family night.

Santino's youngest brother, Kill, lived in a cozy, suburban home. We pulled up to the triple-decker, the front yard scattered with toys, a tricycle, and a small basketball hoop.

Kill greeted us at the door.

He was dressed in jeans and a leather jacket, his dark hair messy and falling over his eyes. Family photos added a splash of color to the black-and-white palette of the house. A buttery scent wafted through the air.

Violet bustled from the kitchen and grabbed me in a hug. "Come on in, make yourselves comfortable. We're about to play UNO."

In the living room, I spotted two of Santino's sisters with Jack. He was deeply engrossed in his game of stacking blocks. Santino ruffled the boy's hair.

Jack looked up and grinned. "Uncle Sonny! Are you playing cards with us?"

"Absolutely, buddy," Santino replied.

We settled around the dining table. Kill took his place while Violet handed out the cards with a gleam of excitement in her eyes.

"Alright, folks," she announced with a playful grin. "The rules are simple. Loser has to eat from the Bean Boozled jelly bean tin."

Santino groaned.

I raised an eyebrow, curious.

"Oh, you'll see," Violet said, her eyes twinkling.

The game quickly turned raucous, laughter and teasing filling the room. It was clear this was a tradition for them, a way to unwind and enjoy each other's company. I found myself relaxing, caught up in the absurdity of the game.

As the rounds went on, the Bean Boozled tin became a source of both dread and hilarity. The jelly beans ranged from delicious to downright disgusting, with flavors like "Stinky Socks" and "Rotten Egg." Each time someone lost, there was a collective groan and a burst of laughter as they ate the awful flavors.

Violet slid the tin toward me. "You're up!"

I hesitated, eyeing the colorful beans warily. "Do I have to?"

"It's a family tradition," Santino teased.

Sighing, I reached into the tin and picked a bean. The moment I bit into it, a wave of nausea hit me. It was "Dead Fish," and it was every bit as terrible as it sounded. I made a face as everyone laughed.

I gagged.

Santino patted my back. "You alright?"

I nodded, cringing. My stomach churned. As the game continued, I couldn't shake the queasiness. It had to be the stress of everything that had happened recently.

Like Luca.

I couldn't shake the image of Santino's grief when he looked at the photograph. He had no idea who Luca really was. How could I tell him the truth? How could I break the news that his cousin, the boy he still mourned, had grown up under the thumb of the Bratva? And more importantly, why hadn't Luca ever told me about his past? Why hadn't he escaped?

Memories of our childhood flashed—cold nights in Providence, huddled together, passing a bottle back and forth, trying to escape our demons. We had been close, yet he'd hidden a huge part of himself from me.

I needed to tell Santino, but the timing had to be right. The alliance with my family was on shaky ground, primed to blow up at any second. Santino had a right to know, and the longer I waited, the worse it would be. I grabbed my phone and disappeared to the bathroom, bringing up Luca's number. My finger hovered over the call button.

I pressed the button and brought the phone to my ear.

The line rang once, twice, and went to voicemail.

Luca wouldn't return my calls. I couldn't get ahold of him, and I was losing my mind. My stomach roiled from keeping the secret. But I needed more proof before I told them anything.

The next morning, I combed through Santino's photo albums. I pored over pictures and agonized over faces that might be Luca. After an hour of this, Santino strolled into the living room, where I'd laid out the books.

He sank onto the couch with a wry grin. "Writing an autobiography about my life?"

"Something like that."

He cocked his head. "What are you up to?"

I stabbed at a photograph. "Who are the people in this picture?"

He leaned over. "No idea."

I frowned, pointing at another. "This one?"

He shrugged. "The neighbor's kid."

"Are you sure?"

"It was a million years ago." His smile widened when I sank back onto the couch. "Why do you care?"

"I'm just trying to get to know you."

Santino's gaze sharpened, but then he sighed, running a hand through his hair. "You don't have to dig through old photos for that. Just ask."

"I like visuals. It helps me connect the dots."

Santino flipped through a page, chuckling. "I haven't

looked at these in a while. Jack looks just like my brother. Unreal."

I leaned into him. "Is that Luca?"

He tapped another face. "No, that's him."

I examined the picture, but I couldn't say he was a dead ringer for the adult version. "Can you show me more photos of him?"

Santino hesitated and pointed to three boys opening presents under a tree. I squinted, trying to determine if he had a birthmark under his eye.

His smile faded as he reached the end of the album. Then he closed the cover and seemed to realize I had more of them underneath. He gave me a strange look. Finally, he let out a huge sigh.

"There's something you should know."

I clutched my hands, waiting.

Santino's eyes never wavered from mine. "The fire that killed my aunt, uncle, and cousin? It was orchestrated by the Romanovs. Luca was caught in the crossfire of a long feud between our families."

The ground fell away beneath me. I felt sick, the room spinning around me. My family had done this?

"Why would they do something like that?" I whispered.

"Years ago, the Romanovs were in Boston. There was a turf war. Territories in Southie were up for grabs, prime real estate for any family willing to spill blood for it."

My breath caught. "And my family...?"

He nodded grimly. "Your grandfather wanted control

over the docks. He wanted to send a message to anybody who thought they could operate on his turf."

"So, they set a fire?"

"Yes. They thought my uncle was becoming too influential. He had connections. Your grandfather believed eliminating him would scatter his allies and solidify the Romanov's control."

That chilled me to the bone. "But Luca was just a child."

Santino's expression darkened. "Collateral damage."

The albums suddenly felt like relics of a past soaked in blood.

I felt sick. "And now?"

"I'm telling you this because if we have any chance together, you need to know the whole story."

The photos blurred as tears welled in my eyes. The idea that my family could be responsible for such heartless brutality was overwhelming. As I sat there, a desperate thought flickered in my mind. The Luca I knew could really be Santino's cousin.

"Is there any chance Luca could have survived the fire?"

Santino's eyebrows knitted together. "Everybody died."

"How do you know that?"

He shrugged. "They're all gone."

"But what if—"

He sighed. "Delilah, let it go."

My heart hammered. "Santino, I think he's still alive."

"What are you talking about?"

"I've seen him before—"

"Baby, that's just not possible."

Santino kissed my cheek. I barely felt the warmth on my cold skin. His family believed he was dead, but Luca was very much alive. I needed to make him listen.

My phone shrieked.

I sat up, grabbing it from the nightstand. Notifications popped on the screen. Dozens of them from the security cameras mounted at the store. My heart hammered as I opened the live camera feed filled with swirling plumes of black smoke. Flames ate up the freshly painted walls.

My store was on fire.

THIRTY-TWO
DELILAH

We got there too late.

The boutique was a charred husk, the half-finished mural smeared with soot and streaks of water. Firefighters milled around, packing up hoses and equipment, the last wisps of smoke curling into the blue sky. I stumbled out of the car, my heart sinking as I took in the devastation.

Santino grabbed my arm, steadying me. "Delilah, wait."

I couldn't. I pushed past him and into the store, my boots crunching on shattered glass and debris. The air was thick with the acrid stench of burned fabric and paint. Everything was ruined—racks of vintage clothes were reduced to damp, smoky tatters, and the beautiful fixtures I'd handpicked were scorched beyond recognition.

Only a few boxes in the back, somehow shielded from the worst of the fire and water, had survived. It wasn't enough. Not nearly enough. Tears blurred my vision as I surveyed the wreckage of what was supposed to be my new beginning.

Santino's hand settled on my shoulder, his touch gentle.

I shook my head, despair hollowing out my voice. "It's all gone."

He didn't respond right away, just stood there with me in the ruin. "This isn't the end. We'll rebuild everything."

I looked up at him, trying to breathe through my tears. "From what? Everything is destroyed. All the vintage clothing I spent *months* sourcing. How do I even start over from this?"

"We'll find out what happened." His jaw tightened, anger simmering in his eyes. "And I'll punish the bastards responsible."

"Dimitri did this. He wants to punish me for leaving him. He knew this would break me."

"He won't get away with this."

I nodded, wiping away tears. "But even if you find him, it's gone, Santino. All my work...my sketches."

"I'll help you. We'll make it even better than before."

A different kind of ache began to gnaw at me. The kind that whispered for a quick fix that could wash away the day's horrors. My gaze drifted toward the remnants of the boutique's cash register, where, once, I'd hidden a bottle.

"I need to get out of here."

I turned away from the wreckage. The destruction was pushing me toward an edge I'd promised myself I'd never teeter on again.

Santino caught my elbow gently. "Let's go home."

The drive back was silent. Santino kept glancing at me, his eyes filled with concern. By the time we reached his penthouse, the craving was a live wire inside me.

In the elevator, I leaned against the wall, my thoughts racing as we ascended. Santino stayed close. As soon as the doors opened, I paced into the kitchen. My hands trembled as I grabbed a glass of water, the cool liquid barely quenching my thirst.

"Principessa, talk to me."

"All I want is a drink. To forget just for a little while."

"You know you can't do that."

I gritted my teeth. "What if it was just one?"

"You know what happens when you do that. Not an option." Santino pulled out his phone, texting someone. "My brother's wife will keep you company while I deal with this."

"I don't need a babysitter."

"She's coming over," he ground out. "Stay here and don't do anything crazy."

I need a drink.

The thought shot across my mind every five minutes as Violet and I played a board game called Azul. Jack, Kill's four-year-old son, bounced around the room, periodically trying to add his own tiles to the game, which only made things more chaotic. Violet laughed, her Southern drawl thickening as she scooped him into her lap.

He giggled, squirming in her grasp before settling down to watch us play.

Violet caught my distracted glance as I fumbled with a tile, her eyes softening. "Jack's been gettin' into everything lately. He's at that age where curiosity's got him pokin' around where he shouldn't."

I forced a smile. "Kids are like that, right? Always exploring."

"Yeah, just the other day, I found him tryin' to climb the kitchen cabinets to get to the cookies I hid. Had to give him a stern talkin' to, but it's hard not to laugh sometimes."

"Sounds like a handful." I placed a tile and tried to keep my hands steady. The smell of smoke seemed to linger, a phantom scent that refused to leave my nostrils.

"He is, but he's also the sweetest boy. Loves to bring me flowers from the yard. Just the other day, he picked a whole bunch of dandelions and said they were for the 'prettiest lady in the world.' Melted my heart."

I smiled, a genuine one this time, as I pictured little Jack with his armful of yellow flowers. "That's so cute."

"Jack here has always been a light in my life. Times were tough, but he always found a way to make me smile. Kids have that magic, you know? Back home, it's all about community, helping each other out. It takes a village not just to raise a child but to keep going through hard times."

Her words struck a chord within me. Maybe I needed to lean on others more and try not to handle everything on my own.

"Delilah, you ain't alone here. Family, new or old, are here for you. And if that scumbag did what you think he did, well, he'll have more than just you to answer to."

I blinked back tears. "Thanks."

"Sometimes life throws us these curveballs, and we just

have to keep goin'. Focus on the good, no matter how small it might seem."

I nodded, my throat tight.

Violet's phone buzzed on the table. She glanced at it, her face tightening as she read the screen. "Sorry, I have to take this."

I watched her step away, her voice dropping to a whisper as she answered the call. A minute later, she came back, moaning. "Oh no, I completely forgot! I was supposed to take Jack to gymnastics. I'm so sorry. I need to rush him over there, or he'll miss it."

I smiled. "No problem, go ahead."

She gathered Jack quickly, ushering him toward the door. "Thanks for understanding, Delilah. Santino's on his way."

They hurried out, and a sense of isolation crept over me, the shield of companionship fading as she closed the door.

Alone again.

The board game lay on the table, the colorful tiles blurring. My hands trembled slightly, and a haunting urge whispered seductively in my ear.

Just one drink.

The boutique was gone. My dreams, reduced to ashes. A drink would dull the pain clawing at my chest. I wandered toward the kitchen. I glanced at the cabinet, where I used to keep a bottle. My throat tightened, my body craving the warmth that alcohol would bring.

No one has to know.

I reached for the door, the cool metal of the handle under my fingertips.

"Delilah?"

Santino's voice echoed through the penthouse, pulling me out of the haze. I froze. My pulse roared in my ears.

The door swung open behind me, and his heavy footsteps filled the space. I didn't turn around.

"Delilah, what are you doing?"

"I wanted a drink."

He gently pulled my hand away from the door and spun me to face him. He didn't say a word, just pulled me into his chest.

I buried my face against him. The store, the fire, Dimitri—it was too much. But Santino was there, keeping me grounded.

"It's okay," he murmured into my hair. "I'm not going to let you fall."

THIRTY-THREE
DELILAH

My phone buzzed again, this time flashing another message from the contractor about the repairs. I sighed, silencing it as I stood in the middle of the kitchen, staring at the overwhelming stack of papers on the counter—quotes from suppliers, emails from vendors, and a never-ending to-do list that kept growing.

The fire had gutted everything. All the vintage clothing, the displays, the custom fixtures I'd spent months curating... gone. I'd spent hours on the phone with the insurance company, trying to explain the loss, compiling lists of everything I'd owned, and sorting out the renter's insurance claim for the merchandise and fixtures. The insurance company dragged their feet, holding off on payouts because of "suspicious circumstances."

It was arson. Santino's people had already told me that much. They were handling it quietly, out of sight from the cops, but not knowing who was behind it for sure ate at me.

Luca's face flickered through my mind again, but I

pushed it aside. I couldn't focus on that right now. I had enough on my plate without adding another layer of stress.

I shuffled through the paperwork again, my head spinning. The fire. The inventory. The money I'd lost. Luca's reappearance. Everything was tangled up together, and I was barely keeping my head above water.

Santino entered the kitchen. "What's wrong?"

"I'm thinking about the inventory I lost. I don't think I can replace it all."

Santino stepped closer, his hand resting on my back. "We will."

I forced a smile, but my mind was still reeling. I needed to focus on something else to keep from spiraling.

"You haven't been eating much lately. Are you feeling okay?"

I shrugged. "I haven't had much of an appetite."

Santino's brow furrowed. "You sure that's all it is? You've been a little different."

"How?"

Santino reached out, tilting my chin so I met his gaze. "You're more tired than usual. And you've been avoiding food. That's not like you."

I sat up. "Maybe I'm not in the mood to eat."

"Delilah, I think you should take a pregnancy test."

My heart skipped a beat.

He traced circles on my back. "I mean, it could explain a few things, right?"

I nodded, my stomach churning.

My period was a bit late. Two weeks. I didn't want to examine what that meant. The thought of being pregnant was not something I wanted to contemplate. Life was too crazy right now: my store burned down, missing cousins had reappeared, and my ex still wanted to kill me.

Santino nudged my back. "There's a test in the bathroom."

"I'm not taking it. It'll just be another thing on my plate."

"Ignoring it won't change the truth."

"No, but it'll make me feel better."

Santino pulled me closer, his arms enveloping me in a tight hug. "You're not alone. We'll do this together. Let's just start with knowing for sure."

I turned, my legs shaky, and walked to the bathroom.

I found the test in a drawer and unwrapped it, my hands trembling. After I did my business, I leaned against the sink and waited for the results. A single dark line formed in the small window and stayed solid.

Not pregnant.

My lungs deflated, and my whole body sagged. Why wasn't I pregnant? I caught myself on the edge of the sink, my eyes stinging. Was I *crying*? Because I wasn't pregnant?

I threw the test in the trash.

Santino looked up, his eyes searching mine.

"It's negative," I said.

I should've been thrilled, right?

A lead weight formed in my stomach as I climbed into bed. I disappeared into the sheets, yanking the duvet to my chin. I couldn't make sense of the emotions raging in my head. I wasn't going to become a mother. Relief warred with a strange sadness.

Santino smoothed my hair from my face. "It's okay to be disappointed."

My insides splintered.

Santino's hand rested gently on my arm, his presence grounding me, but even he couldn't stop the storm that had settled in my chest. I needed to tell him about Luca. I'd tried to, but I had to insist he heard me out. Every day that passed, it got harder to say the words, harder to explain why I hadn't said anything sooner. And now it felt like everything was slipping beyond my control.

"I don't know what I'm doing."

Santino shifted beside me, his hand still on my arm. "You don't have to figure it all out right now."

"It feels like everything is falling apart."

His grip tightened slightly. "You haven't lost anything, Delilah."

I shook my head, tears stinging the back of my eyes. How would Santino react if he knew the truth about Luca? About the man he became in the shadows of the Bratva? I had no idea what his family would do once they found out.

I couldn't do anything about the store, but I could help them.

His family was a close-knit group. They'd endured so much together, and now I was a part of that. Luca's shadow loomed over us, a secret that threatened to unravel everything. I owed these people.

My father was the only one with answers.

THIRTY-FOUR
SANTINO

It took longer than I thought to get footage from the surrounding businesses. The store across the street showed several masked men breaking into her store. They hid their faces but stupidly wore jean jackets with a horned animal's skull on the back.

The Animals.

So he'd hired out for the job. I'd scoured Boston for Dimitri, but like a rat scurrying in the sewers, he'd disappeared. The news had a field day with the fire. Headlines decried the out-of-control crime, and the mayor called my boss, threatening to hire the National Guard and shut the city down if things kept spiraling out of control. It pissed me off to no end. The boutique was Delilah's dream, and it'd been torched because of me. Dimitri couldn't touch her directly, so he went after what she cared about most.

The next day, police raided my warehouse. An anonymous tip claimed that I was holding someone hostage. A SWAT team burst into my underground fighting ring.

Luckily, I'd canceled Thursday night's fight in anticipation of a move against me. They found nothing, but the disruption was another message from that shit stain.

And Delilah was acting strange since the fire. She spent a lot of time in bed, barely moving. She didn't sleep. Barely ate. I hired a personal chef and made her cook Russian food. Those little dumplings filled with beef. What were they called? Pelmeni? They sat in a bowl by the bed, untouched. I watched her curl under the blankets, her eyes rimmed with red, her lips and nose red.

Seeing her like this fucked me up inside. I had no idea how to fix this part. At least her drinking problem had actionable solutions—rehab, doctors, support. I didn't know what to do about *this*. She was pissed at me. I couldn't blame her. I'd let her down so badly. She blamed me for her store burning down, and guilt gnawed at me. I didn't know what to do with that, either.

On the third day, she showed signs of life. She dragged herself out of bed, did her hair and makeup, and sat in the kitchen, sketching in a notepad. Shafts of golden light poured into the room, painting her beautiful face. She stopped when I walked in, her cheeks staining pink like I'd caught her cheating.

My arm curled around her waist, and she stiffened. "I'm glad you're out of bed."

She shrugged. "I have some errands."

"I can take you to them. I'm about to head out."

"No thanks. I-I'd rather do them alone."

I nodded, and she pulled out of my reach. "See you at dinner?"

"For sure."

For sure.

I hated that. It sounded like something I used to say in my manwhore era when I was ready to ghost someone.

Except then, Delilah gave me a radiant smile, the one she always used when she wanted something. She leaned forward, grasped my shoulder, and kissed me. Her kiss was slow and thorough, and so were her hands. Gliding down my ass, circling the front of my hips, her finger tracing the head of my stiff cock.

I groaned.

She hadn't kissed me like this in a while. Her tongue flicked mine, teasing, as she pulled away. Her fingers gave my cock another squeeze, then she smirked.

"Bye, handsome."

She grabbed her car keys and wiggled her little fingers. Then she disappeared out the door. A dark suspicion started to weave through my head. Delilah using sex to get what she wanted didn't surprise me, and my wallet was intact.

What was she playing at?

This. She wants you standing at the door with your dick in your hand.

I grabbed my coat and car keys.

She got into her car. So did I. I waited a few minutes before following, using the tracker I kept on all my cars to guide me onto 95-S. She kept driving past Milton and Foxborough.

She was heading back to Providence. My gut tightened.

That city was a damn minefield for her, and she knew it. What the fuck was she thinking?

Delilah's car turned into a quiet, residential area with manicured lawns and cookie-cutter houses. Every turn she took felt like a twist in my stomach. She stopped in front of a big house I'd visited not long ago. The gate opened for her, and she drove in.

I parked a few houses down, staying hidden but with a clear view of her. She got out of the car and headed toward her father's house.

What are you doing, Delilah?

She walked up to the front door, and my heart hammered. My grip tightened on the steering wheel as she knocked. A man opened the door, older, with a presence that filled the doorway. Her father.

My mind raced with a thousand possibilities. Was she running back to her old life? Or was there something else, something deeper she hadn't told me? My vision blurred as I watched them exchange words. Mikhail stepped aside, letting her into the house.

Fuck this.

I got out of the car, my fists clenching as I approached the gate. The sight of Mikhail's smug face made me want to tear the door off its hinges.

What the fuck is going on?

THIRTY-FIVE
DELILAH

"Are you alone?"

I nodded, but Dad glanced over my shoulder.

"Alright. Come in."

I walked inside, and he patted my shoulder. Dad was never one for big displays of emotion. I hadn't seen him since the wedding nearly four months ago, and he looked like he'd aged years. Bags hung under his red-rimmed eyes. A grim disappointment set his jaw.

The air was thick with the tension of our strained relationship. He brought me into the living room, the scent of leather and cigar smoke mingling with my stepmother's perfume. Zofia sat in her usual chair, her eyes narrowing.

"Well, if it isn't the runaway bride," she sneered, her voice dripping with disdain. "Vodka?"

She poured me a shot from the bottle on the table, not even bothering to wait for a response. She'd always been a horrible human being. I sat in the chair furthest from her and focused on my dad.

He sat in front of me, his gaze hard.

"Running away from Dimitri was the most foolish thing you've ever done. Do you have any idea the chaos you've caused? The shame you've brought on this family?"

Zofia sat back, crossing her legs. "*Solnyshko*, we only want what's best for you. You know that, don't you?"

"Not really."

Zofia smiled. "You've always been headstrong. It's just...sometimes, *solnyshko*, we need to think about more than just ourselves. Our actions affect everyone around us."

Classic Zofia move—a compliment laced with criticism.

"Family is everything," she pressed on, leaning forward, her eyes locked on mine. "And sometimes, family requires sacrifice. We all have to do things we don't like for the good of the family. It's time you start thinking about your role in all this."

She framed submission as duty and manipulation as love. It was a skill she'd perfected over the years, making you feel guilty for wanting something different.

"And we can forgive, you know," she added softly, almost a whisper. "We can move past this incident. We can put it all behind us if you apologize."

I looked from her to my father, seeing the same demand for compliance in his eyes. "I'm not here to apologize about my decision. I don't regret leaving Dimitri, not for a second. I came to ask you about Luca."

My father stiffened. "What about him?"

"I need to know the truth about him, Dad. I think I know who he really is, and I think you do, too."

Zofia pursed her lips, glancing at my father. "What is she talking about?"

He waved a hand. "She's babbling nonsense."

"Dad, I've seen pictures of him at Santino's house. He carries a photo of him in his wallet. Did you really think you'd get away with this forever? That you could...steal a fucking child?"

Zofia's tinkling laughter broke the silence.

Dad shook his head. "I've never heard such *chepukha* in my life."

"Tell me the truth. Who is Luca?"

Dad's voice was flat, almost bored. "Luca is no one important. Just a boy that your imagination has turned into something else."

Heat flared in my chest. "He's not just some boy. He's Santino's cousin who supposedly died in a fire you started."

Zofia laughed again. "Such wild fantasies."

I ignored her. "Dad, I need the truth. This isn't just about family feuds or old crimes. People's lives are at stake."

"If you like living, you will drop this. Forget about Luca."

I swallowed hard. "I can't do that."

He stood abruptly, his chair scraping back hard. "Then you are no daughter of mine!"

I stayed seated. "What the hell have you been doing to him?"

"I didn't do anything to him," he snapped. "I saved him. His family was killed, so I gave him another one."

"You stole him from his real family and raised him in a world of lies. Why?"

His face flushed. "His family was a threat. Taking him in was the only way to neutralize them."

"By turning him into one of us? By keeping him hidden all these years?"

"A dead child holds no value. But a living one who believes his family left him for dead, that's useful. Luca isn't here because he doesn't remember who he is. He's here because I made him believe there was nothing left to go back to."

I stared at him, horrified. "You made him think his family abandoned him?"

"It wasn't difficult. He was young and scared. He believed me because he had no other choice." Dad glared at me, his voice rising sharply. "I saved his life."

"After killing his parents!"

My father's gaze hardened. "Luca is an adult. If he wanted to leave, he would have. But he hasn't. He knows who I am, and what I've done for him. Don't kid yourself into thinking you can change that with a few words. And if you try to change his mind, you'll be the one who suffers."

A sick feeling settled in my chest. "You turned him into one of us, made him live a life he never asked for. And for what? To keep your enemies close?"

He didn't respond, his silence confirming everything. My stepmother shifted uncomfortably in her chair.

"Where is he?" I asked.

"I won't tell you that."

"Dad, come on. You must've known this day would come."

"Which is...what?" My father grabbed the shot I

refused to touch, downing it. "What makes you think he'll want to go back?"

"You killed his parents."

His shameless gaze stabbed into me. "I did what was necessary for our family. You wouldn't understand. You've lived a sheltered life."

"I've lived a lie, surrounded by *murderers* who justify their sins as survival tactics!"

Dad laughed. "And what do you think your *makarony* is?"

"He's not a selfish asshole!"

"Don't talk to your father like that," Zofia shouted.

I glared at her. "It doesn't surprise me that you're defending how he kidnapped a child!"

"Luca is an adult," my father seethed. "If he wanted to go home, he could have."

"I'm finding Luca, with or without your help. And when I do, I'm telling him the truth."

Dad's face twisted. "You're no longer part of this family, you worthless *suka*! You're on your own, so don't you dare come back here begging for help when Costa tires of you and throws you to his men!"

I headed to the door.

My father followed, shouting. I blocked out most of what he said, but a few of his insults managed to penetrate the wall in my head.

Whore, whore, whore.

I left the house, slamming the door behind me.

When I told Santino about Luca, he'd be furious. He

might not want me anymore. What if telling Santino the truth was the thing that finally drove him away?

I'd fallen for him in a way I never expected. He wasn't just protection from my twisted family; he was the man whose arms I craved. He talked about how I hooked him, but he'd seduced me that first night. Every encounter with him built me up, even the ones on my knees. Because he'd been the one to push for a relationship. He'd told me that he wanted more. He'd shown me what it was like to be cared for.

But this secret had the power to destroy everything.

I drove back home, dazed. Then I parked the car and headed up the elevator, dreading the moment those doors opened.

THIRTY-SIX
SANTINO

Delilah walked to her car, her pace quick but composed. She paused beside the driver's door, taking out her phone. She typed something, then put the phone away and drove off.

My phone vibrated. I pulled it from my pocket.

PRINCIPESSA
Done with errands, heading home now.

My jaw tightened. What was so important that she had to see her father without telling me? What was she hiding?

I started my car and followed her. The drive back was a blur of dark thoughts. Every turn reminded me of the distance growing between us.

I parked my car in our building's garage and headed up to our floor. I stormed into our bedroom, yanking open the door to the bathroom. I opened a drawer. I grabbed another pink box, and then I noticed the stick in the trash.

Two lines. Clear as day.

My heart spasmed.

Pregnant. She was pregnant.

She must've taken another test. When? Why did she take a test without telling me? She was keeping secrets. Was the pregnancy only one of them?

Delilah walked in, her face pale. Her gaze flicked to the pregnancy test in my hand.

"Why the fuck didn't you tell me?"

She flinched. "I just found out."

"Jesus, enough with the lying. I found it in the trash." I slammed it onto the counter.

She picked it up, her expression impassive. "I was going to tell you."

"Your lies are getting more desperate, principessa."

"I'm not lying!"

"You've been keeping things from me. First your father, now this. I thought we were past this shit."

Delilah's fierce gaze stabbed into me. "I had to ask him something."

"Like for his help getting away from me?"

"It wasn't about you."

Sure, I believe that.

I sneered, cornering her against the counter. I reached into my jacket and pulled out the box. My thumb popped it open, and I grabbed the ring. Then I took her wrist and slid it onto her finger.

"We're getting married in a month."

She bared her teeth. "That's not a proposal."

"We are having a baby. We need to get married."

She took off the ring and put it on the counter. "First of

all, no, we don't. And secondly, I don't want to get married while our families are at each other's throats."

"It's the right thing to do."

"For who?"

"The baby," I fumed. "You'll wear my ring, walk down the aisle, eat some cake, and smile for the photographers. And then, when it's all over, you can go back to lying with every breath."

"You're being an unreasonable prick!"

"You think I'm bad now? Just wait until our kid is born."

She paled. "I took the test today. I was going to tell you, I swear."

"That's convenient."

Her eyes misted over, probably upset I'd caught her in a lie. It took a lot to make her shed tears. I'd only seen her this upset the time she came into Afterlife. She'd bypassed the line of peasants and demanded a private audience. I took her into a different room, and as soon as the door closed, she fell apart. So many people approached me with a sob story, lying their asses off, that I was prepared to just dismiss her outright.

Delilah hadn't lied about her story, but she had withheld information. She pretended to be into me and used her body to get what she wanted. And it worked every fucking time. I belonged to her. I thought that meant we were good together.

Maybe I was wrong.

A fat tear rolled down her flawless cheek. "Santino, I'm not trying to leave you."

"Yes, you are."

"No, I swear—"

I let go of her chin, sneering. "It's like you said. This relationship was always about money. Securing *your* future."

"That's not fair."

"Do you even care who you're fucking? As long as *you* get what you want?" A dark flush spread across her cheeks, and a mean flare of victory heated my chest. "I did see this coming. It's not like I didn't know exactly what you are."

The second those words landed, I knew they'd hurt. I felt the pain inside me as I saw it reflected on her face.

"That's rich, coming from you. You used your money to control me from the beginning, and now you want to act like I'm the one to blame?"

"You didn't hesitate to take it. You've been using me since the start."

Delilah's eyes flashed. "I *needed* you. There's a difference."

"Is there?" I stepped closer, towering over her. "You wanted me to think you were a gold digger, and now you're pissed when I throw it back in your face? That's on you, Delilah."

Her lip trembled, but she clenched her jaw. I should've stopped, but I couldn't. The rage burned too hot inside me.

"You want to talk about trust? You've been lying to me since the day we met. Hiding things, going behind my back, always keeping your secrets close. What else are you hiding from me?"

I saw the exact moment I crossed the line. It hit something deep inside her. She shut down, her entire body tensing like she was trying to protect herself.

"Delilah."

It was too late. I'd already lit the fuse. Delilah stepped back, her body rigid. Nostrils flaring, she stormed out of the room. Banging sounds erupted in the kitchen. She'd thrown open all the cabinet doors and was rifling through the shelves in the pantry, searching desperately.

My heart ached. "Fuck."

She set aside bottles of olive oil and canola, probably looking for cooking wine. No use. I'd thrown all that shit out. Regret formed a ball in my throat.

"Can we talk about this?"

"Why bother? I'm just a whore to you."

I winced. "I didn't say that."

"You say I'm the one using you," she hurled back, her arm knocking over the bottles of cooking oil. "But you act like you can buy me, like I'm not even a real person."

I rubbed my face. "Delilah—"

"Just leave me alone, Santino."

Guilt sat heavy in my lungs.

"Delilah, there's no alcohol in the house."

She wasn't listening. She still rooted around, searching behind cans of garbanzo beans for a drop of alcohol that didn't exist. Finally, she stopped, slumping on the kitchen floor. She bowed her head in her hands, and her shoulders shook.

I couldn't stand this. I was crumbling inside. I opened my mouth to fix the rift tearing us apart. But what could I say? That I was scared? That every fear was tied up in her?

That I didn't know how to love without also trying to control?

Delilah wiped her cheeks, her gaze hardening. "If I'm just a gold digger to you, then maybe you're right, and there's nothing left for us here."

My stomach sank. "Do you remember when we first met?"

She nodded, sniffing.

"When you walked in Afterlife, you changed my life forever. You were all dressed up. Tight skirt, hair done up, makeup. So beautiful. I'd never seen anything so perfect. And when you told me your last name, I couldn't believe you'd come to me. You walked right up to me. I didn't just see a beautiful woman who needed to be saved. I saw bravery. You were fierce. I've watched you struggle and fight. You never back down. Then, when you arrived at the hotel, dressed up like a bride..." I smiled, the memory glowing in my chest. "Right then, I knew I'd met my match."

Delilah scoffed. "You used me for sex."

"I was just trying to hold on to you. I used what I had—money. I thought if I could get you to stay, maybe you'd see something worth staying for."

She snorted. "You dangled money in front of me, used my body like it was your right, and now you're telling me it was because you cared?"

I met her gaze head-on. "I grew up in a world where you take what's yours and hold on to it with both hands. And yeah, I used what I had to keep you. But that's because I knew you were worth it."

Delilah's glare softened for a moment. "You don't get it.

This isn't about whether I'm worth it to you. It's about whether I'm safe with you."

"You are."

Her lips quivered, and she shook her head. "Get out."

My chest caved in. "What?"

"You need to leave. I need to think about what's best for me."

"You want me to go?"

She nodded, her eyes filling with tears. "Please."

A stabbing pain throbbed in my gut. I'd always been afraid of this. She saw me as just another version of the men who'd controlled her. It was like everything I'd done had become unrecognizable. She saw me as a threat, not a refuge.

I loved her more than anything. She wasn't just a means to an end. She was the center of my world. How could I make her see that?

"I'll go. If that's what you need."

"It is," she ground out.

I turned around and headed out. Part of me wanted to fight, but it wouldn't make her see me any differently. I paused at the door, hoping for some sign of change, not the silence filling the space between us. Then I stepped out, closing the door behind me.

THIRTY-SEVEN
DELILAH

I spiraled the moment he stepped out.

I sat alone in Santino's penthouse. Every word he'd hurled at me echoed in my ears as I replayed our fight. The only thing stopping me from a trip to the liquor store was the tiny life growing inside me. I couldn't be more than a few weeks pregnant. The baby was only a speck at this point, but it already had a hold on me.

Just a few days ago, the idea of being pregnant terrified me, but now it was the only thing keeping me sane. The ache in my chest deepened, and I squeezed my eyes shut, willing the tears to stay at bay. I couldn't afford to fall apart. This baby...our baby deserved better than this. It deserved parents who loved each other.

Someone knocked.

I got up from the couch, flying to the door. When I opened it, Santino's brother stood in the doorway. His expression was unreadable as always, his cold gaze sweeping over me.

"Can I come in?"

I nodded, stepping aside.

The door closed silently behind him, and Kill crossed his arms.

"I heard about the fight," Kill deadpanned.

"It's none of your business."

Kill didn't move, his gaze boring into me.

I clenched my jaw. "He shoved a freaking ring on my finger and *told* me we were getting married. He didn't even ask. He wouldn't let it go, so I kicked him out."

"He doesn't do things halfway. You should know that by now."

A bitter laugh escaped me. "Yeah, I do."

"You're important to him," Kill said, his baritone surprisingly gentle. "Maybe more than you realize."

His words stung because I wanted to believe them. It'd be nice if Santino's obsession with control was rooted in love, but every step forward felt like falling more into a trap.

"He's just so... intense. Like he's trying to control everything."

Kill studied me for a long moment. "Santino's not like your dad, and he's not Dimitri. He's got his own demons, sure, but he'll never hurt you. He's protective. Sometimes, he just goes about it in a fucked-up way."

"He's unhinged."

"We all are."

"Yeah, but he's done a lot of messed up things."

Kill used to murder people for a living. He wouldn't bat an eye if I told him about the kidnapping, the birth control pills going mysteriously missing, or the man at the fighting ring he'd probably beaten to death.

"If he's done some bad shit, it's because he likes you so much."

"You're just here to help out your brother."

"Santino isn't the type to fly off the handle for a girl, but with you, he's different. He's..." He shook his head, smiling. "*Whipped.*"

"He sure has a funny way of showing it."

"He's never been good with feelings. Doesn't mean they're not there. And I've never seen him like this."

I swallowed, my throat tight. "Then why doesn't he just say it? Why does everything have to be about control?"

Kill shrugged. "Because that's how we protect the people we love."

I looked up at Kill, searching his face for any sign of deceit. I wasn't angry anymore, just confused. Could it really be that simple? That all of this intensity was because Santino felt something deeper than he could admit?

"You think he loves me?"

Kill nodded. "I've never seen him this tortured over a woman in my life. And I've never seen him leave when things get tough. Not until today. And that's only because you asked him to."

All this time, I'd been so focused on my own fears. I hadn't seen what was right in front of me.

"He's scared," Kill continued, his tone softening. "He's terrified of losing you. And that makes him do stupid things. But it's because he wants to make sure you're with him. Always."

I swallowed hard. "What if I'm too broken for him?"

"We're all broken. That doesn't mean we're not worth fighting for."

That settled over me like a warm blanket. Maybe he was right.

"I don't want to lose him," I whispered.

"Then don't. Talk to him."

"Where is he?"

"He's at the fighting ring."

My throat tightened. "What's he doing there?"

"Causing trouble. Not just with the talent, but civilians too. It's getting out of hand. Someone needs to pull him back before he does something crazy."

My stomach clenched. "I'll go to him. I'll talk sense into him."

Kill opened the door. "I'll take you."

I grabbed my coat, and Kill led the way. As we headed out, my heart pounded. This wasn't just a rescue mission. It was the last chance to salvage our relationship or, at the very least, bring him back from the brink before he destroyed himself.

"Thanks for coming with me," I said as I got into his car.

"It's what family does." Kill started the engine and drove out of the parking garage.

When we arrived, the place was buzzing with the usual nighttime crowd. I followed Kill, his presence clearing a path through the crowd.

Stepping inside the room that held the ring was like entering a world where the rules of the outside didn't apply. The stench of blood and sweat saturated the air. I scanned the crowd, searching for Santino.

Kill nodded toward the far corner. A group of guys shoved each other. Santino stood in the center of the commotion, his fists balled and his shirt ripped. Men in suits formed a ring around him, blocking from a shirtless man wearing red boxing gloves. Santino was fighting the only way he knew how.

I'd done that to him.

I'd made him feel unwanted, too scared to admit I loved him. I hated that I'd shown it by pushing him away. I'd been so focused on not getting hurt that I didn't see how I was hurting us both, maybe beyond repair.

My whole life, I'd been discarded. I entered a relationship with Santino, expecting him to let me go after he had his fill. Instead he'd kept me around. Offered me a life with him. Practically begged me to say yes. And I'd been too caught up in my demons to realize that we belonged together. My heart ached to see him so lost and desperate.

I had something beautiful with this man.

But if I didn't claim him now, I'd lose him.

"Santino!"

My voice barely cut through the din of the crowd.

His head snapped up, eyes locking onto mine. For a split second, everything around us faded—the noise, the chaos, the ring. He didn't move.

Kill sighed. "Let me talk to him first. Stay here."

He approached Santino, placing a firm hand on his shoulder. Santino turned, his expression bestial. They exchanged a few words, too low for me to hear over the music, and then Santino's posture relaxed.

Kill motioned for me to come over. I took a deep breath and moved forward, my heart pounding. Santino was battered but still so damn beautiful. His eyes met mine, a mix of emotions flickering across his face—anger, confusion, and something that looked painfully like regret.

I pushed through the crowd until I stood in front of him.

His lips flattened. "Go home, Delilah."

"*No.*"

His nostrils flared, and a few of his men winced.

I ignored them. "We need to talk."

I took his hand, drawing him away from the men. He resisted. His black eyes blazed with need, but something kept him from falling into my arms like he usually did. Pride, maybe.

So I kissed him.

I linked my arms around his neck and poured my feelings into a kiss. My hands framed his face. He tasted like whiskey, and it made me crave every sweep of his tongue. His mouth softened, and his arms wound my waist, anchoring me to his body. I pulled back and gently took the lead again. I tugged on his hand. He followed, grabbing his jacket from a chair.

Once we stood outside, alone in the parking lot, I ran my fingers over his bloody hand.

"Your knuckles are all ripped up."

"I got into a fight."

"I'm sorry," I whispered, my arms tightening around

him. "I'm sorry for all the times I pushed you away. It's not because I don't care—it's because I care too much. And I... there's something I need to tell you. I tried to tell you earlier, but you brushed me off."

Would this be the last time he looked at me like this?

Santino stared at me, unblinking. "What is it?"

Taking a deep breath, I gathered all my courage. My heart screamed to tell him how much I loved him and how desperately I wanted us to build a future together. Instead, I focused on the other truth that needed to be shared.

"Luca is alive, and he's in Providence."

THIRTY-EIGHT
DELILAH

I handed Santino my phone.

The screen illuminated a candid photo of Luca and me at Christmas, wearing sullen sneers as someone, probably my aunt, harassed us to smile. I scrolled to another, each image a piece of a puzzle I'd been too scared to solve until now. All of them showed Luca, not as a memory lost to a fire, but as a boy who grew up with me under the Romanovs.

I'd spent hours digging through digital albums, looking for evidence tying the man I knew to the child everyone believed perished in the fire. Slowly, I'd gathered photos from my childhood and a few rare ones where Luca and I were together, his features unmistakably similar to the boy in Santino's photograph.

"He was never in the fire, Santino. My father told me everything. He went over there and killed his parents but couldn't go through with it when he got to Luca's bedroom.

He took Luca out of the house that night and gave him to a relative to raise—one of my aunts with two other boys."

Santino lowered the phone, his jaw slack. "He took my cousin?"

"Yeah, and brought him to Providence."

"I don't believe it," he murmured, grabbing the photo in his wallet. "You're saying this is the same kid?"

"*Yes.*"

His jaw clenched. "Are you fucking with me?"

"It's him. He even still goes by Luca."

Santino raked a hand through his hair. "Everybody knows this?"

"I'm not sure. I didn't put it together until you showed me that picture in your wallet." I sucked in a deep breath as Santino scrolled through the gallery. "Dad never told me anything about Luca, but he always stuck out like a sore thumb. Black hair and olive skin and speaking Russian."

"He speaks *Russian?*"

"Yeah," I whispered, heart hammering. "They must've taught him."

Santino's fist tightened on my phone as he got to an image of Luca at seventeen, looking cool and detached, flipping off the camera. "Your father confessed?"

I nodded. "That's why I went to Providence without you. I had to ask him about Luca. I didn't tell you because I didn't want to give you false hope."

Santino didn't say anything. Then he put the phone back in my hands, clasping my shoulder with a biting grip. He looked at me, fire smoldering in his black eyes.

"Take me to him."

"He works here?"

Santino turned in the car seat, casting a doubtful look at the Eastern European grocery store, an unassuming building sandwiched in between a divorce lawyer and a carpet cleaning service. The strip mall was innocuous.

I nodded. "It's one of my dad's money-laundering businesses."

Santino's brow furrowed. "What does he do?"

"Besides ring up customers, you mean? I'm not sure. He might handle some of the back-end work, too—accounts, maybe. But he's always kept a low profile, exactly the way my dad wanted him to. Low enough that your family would never realize he was still alive."

Santino's gaze hardened. "So they raised him to think that he was abandoned. Did they brainwash him or something? What have they been forcing him to do?"

"I don't know. I wish I could tell you more."

Santino let out a frustrated sigh.

He'd grilled me on the drive to Providence, but most of my answers consisted of *I don't know*. He'd been especially curious about why Luca hadn't escaped in fifteen years of captivity. Again, I had no explanation to give him. I had no idea if Luca had been threatened or was Stockholmed into compliance.

All the answers to Santino's burning questions were in that store, but Santino couldn't walk into a Bratva-owned business without getting shot on the way out.

He started to unbuckle his seatbelt.

Alarmed, I grabbed his forearm. "Where do you think you're going?"

He paused, halfway out of the seat. "I need to talk to him. Face to face."

"Okay, but *how* are you going to do that?"

He jerked his head toward the store.

"*No.* Hell to the no. That's a *really* bad idea. He's not going to be alone. And I guarantee you he has a gun behind the counter."

"It'll be fine."

He opened the car door.

I watched him stroll to the entrance of the grocery store, biting my lip. Then I got out and ran to him. My ballet flats slapped the pavement as I hooked my arm through his. Santino didn't stop walking, but he slowed down.

We opened the door, and a bell chimed. We turned right into an aisle of canned goods. I grabbed a basket and walked around, filling it with a few items—corkscrew pasta, sour cherries, sausage from the fridge. Santino reached for an item on the top shelf as his attention wandered to the cash register.

Behind it, there was a small kitchen. A tall, stainless steel pot simmered on the stove, and a satellite radio blared sports commentary of a Russian soccer league. Low voices rumbled behind a plastic curtain.

My throat tightened as Santino approached the counter. His palm slapped the bell.

The plastic curtain rippled, and Luca walked through. He looked just like a typical street thug, fade haircut, eyebrow slits, oversized hoodie, and tattoos on his hands and knuckles.

"Ready to check out?" he asked.

Santino nodded.

I waited for a sign of recognition as Santino pushed the basket toward him, but Luca didn't glance in my direction. Santino's knuckle rapped the thick plate of plastic glass in front of the register.

"What's this for?"

Luca hit the keys on the cash register. "Protection. Lots of crime in the area."

"Oh yeah? Shame."

Luca finally looked at me, swallowing hard. His hands paused, and his eyes flicked up to meet Santino's before returning to the register. "Did you find everything you need?"

"Yeah."

"Good," Luca deadpanned. "That'll be twenty fifty-eight."

Santino glanced at me. I shook my head slightly, my stomach twisting with nerves. He turned back to Luca, his expression unreadable. He handed over cash, and the register sprang open. A small machine spat out a receipt, and Luca ripped it off, shoving it and Santino's change into his palm.

Luca bagged the groceries and handed the bag over the counter. "Have a good day."

Santino took the bag but didn't move. "Do you know who I am?"

Luca's pointed glare drifted to me. "I have no idea."

"Okay, Luca."

Luca completely ignored Santino, taking his time closing the register. His attention darted to the security camera angled above the counter, then back to Santino.

A man in the back shouted in Russian. *"Are they done? What's taking so long?"*

Luca tensed. *"They're asking for directions."*

Santino leaned in closer. "Luca, what the fuck?"

"You need to go." Luca pointed toward the door. "Now."

Santino's jaw worked. "Do you remember me?"

"Sir, I think you're confused. I'm just trying to work here. Please leave the premises before I call the authorities."

I grabbed Santino's hand.

Reluctantly, he let me lead him outside. As we exited the store, the door closed with a soft jingle. I looked over my shoulder as we reached Santino's car, but Santino kept his gaze forward.

"He acted like he didn't recognize me. Something is very wrong. He seemed tense and wary of the cameras, the surveillance...I've never noticed that with him before."

Santino glanced at the store again. "Fifteen years, he's been in my backyard. *Alone*. Enduring God-knows-what. Did they torture him?"

"I-I don't think so." Part of me wanted to say that my dad wasn't capable of that, but honestly? I wasn't sure anymore. "Luca was just a kid when he was taken."

"I need to figure this out. I can't leave him in this situation."

"We won't."

I intertwined my fingers with his, and the tension in his jaw softened.

"This will change everything with your father. My boss will want him dead. We have to get him out of town."

"You'd do that for me?"

He smiled wryly, and a lightness fluttered in my heart. "You don't want his blood on your hands, principessa. That's not something you can walk away from. If I have to keep him alive for you, then that's what I'll do."

"I don't want you to risk your life for my father."

His eyes blazed with black fire. "What do you want?"

"You," I whispered. "Just you."

He stared at me, the harsh lines of his face softening. He broke into a small but beautiful smile. He reached out, his fingers trembling slightly as they brushed against my cheek.

A harsh cough echoed through the quiet.

We looked over. Standing outside the entrance of the grocery store were Luca and several other burly men, each with a gun pointed at us.

THIRTY-NINE
DELILAH

They frisked Santino, taking the gun from his jacket. Then they confiscated our phones and dumped them. My father's men stuffed us into Santino's car, and Luca sat in the driver's seat, showing no trace of discomfort as he drove to my father's house.

The lights turned on as the garage door rolled up, and we went inside. Many people had disappeared after entering my father's garage. I knew because the ductwork from the garage led to a floor in the upstairs bedroom. Growing up, I sometimes heard strange noises. When I mentioned it, Dad told me that his men liked to watch scary movies in the garage. But one day, I worked up the courage to sneak inside the garage, and I only saw concrete, rusted tools, and lawn equipment.

Santino didn't react as they hauled him out, prodding him in the back with a gun toward a chair in the middle of the room. My father was behind it, arms crossed. Beside him stood my loathsome ex-fiancé. A sick feeling pitted my stomach as his wrathful gaze zeroed in on Santino.

That was it.

I'd never see Santino again.

I wanted to clutch onto his arm and scream, but my lungs didn't work. Santino didn't even glance my way. He lounged in the chair, legs spread, the muscles in his arms taut.

"Good boy, Luca."

Dad patted Luca's shoulders like he was a golden retriever. Luca's dispassionate gaze swept over me as he stood in the corner. Well, he had warned me not to trust anybody.

"Delilah, come," my father said, beckoning me forward. "You don't need to see this."

"I'm not going anywhere without Santino."

Dimitri shot Santino a glare. "What did you do to my fiancée, you prick?"

Santino shrugged, his mouth twitching. "Just had some fun with her, that's all."

My heart twisted. I knew Santino too well by now and could see the lie for what it was—a desperate attempt to shield me from the worst of what was coming. He thought he was done for, and this was his way of making sure I wasn't dragged down with him.

Dimitri sneered, fists clenched at his sides. "You think you can just walk in and take what's mine?"

"I already did. I had your girl wrapped around my finger."

My stomach churned as I looked around for an escape.

Santino was trying to buy time. Dad gestured to one of his men, who grabbed Santino's hair and wrenched his head back.

"Enough," my father growled. "Delilah, come here. Now."

Santino's throat bobbed, but his lips turned up in a smirk. A silent plea gleamed in his eyes. He wanted me to go.

I latched onto the back of Santino's chair, refusing to let go, my fingers digging into the worn leather as if it could somehow anchor him to this world. My father's gaze hardened, and Dimitri's face twisted with fury.

"You dumb bitch. You're defending him? After everything he's done?"

Santino's jaw tightened. "She's just confused. She doesn't know what she's doing."

"I know exactly what I'm doing."

Dimitri snorted in disgust and raised his gun to Santino's temple. "If you want chunks of brain in your hair, fine by me."

There had to be some way out of this.

I caught my dad's gaze. "Please don't do this."

Dad glowered. "Get out. This is no place for a woman."

"What will you do with him?" I pleaded.

"Oh, we're gonna take our time," Dimitri snarled. "I'll make a soundtrack of his screaming and play it during our wedding night."

Santino's throat bobbed as he swallowed. His eyes said only one thing—run. I probably could. I'd disappear into the night, hole up with Santino's relatives in Boston, and raise Santino's baby in peace, far from the reach of my father.

I'd be miserable for the rest of my life. No, leaving Santino was unthinkable. I couldn't force myself to go any more than I could stop breathing. Everything in me wanted to fight.

But how?

Three men surrounded us, plus my father. Everybody had a gun. Santino probably carried a knife. After we had sex, I'd watch him strap on his weapons. Each holster and blade.

My heart pounded.

He always had a small switchblade tucked into his boot. I remembered him joking once, saying it was his "good luck charm." Could they have missed it?

I glanced at his boots, trying to gauge if he was prepared to use it. His eyes met mine, and he subtly shifted his stance. Santino wouldn't go down without a fight. If he was going to make a move, it had to be soon. My father and Dimitri were eager for blood. I could see it in their eyes. They'd make him pay for daring to touch me.

I swallowed hard, my mind racing. If Santino had the knife, he could take out one of them. But then what? There were too many guns. We'd both be dead in seconds.

Santino's gaze flicked to me. He knew the odds, but he wasn't going to give up. Not if there was a slim chance of getting us out of this alive.

I had to act. I couldn't stand here and watch him get torn apart. My mind raced. I needed to create a distraction, something that gave Santino the opening he needed.

Santino's hand twitched. The knife was still there, hidden and waiting. He just needed a brief moment of chaos to tip the scales in our favor.

I had to create that moment.

"Boris," my father snapped. "Take her out of here."

A bald man grabbed my arm, pulling me toward the door. I elbowed his chest and scratched at his arms, screaming my throat hoarse. The man shoved me toward the door. I stumbled, grabbing a tire iron off the wall. I turned, swinging it hard.

It slammed into Boris's face. He staggered, clutching his cheek. Then I lunged forward, grabbed the edge of a table, and flipped it over, sending a toolbox crashing to the floor.

Santino's hand flashed to his boot. Then he plunged silver into Dimitri's thigh. Dimitri screamed, clutching his leg. His gun clattered to the ground. Santino dove for it. He grasped the handle—

Two loud bangs erupted.

My eyes widened as Boris crumpled to the ground, a neat hole between his eyes. Luca held a gun, his narrowed gaze focused on my father. My father staggered, blood blossoming on his shirt. Dimitri struggled on the floor, writhing in his blood. Santino emptied his clip into Dimitri, the shell casings pinging the concrete.

People inside the house shouted. Luca hit the garage door opener, and the sound of the motor drowned out the shouts of confusion. Santino grabbed me, opening a car door and shoving me inside as Luca scrambled into the driver's seat.

The door flew open.

Men burst into the garage, guns drawn.

A hail of gunfire cracked the windshield as Luca turned the car on. The engine roared to life, and Luca peeled out of the garage, tires screeching. Santino forced my head all the way down. He didn't let up until we'd merged onto the freeway.

Santino raked a hand through his hair, grinning. "How does it feel to be free?"

Luca growled something indistinct. He didn't say another word, his face a mask of concentration. The blood on his shirt and the wild look in his eyes were the only signs that he'd shot his way out of a death trap.

"Luca," I said, my voice cracking.

He glanced at me in the rearview mirror. "We'll talk later. We need to get somewhere safe."

Santino squeezed my hand, drawing my attention back to him. "Everything will be alright."

Luca took a sharp turn, the tires squealing as the car sped onto a side road. We made it out alive. Survival was just the beginning.

FORTY

SANTINO

Luca balanced a glass of water on his knee as he sat on my couch. "You got anything stronger than this?"

I shook my head. "We have seltzer and diet soda."

"Huh. You're a lot more boring than I remember."

"That's my fault," said Delilah from her seat beside Luca. "I'm sober now."

Luca's mouth twitched. "Makes one of us."

He inhaled the rest of the water like a shot, then he set the glass on the coffee table. Delilah slid a coaster underneath the glass, her eyes glazed over and raw.

Having him back was supposed to be euphoric. This was a fucking miracle. And yet, it didn't *feel* like one. Maybe because I didn't recognize the man sitting in front of me.

Sure, he looked like my cousin. I observed him from my leather armchair, cataloging the details. The oversized sweatshirt, baggy jeans, sneakers. Fade haircut. He had the hard look of a street thug, complete with the dead-eyed stare. His black eyes drilled holes into my head. His accent had changed from the working-class slang of Boston to a hint of Russian. My stomach hardened. What else had they changed about him?

I couldn't stop staring at him. I hadn't been able to tear my eyes off him since we got into my house, like he'd vanish into thin air if I blinked.

"Did you recognize me in the shop?"

"Obviously," he said, drumming his fingers on the couch. "I tried to get you out of there. You had no idea what you walked into."

Heat flushed my chest. "I didn't believe her when she told me you were alive. I had to see you."

Luca leaned back into the couch. "I figured you wouldn't. Everyone thought I was dead."

Why didn't you tell us you weren't?

The question lodged in my throat. I had so many questions, but I wasn't sure what he'd been through. I didn't want to grill him, but I needed to know. *Now*.

Delilah slid a hand over his shoulder. "You're family, and Santino cares about you. We *both* do."

Luca shrugged. "So now what?"

"I need to make some calls to Vinn. He needs to know what happened, but first, I have to figure out what I'm going to say to him. To everyone. My mom's going to lose her fucking mind. She still cries every year on the anniversary of your death."

His brows softened. "Does she still make espresso biscotti?"

"Yeah, she's always in the kitchen. Though, now that Kill has a kid, she's busy with babysitting."

Luca blinked. "He had a kid?"

"Yeah, a boy. He has another one on the way." I opened my phone to the shared gallery of Jack, showing him pictures. "Here."

Luca leaned forward, gazing at them.

I pointed at a photo of father and son. "Jack looks just like Kill, doesn't he?"

"The last time I saw Kill, he was about this big." Luca held out a hand, miming the height of a child.

"Luca, I need you to tell me what happened. I want you to go back to the beginning. Give me every detail you can. Start by telling me what you remember about the fire."

Luca sat back, the light leaving his eyes. His fingers restlessly drummed the armchair, mimicking the twitchy behavior during Delilah's withdrawal. She'd mentioned they used to pass a bottle of vodka back and forth like it was soda. Was he an alcoholic like her, or something worse?

"I don't remember much about that night," he muttered.

Bullshit. "They weren't my parents, and I still have that image of your house on fire seared in my brain."

His sharp gaze met mine. "I said, *I don't remember*."

"Why are you dodging the question?"

"Santino is just trying to understand what happened," Delilah said in a louder voice. "Just start with the things you do remember."

"The itchy blanket," he murmured. "They brought me

to someone's house and put me to bed on this hard mattress, and it had this wool, scratchy blanket."

"What about before that?"

Delilah shot me a vicious look, and I closed my mouth.

"I told you, I don't fucking remember. It's all clouded in confusing images. I remember heat and smoke. I remember a strange man pulling me from the house. I blacked out before I got to the car. And then...I woke up in a strange bed. A woman and a man introduced themselves to me—Ilya and Svetlana. They told me a fireman had saved me. That my parents were dead, that the house had burned down. They told me a heated blanket in the living room caught fire."

"That's a lie—"

"I know. I mean, I figured that out later, but..." His voice trailed off, and he tensed. "For the longest time, I believed them. I used to crawl under the blanket, turn it on, and read. I figured I'd forgotten to turn it off. They made me think that I'd made a mistake, that it was *my* fault."

Heat curled around my throat.

Luca inhaled, his breath hitching. "I thought someone would come to get me. One of my aunts or uncles, a grandparent, *someone*, but nobody ever did. They locked me in a room and said it was for my protection. I was so scared at first, but they were patient. Told me they were my new family. I didn't have a choice but to trust them. For a while, they treated me well—fed me, clothed me, taught me Russian. They said it was for my own good, so I could understand their world. And I believed them because I was just a kid. What did I know?"

My stomach churned. "They manipulated you."

Luca glanced at me, his eyes hollow. "Yeah, but I didn't know that back then. They made me believe everybody had abandoned me. That I had no one else. I started to accept it. They made me part of their...family."

"Is that why you never reached out?" I pressed.

"I couldn't have even if I wanted to. They kept me locked up. I wasn't allowed access to anything where I could look up my family. All I could do was focus on trying to survive. I knew my situation wasn't normal, but I thought I deserved it for killing my parents. My mind still found ways to blame myself for their deaths. By the time I was old enough to know better, I was a shell of a person. I didn't *want* to come home." Luca paused, his gaze fixed on the floor. "I'd accepted that I didn't belong anywhere else."

I raked a hand through my hair. "Jesus."

"I was becoming a problem. When they let me out, I started fights with anybody, I smashed up things, and I drank until I puked. The only person I got along with was Delilah, who was trapped in her own prison. When they locked me up, I had nothing to do but stare at the four walls of my prison. Then Mikhail stepped in and gave me a job." He exhaled sharply, the sound almost a laugh, but bitter. "That's when it started. I worked my way up the ladder. I had to be useful. I learned how to do things for them—small errands at first, but eventually, they let me do more. It was the only way I could earn some kind of freedom. I convinced myself it was the right move. It was easier than facing that I was stuck."

I leaned forward. "Is that when you decided to get revenge?"

"In the beginning, it was just about survival. Keeping them off my back, avoiding punishment. But the more I worked for them, the more I started to see things differently. I watched how they operated. I saw the lies. It was like a switch flipped. I realized what they'd taken from me." He clenched his fists. "I thought about the family I'd lost, about you. I knew you were out there, living your life while I was trapped. That's when everything changed. It stopped being about surviving and started being about getting even."

"I had no idea," Delilah whispered. "Why didn't you talk to me?"

Luca's lips thinned. "You were the Pakhan's daughter. I couldn't take that risk."

Silence filled the room. I studied his face, piecing together the cousin I once knew from the man sitting across from me. The transformation was unsettling, and yet...I understood it.

Luca stared at his hands. "I had to prove that I was more valuable alive than dead. I was nothing to them at first. Just a tool. But I made myself indispensable. I watched, I learned, and I waited."

Delilah shifted beside him. "How did you stay under the radar?"

"I became one of them," Luca replied, his voice cold. "I blended in. I kept my head down and never gave them a reason to suspect me. It took years. Every time I thought I was getting close, they'd test me, push me to see if I'd break. I had to play the part perfectly, or they'd kill me."

He lifted his gaze, meeting my eyes. "I waited for the right moment. I thought, maybe if I got close enough, I could take out Mikhail, especially after seeing how he treated Delilah. But then..." His jaw tightened, and he glanced at Delilah. "Then you two walked into that shop."

My chest tightened. "What changed?"

Luca shook his head, a bitter smile forming on his lips. "I realized the perfect moment would never come. I'd spent so long planning, convincing myself there'd be this flawless opportunity, but there's no such thing. When I saw you both, I knew I had to act, or I'd lose my chance forever. Revenge wasn't going to wait for me to be ready."

"So you made your move."

Luca nodded. "I had to. I wasn't going to let them take anyone else from me."

"I get it," I whispered. "You got close to Mikhail and bided your time until you could make a move, but I need you to hear me on this—you were never forgotten. Not a day went by that this family didn't think of you. We put up candles, said your name at dinner, and raised our glasses to you every Christmas. My mom, all of us... we never stopped thinking about you."

I fished out my wallet, showing him the portrait I kept tucked inside.

He swallowed hard. I could see the storm of emotions twisting up inside him. Rage, regret, maybe even hope.

"You're family," I said, tucking the photo back inside.

"You'll always have a place here. That doesn't change, no matter how long you're gone."

Luca's eyes went glassy, but he blinked, hardening. "You don't know what I had to do for them."

"I don't care."

His face flushed. "You say that now...but you might not like who I am."

I shrugged. "We take care of our own, no matter how fucked up they are."

Delilah sighed. "What Santino means to say is that he loves you unconditionally."

"I can speak for myself, principessa."

She raised a brow. "Could've fooled me."

Luca looked away, his jaw flexing. Delilah reached out and squeezed his shoulder. His eyes dropped to the floor. Delilah wrapped her arms around him, pulling him in tight. Luca stiffened, then leaned into her embrace, his chin dropping to her shoulder.

I hesitated. Then I moved to the couch and placed a hand on his back. "You're not alone anymore."

Luca tensed, then glanced up, a faint, almost defiant smile forming on his lips. Then I saw him—the cousin I used to know, still in there, fighting his way back.

FORTY-ONE
DELILAH
TWO WEEKS LATER

"Are you Delilah?"

I hitched a smile. "Yes, I am."

An olive-skinned man with wild hair shook my hand. "I'm Tony. It's a pleasure to meet you."

I nodded. "Likewise."

"This is my wife, Evie," he said, gesturing toward a young woman in jeans and a leather jacket. "I just wanted to thank you for what you did for our family. If you ever need anything, give me a shout."

His ringed hand patted mine, and he disappeared into the party. As soon as he left, yet another member of the family introduced himself to me. Michael. Or was it Alessio?

Santino had thrown a party to celebrate Luca's miraculous return. Relatives, friends, and allies kept filtering into the living room and wringing my hand. The atmosphere was ecstatic. Santino's mom had collapsed against me, thanking me through a stream of tears. They wanted to hear what happened to Luca. What his life had been like. They begged me for stories. Everyone wanted to meet the woman who'd brought Luca back to life.

Santino was by my side most of the time, his hand a constant presence on my lower back. He drank seltzer in his tumbler. The whole party was alcohol-free. I tried to make him change his mind, but he said he cared more about me than his guests' comfort.

"You okay, principessa?"

I needed a moment to breathe. "I can't believe all these people want to meet me."

Santino smiled, shaking his head. "Even Tony crawled out of his cave to see the girl everyone's talking about."

It was overwhelming, the constant stream of people, the noise, the praise. I felt like I was suffocating under the weight of it all. My chest tightened. I needed to be alone.

Santino's hand moved up to my shoulder. "You sure you're okay?"

"I need a little air," I said, trying to keep my voice light, not wanting to worry him. "It's a lot, you know?"

His eyes softened. "Go on, then. I'll cover for you."

I slipped out of the main room, maneuvering through the maze of people. The chatter faded as I found a quieter hallway. I wandered down, the sounds of laughter fading. I wasn't used to being the center of attention.

I climbed to the second floor, turned a corner, and noticed a door slightly ajar. Light spilled out from the crack, and movement rustled inside. I approached the door quietly, peeking inside.

Luca stood in the center of a small study. He stared at a

wall covered with old photographs, his back to me. The light from a nearby lamp cast a warm glow over the room, highlighting the tension in his shoulders.

I hesitated. "Luca?"

He didn't turn around immediately, but his shoulders relaxed. "I didn't hear you come in."

I stepped inside. "I needed a break from the party."

He nodded, still not looking at me.

I stood beside him. The old photos on the wall showed children playing in the yard, family gatherings, holidays. I glimpsed a younger Santino in some of them, always with that same intense look.

Luca's gaze fixed on a group shot of the family taken years ago. He was in it, a small boy standing in front of his parents, a wide smile on his face. The kind of photo that'd break your heart if you knew the story behind it.

"It must be strange," I said softly, "seeing all of this after so long."

Luca finally looked at me. "I don't belong here anymore."

"You do. You're family."

He looked back at the photo, his jaw tightening. "I was turned into someone else. How do you come back from that?"

I didn't have an answer, so I stayed silent.

"They don't know me. They see me as that boy in the picture, but I'm not him anymore." He laughed bitterly. "I don't fit in. I speak Russian, not Italian."

"Give it time."

"I don't even know who I am, so how can they?"

I reached out, placing a hand on his arm. "You're Luca, and you're not alone. You have people who care about you and want to help you find yourself again."

Luca crossed his arms, still tense. He looked down at my hand on his arm, then up at me. There was a vulnerability in his eyes that I hadn't seen before, a rawness.

The door opened.

Santino strolled in. "I figured you'd be hiding together. They're looking for you downstairs." He gripped his cousin's shoulder.

Luca wormed out of Santino's grip and left the room.

Santino frowned, staring after him. "He's been weird all night."

"Considering what he's been through, he'll probably be weird for a while."

Santino rubbed the back of his neck. "Yeah, I guess you're right. It's just hard seeing him like this."

"He'll get there. He just needs space to figure things out."

Santino turned to me, his expression softening. "What about you?"

I shrugged. "I'm managing."

My ex died in the shootout. There was no obituary or funeral, but he'd mysteriously disappeared. That meant the Bratva had handled his body privately. My father was in the hospital in a medicated coma. He probably wouldn't wake up. I kept waiting to feel devastated, but all I felt was relief that I'd escaped him for good.

I only wanted him to wake up to answer for his crimes. I'd hoped that his saving Luca had been an act of mercy, but I knew better. Mercy wasn't in my father's playbook. Turning one of their own against them was the ultimate display of power over the Costas.

Seeing Luca brought the reality of my relationship with Santino crashing down. I'd exposed my father as a monster who kidnapped a child, and I had no idea if Santino's feelings toward me had changed. Nobody in their right mind would still *want* me after everything. We'd barely even addressed the pregnancy.

Santino stepped closer, his hand gently tilting my chin so I had to meet his gaze. "Want me to kick everyone out?"

"No, I'm enjoying myself. It's just strange to be liked by so many people."

"You brought Luca back." Santino threaded his fingers through my hair, stroking me. "And you made me look really good in front of the boss."

"Oh yeah?"

He nodded slowly. "Getting him back scored me major points."

"You're welcome."

Santino chuckled. "You're becoming pretty popular with my family."

"I thought they'd be wary of me."

He shook his head, still smiling. "Not even close. You've earned their respect. My mom can't stop talking about how brave you are, and even my hard-ass uncles are impressed. They see you as someone willing to stand up for what's right, even when you had to abandon your family."

"They weren't much of a family."

"Yeah, but still. It's impressive. You're tougher than half the men here," he teased, pulling me closer. "And they all see how much you mean to me. What you've done for Luca. That goes a long way with the Costas."

I smiled. "I guess I didn't think I'd fit in."

"You fit in better than you realize. And you've done something for us that no one else could. Giving Luca back to us is something none of us will ever forget."

"Huh. Does that mean my debt to you is wiped clean?"

He smiled. "You think you can get rid of me that easily?"

I raised an eyebrow. "Well, considering everything, I'd say I've more than paid my dues."

He chuckled. "Maybe so. But since you're carrying my kid, I'm not going anywhere. In fact," he leaned in closer, his breath warm against my ear, "I'm going to be in your business even more. So you better get used to the attention."

My heart fluttered. "Oh, great. So now I'm stuck with you?"

"Damn right, and just to make sure you don't forget it..."

He pulled back and reached into his pocket, producing a small envelope. He handed it to me, grinning.

"What's this?"

"Open it and see."

I tore it open. Inside was a set of keys and a small card with a note written in Santino's bold handwriting.

For Retro Rose Boutique. It's all yours, Delilah. Now you really have no excuse to leave me. Love, Santino.

"You bought me a building?"

Santino nodded, his gaze steady on mine. "Pulled a few strings, called in some favors. It's on Newbury Street. Prime location. Bigger space, too, about twenty-five hundred square feet. You've got room to expand and add whatever you want."

"When did you even have time to do this?"

"I've been working on it since the fire. I didn't want you to worry about it, so I kept it under wraps. Everyone pitched in—my brothers, uncles. They all wanted to help."

"They did?"

"You're part of us now. We take care of our own."

My eyes burned. "I don't know what to say."

"You don't have to say anything," Santino murmured, his thumb brushing away a tear that had slipped down my cheek. "Just know that it's yours. Your name's on the title. You own it."

I stared at the keys in my hand, speechless.

He leaned in, his forehead resting against mine. Silence hung between us, the quiet hum of the distant party noises worlds away. Santino shut his eyes and opened them, taking a deep breath.

"And if you ever want…if you need your own space, I'll help you. Just yours. No strings."

My heart sank a little. Was he giving me a way out? Did he think I'd want one? Did *he* want one? The warmth of his body so close suddenly felt like a thousand miles away.

My stomach sank. "You're letting me go?"

He nodded, his eyes burning.

"You don't want me anymore?"

Santino's brow furrowed. "It's not that. I don't want to be another thing tying you down. This thing with Luca made me think. If you're here, it should be because you want to be. Not because you feel stuck."

"I don't feel stuck. I don't want to be anywhere else."

He softened. "I messed up. Made you feel trapped. That's on me. But if we're doing this, it's gotta be real. I want it to be right."

"I knew what you are. I chose you. And this shop is more than I ever expected. But I don't want it if it means not having you."

His hand came up to cradle my face, his thumb tracing the line of my jaw tenderly. "You have me, principessa. Always. If you want me."

"I do. More than anything. I love you," I blurted, the words rushing out. "I love you, and I'm scared of how deep this goes, scared of what it means for us both. I should have told you sooner how I felt, but I was afraid that loving you this much could destroy me."

"I love you, too, Delilah."

Tears welled up in my eyes, blurring his face, but I could hear how much he meant those words. My heart pounded. Hearing him say he loved me—it was everything I needed.

Santino raised his brow. "So, you'll marry me?"

"Yes."

"*Yes?*"

I smiled and nodded.

Santino got the box out of his jacket. I held up my hand, and he slipped the ring onto my finger. Then he pulled me into his arms, holding me tight against his chest.

EPILOGUE
DELILAH

Wedding bells chimed.

Santino and I stepped down the stone steps, hand in hand. A cloud of bubbles floated around us, courtesy of Jack and the other children, their laughter mingling with the cheers. The scene felt like something out of a fairy tale, surreal and magical but undeniably real.

The ceremony had been simple. Only close family and a few friends. We'd come so far from the moment I fled Dimitri to this moment when I chose Santino to be mine forever.

As we reached the bottom of the steps, I spotted Violet fussing with a tiny bow on her newborn's outfit. Kill stood beside her, arms crossed, a bemused look on his face. A few feet away, Romeo bantered with his sisters, his hands gesturing wildly.

Right in the middle of them stood Luca, grinning as he held Jack up on his shoulders. Luca's eyes flicked over, catching my gaze, and he gave a small nod.

Santino opened the car door for me.

"Ready to go, Mrs. Costa?"

I smiled at him, my heart full. I climbed into the car, and this time, the dress cooperated. Santino got in beside me and kissed my cheek.

As we drove away, the cityscape of Boston passed by in a blur. I leaned back, feeling the gentle pull of the car as it sped toward our future. Santino's hand never left mine, his thumb tracing my wedding band.

"Do you remember the second time we met?" I asked, a playful smile tugging at my lips.

"You were the hottest runaway bride I'd ever seen."

I laughed softly. "Now, I'm all yours."

He pulled me into his arms, kissing me. Leaning in, I stuck my hand into his moussed hair. When I parted my mouth, he groaned and kissed me. He cupped the nape of my neck, his body crowding mine. A surge of warmth spread through me, electrifying every nerve. Each kiss was a promise that he'd never let me go.

When I ran that day, I wasn't just escaping. I was running toward the man who'd become my true home.

ACKNOWLEDGMENTS

I've always wanted to write a gun moll heroine, and this book allowed me to do just that. It was such a thrill to dive into the mindset of a strong woman who believes she has the hero wrapped around her finger. Writing this book brought me so much joy, and I hope you enjoy the ride as much as I did.

A huge thank you to Molly Whitman and Christine LePorte for your incredible editing work on this book. Your keen eyes and thoughtful feedback helped shape the story into what it is now, and I couldn't have done it without you.

Special thanks to Madison for beta reading. Your insights and suggestions were invaluable, and I'm deeply grateful for your dedication in helping this story shine.

Kevin McGrath, you've outdone yourself with the stunning cover, and Michelle Lancaster, the photo captures the hero perfectly.

To all my readers, words cannot express how much your support means to me. You are the driving force behind every word I write. I'm beyond grateful for your enthusiasm to my stories. It's what keeps me inspired every day.

With all my love,
Vanessa

ALSO BY VANESSA WALTZ

Dark Billionaire Romance

Monster: An Arranged Marriage Enemies-to-Lovers Romance (Filthy Rich Villains #1)

Tyrant: A Dark Second Chance Romance (Filthy Rich Villains #2)

Devil: A Dubcon/Kidnapping Romance (Filthy Rich Villains #3)

Dark Mafia Romance

Tempted: A Free Dark Romance Prequel (Sinners of Boston 0.5)

Arranged: An Arranged Marriage Romance (Sinners of Boston #1)

Taken: A Forced Marriage Romance (Sinners of Boston #2)

Faked: A Fake Engagement Romance (Sinners of Boston #3)

Claimed: A Secret Baby Romance (Sinners of Boston #4)

Mafia Romance

High Stakes (Vittorio Crime Family #1)

Double Blind (Vittorio Crime Family #2)

End Game (Vittorio Crime Family #3)

His Witness (Vittorio Crime Family #4)

Spicy Mafia Romance

Married to the Bad Boy (Cravotta Crime Family #1)

Knocked Up by the Bad Boy (Cravotta Crime Family #2)

Tied Down (Cravotta Crime Family #2.5)

Property of the Bad Boy (Cravotta Crime Family #3)

Owned by the Bad Boy (Cravotta Crime Family #4)

Campy Dark Mafia Romance

Hitman's Bride

His Secret Baby

Billionaire Romance

The Cinderella Arrangement: A Fake-Dating Romance

The Roommate Arrangement: A Brother's Best Friend Romance

The Secret Arrangement: A Marriage of Convenience Romance

The Guarded Heart: A Bodyguard Romance *as Blair LeBlanc

Romantic Comedy

The Mechanic: An Accidental Pregnancy Romance

The Detective (Fair Oaks #2)

Jingle Balls: A Christmas Romance

The D: A Student/Professor Romance

Royal Romance

Dirty Prince: A Marriage of Convenience Romance

Love Triangle Romance

The Marriage Debt

Psychological Thrillers *as Rachel Hargrove

Not a Normal Family

The Maid

Sick Girl

The Wrong Patient

My Sister's Lies

ABOUT THE AUTHOR

Vanessa Waltz is an author of Dark Bad Boy Romance and lives in Seattle with her two ill-behaved cats.

Before she settled in Seattle, she lived in Northern California where she studied English Literature at San Jose State University. She pursued a career in medicine before making an about-face to write full-time. She also pens psychological thrillers as Rachel Hargrove.

Vanessa is represented by Jill Marsal of Marsal Lyon Literary Agency.
Vanessa's Newsletter

For more information, follow her here:
www.vanessawaltzbooks.com
info@vanessawaltzbooks.com
Bad Boy Addicts - Facebook Group

Made in the USA
Monee, IL
05 November 2024